Replacing Dad

Replacing Dad

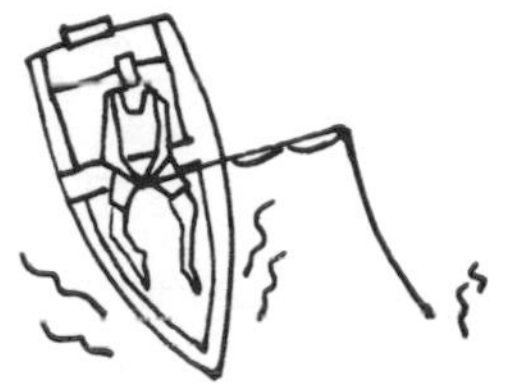

a novel by

Shelley Fraser Mickle

Published by
Algonquin Books of Chapel Hill
Post Office Box 2225
Chapel Hill, North Carolina 27515-2225

a division of
Workman Publishing Company, Inc.
708 Broadway
New York, New York 10003

Printed in the United States of America.
Design by Susan A. Stirling

Library of Congress Cataloging-in-Publication Data
Mickle, Shelley Fraser.
Replacing dad : a novel / by Shelley Fraser Mickle.
p. cm.
ISBN 1-56512-017-5
I. Title.
PS3563.I353W34 1993
813'.54—dc20 92-34209
CIP

10 9 8 7 6 5 4 3 2 1

First Edition

For myself.
—Linda Marsh

For anybody who'll never tell my mother.
—Drew Marsh

Say, my spirit,
How fares the king and's followers?
Confined together . . .
Just as you left them; all prisoners, sir,
In the lime-grove.

—Shakespeare, *The Tempest*

"When Mama ain't happy, ain't nobody happy."
—a sign in a novelty store, 1991

Acknowledgments

I'd like to express my appreciation to Louis Rubin and Shannon Ravenel for their incomparable insights; my family for their support, especially Blake and Paul, who always keep my lingo up to date; Parker, who supports me in many ways without charging interest; Claudia Sabin and Eleanor Blair, who helped me see as a painter might see; Carol Offen and Virginia Holman for making it all smooth; Virginia Barber, my agent; and last but not least, the fictional spirits of Drew and Linda who gave me their stories with such insistence.

Replacing Dad

1.
Drew

I remember thinking that the last thing on my mind ought to be my mother. It was my birthday. I was turning fifteen, and she and I were on our way to the Highway Patrol Station to get me my learner's permit. Now, the thing is, I kept telling myself it was a little nuts for someone like me—fifteen, five foot ten already, and with a few girls already acting like they liked me—to be worrying about my mother. I was wondering what in the hell I could do to get her to just break through where she was. I was sick of her always wearing dark glasses and humming "Don't Worry, Be Happy," and cooking me and Mandy and George brownies every night like she was June Cleaver.

I know about Mrs. Cleaver, because when I was twelve I slipped on my bike in the rain on the main street of Palm Key, and Mr. Tuttle couldn't stop the Wonder Bread delivery in time. I got to stay in bed at home for a good long time with a broken leg and five cracked ribs, watching all these "Leave It to Beaver" reruns. Of course old June cooked all her brownies in the afternoons 'cause she didn't have to work. But I'm not complaining about the brownies—they were out of a mix, guaranteed good, and served warm and gooey like I like them. And I'm not really saying I minded my mother singing "Don't Worry, Be Happy," all the time either, even though her voice is not much better than the sound of somebody blowing a flute with a hole in it. It's just that being around someone who is trying like hell to act like Richard Simmons doing a fat-melting video—when all the time you know that inside, they've hit bottom—didn't fool me.

When you get right down to it, the alternative would have been worse, I guess. But the point is, when someone around you is miserable, even if they do everything in the world to pretend not to be, don't you know?

And so that's where I was: living with June Cleaver. And it didn't fit. It wasn't my mother. It'd been six months since my father had moved out. He was living with this teacher in the same school where I went. She taught fifth grade, was my sister Mandy's teacher. My dad was the principal there—still is—which means he's lord over everything K through twelve, which also means he's lord over not much, since no more than a hundred kids go to the Palm Key School.

So my mother and I were heading up the walkway to the Highway Patrol licensing place—Mom in dark glasses, the curve of her shoulders like she had a fifty-pound backpack tied on, and a smile that Carol Burnett couldn't have come close to. (Saw a lot of Carol reruns, too.)

My mother's short. Even on my fifteenth birthday, she came up to only about my armpit. And in the face we look a lot alike, which can sound kinda weird for a guy to say he looks like his mother. But we both have this dark skin from some Italian great grandmother who decided to turn up just in us, and both our noses are these same long things that look like we've had them sharpened. My mom, though, wears glasses, little wire things. I've asked her several times if she's an old hippie, but all she says is that back when she was in school, everybody was, or at least was sympathetic to the cause: peace and good food and save the Earth and all that. I guess really my mother's hair's too curly to have been a good hippie—unless she'd gone for the Afro look—but the glasses she still wears seem to me to make her look a good bit like John Lennon's lost cousin.

My mother's an artist—at least when she has time—mainly does watercolors. It's my father who was the real hippie, my mother says. He was the one who grew a beard and wanted to do something socially important. Teaching school and then rising to principal of Palm Key High and then moving in with the fifth-grade teacher sure seems socially important.

Outside the Highway Patrol Station, my mother stopped and put her hand on my arm, and I could see the June Cleaver look in her eye, twinkling and carrying on like a damn hyper Christmas light. "Don't worry, Drew, you'll see, this'll be a piece of cake." She touched my arm. (My mother still touched on me quite a lot, even more since Dad had left, like she was afraid any minute I wasn't going to be there either. I gave up touching on her when I was about twelve, had now just started thinking about how it felt: kissing her, mashing my lips up against her cheek when I was five or six, maybe even most recently at ten. (Now, right off, you can tell I'm not normal.) And I could be walking down the street, or working on my fishing boat motor, or just staring at a shear pin—at least everybody was *thinking* that's what I was doing—while inside my head I was wondering if my mother's cheek was going to be anything like touching Heather Wilson or

Mary McVane or any of those other girls who'd been stopping to talk to me when they didn't have anything better to do. The week before, we'd had this sex conference with the coach in the gym. The girls had gone into one side and us into the other, and the coach had said it was time we learned all about diseases and prevention and stuff. He said recent research showed that a seventeen-year-old boy thought about sex once every nine minutes. When I timed myself over the rest of the day, I found out I had that beat by two minutes already.)

Mom walked up the Highway Patrol steps in front of me, then turned and said it all over again. "Now just don't worry about a thing. You can take this test as many times as you want to."

I wasn't sure if that was the truth, or even if I appreciated what she'd said. (My mom could get on my nerves big time.) For quite a while she'd been convinced that I had some kind of wire loose, which made me see stuff backward. She was dying for me to have a learning disability, something somebody could fix. Neither she nor my dad could ever accept the fact that I am slow. Dumb Drew is what I've been called a lot. But I find that most people don't usually get both brains and good sense. They're either book dumb or living dumb. And in that sense, I figure I'm going to be lucky. (If I can at least kick this sex thing. Wonder why, if I'm so slow otherwise, I'm so fast in this other department?)

In fact, in the last few years my mom and dad had been having this ongoing thing about how slow I am. He said I was lazy, didn't care, wanted to do something to rebel against him. She said he was too cheap to get me tested; she was sure I saw words backward and something could be done about it. My father, though, said I was being dumb on purpose, that it was tough being the principal's kid, trying to be perfect like everyone would expect. I hate to disappoint him, but I never was after perfect. (And now it wasn't going to matter anyway. I figured when they found out I was a pervert, my grades were going to seem like nothing.)

So there my mother was, telling the highway patrol cop that I might just read all the words on the test backward, which of course embarrassed the hell out of me. Told the cop she'd like to sit close to make sure I didn't read all the STOP signs as POTS signs. And then she laughed. My mother has this crazy laugh; she's so little that it sounds like she's borrowed a tuba. And I guess by carrying on with the cop, she thought she'd loosen us all up. But he said, "Don't worry, lady, if he can't tell Stop from Pots, he ain't passin' anyway."

That sure filled me with great confidence. So when he put my head into the eye-check machine, I called all the P's B's and all the M's W's, which, if nothing else, proved that my mom wasn't nuts or trying to cheat.

Then the cop pulled out my test score. "Seems to me," he said to my mother, "he sees upside down and inside out, too—or maybe you already know that."

Right away I established myself as a potential driving freak.

When the cop told me to follow him into this room and sit by myself and take the written part of the test the best I could, he left me there and slapped me on the back on his way out. "Shoot, don't worry, kid," he said. "We got eighty-year-olds taking this test and passing."

For a while I wasn't able to do anything or get started. I just sat there counting up all the times I could take the test before I turned eighty. I saw myself on one of those three-wheeled bicycles, carrying groceries back to the nursing home. And I'd always be bumming rides or taking the bus or hitchhiking. I'd have to skip the prom, and I'd never get to take a girl out to the cemetery, where everybody goes to park.

I got myself so worked up I couldn't read any of the questions or have them make sense. I could barely breathe, and my pits were dripping. I counted every third word and chose an answer based on the last letter of that third word. It was a complicated system, but it gave me answers. Then I went out into the waiting room. And while the cop graded my paper, my mother and I prayed.

The thing was, you see, since the divorce my mother had gotten a job at the county dump, was driving an hour every day back and forth, and had had to put George in day care. And there was no way for us to get him before my mom stopped for him on the way home, which was usually close to seven. My father, who Mom calls George the First, wasn't much help. He said he was too busy being the principal. So if I could have gotten a car, any old car, when I turned sixteen, and had my real license, I could be the one to back my mother up. Do all the things she now wasn't home to do. She was counting on me.

"Sorry, kid," the cop said. "Want to take this booklet and sit over there and study it awhile and try again in a few minutes?"

It was almost dark when I got out, walking with my mother back to our car in the parking lot. I'd passed on the third try, after I'd changed my system from choosing every last letter of the third word to the fourth. My mother hugged me. "Wanna drive home?" She handed me the keys.

I opened the door to the car, got in the front seat behind the wheel where I'd been only a few times before, and most often as a kid playing. With a learner's permit, I had to have with me somebody with a license every time I drove, and we both knew that meant mostly her. She looked at me. "Go ahead," she said. Under her breath, high and faint, she was humming, reminding me of the electric buzz of a light bulb about to wear out.

"Guess we better use these." She laughed, pulling out the straps to the seat belt. "It's the law, now, you know," which she said like she wasn't worried a bit about sitting in the death seat.

I turned the key in the ignition, put my foot down on the accelerator.

In a few minutes my hair was blowing back in the wind from the open window. It was a twenty-minute drive to Palm Key, and on the way home we had to stop to get George out of day care and to pick up Mandy at a Girl Scout meeting over at the church. When I turned onto the highway that in about ten miles would lead across the bridges into Palm Key, I gunned it. When I could, I glanced over at my mother. She was gripping the handle of her purse in her lap like she was hanging onto the handle of a trapeze. Yeah, we were really bookin', now. Loose. Our hair wild. I would have driven us straight out of The Here and Now, would have pushed my mother through to the other side of I-didn't-know-what (but had to be better than where we were). If I could.

But when I looked down at the needle on the speedometer, its spidery little hand was hanging on forty, just sitting there like a line I hadn't even known I'd drawn.

2.
Linda

I didn't choose this place; it chose me. We'd been driving down the coast of Florida, George and I; I was three months pregnant with Drew, just enough to know for sure—which I hid from my mother and, God knows, forever from my father. A week later I would tell them I had eloped, then remind them how much a real wedding would have cost. (And for anybody who thinks like my mother, I'd like to add that getting pregnant before the ring is wound around the fourth finger doesn't necessarily mean you're a hussy, slut, or whore. It took me a long time to convince myself of that. And I never did, my mother.)

So George and I were looking for a romantic place where we could be married. The only place we could afford was here, not in a ritzy part of Florida, but on the mud coast, as it is called. Or the Redneck Riviera. I didn't know that then, had never heard it called anything, but it was a place definitely out of the way; and it was the sky at Palm Key that chose me.

Standing on a pier that jutted out into the Gulf, as though with one more step westward we would fall off the earth, George and I looked out at the sky and the late afternoon sun. The tide was in, and the lap of water was all around under me. Two porpoises fed in the gray water just in front of us, breaking through the surface, then disappearing under it, in and out as if they were curved needles sewing the Gulf. And as far as I could turn my head there was sky, all sky. As I moved my feet, turning more, hearing the gentle tap and scrape of my sandals on the gray weathered pier, still there was more sky. It was as though I was standing inside a glass bowl, slate blue, clear, and forever changing. The clouds sat like huge swirls of cream with the sun going down through them in streaks of pink, reminding me of juice dripping from a sliced strawberry, while quietly beside me a big brown pelican landed on a pole near the pier, and looked around, too. For a second his eyes and mine met: the sharp black buttons of a fish hunter, and the girlish pools of a mother-to-be, a little anxious, yet anchored by love.

The sunset was so beautiful it made me know who I was: small and finite, a privileged watcher of porpoises and suns and pelicans landing now and then. And all of this was punctuated even more by the small tender swelling of Drew inside me.

George's arm was around my waist, his hand riding above my hips, his fingers warm against me. So gentle and sweet. Simply, it was, I guess, a sky and place we could not say no to—or leave. And George decided right there and then that he would apply to the local school for a teaching job, while I saw in the sky the colors of paintings that would fill my lifetime. We gave ourselves and our lives to this place so easily, so determinedly, adding the final touches in a ten-minute ceremony at City Hall: married.

The story of the goose who laid the golden egg is suspect. It's what she does when she lets loose with a brown one that's real.

All along I should have been suspicious of how George kept his things. His personal things: his socks and his tools, his books, and his cars. He never let himself have more than two of the same kind, or color, or make. Or loves. George was a barracuda after clutter.

I had Drew here; or at least in the next county. There was no hospital or clinic or anything in Palm Key then. But he grew up here, was my first baby here, was my first offspring of love who got to watch me turn from girl to mother, a sometime playmate or drill sergeant, an occasional fishing mate. It was an easy place to raise him. And it was still easy when Mandy came and then George the Second. No traffic to speak of, no kid-snatching maniacs. There's something special about a place that declares a dog an official speed bump. Our dog, Lolly, got old and had arthritis so bad that he lay out on the warm pavement all day, so cars had to go around him. No one complained; the weekly paper just wrote him up and declared him an official speed bump.

How could I leave a place that was so much a part of me? And yet I could no longer feel it. I could no longer see it as it was. I could no longer bear to see it as it had once been.

I was hanging over Palm Key like a kite that had gotten loose. I knew I should leave, and yet I couldn't. My children's father was here. I couldn't make them leave where once George and I had been as one. I could not bear to think that also here they had witnessed the death of us.

By the time all the lawyers and proceedings got through with me, I didn't have a pot to piss in—as Lucille Duffy said. Lucille ran The Love 'em and Leave 'em Day Care up on Highway 40, where I had to put George the Second when I got a job. I hate to admit this, but when George and I were in college together all I had on my mind was him. And he sure was a pitiful thing to major in, which only shows how dumb I was. I dropped out of college to marry him; of course, I accidentally got pregnant with Drew. I don't ever tell Drew I got pregnant accidentally. He's a smart boy (not book smart but lots of common sense), and he figured out a few years ago that his birthday comes too close to the date of George's and my first anniversary. George's own mother, Drew's grandmother, spilled the beans one Christmas when she reminisced how George and I were married in the spring of 1975, and then of course Drew himself counted up that coming in September of 1975 meant he was either way premature or the spur for the wedding date. Naturally all mothers have times like that when their child comes to them and pumps them for some truth you don't especially want to tell. So what do you do? Make up a story that is not only truer than the real one but also way the hell better. So I told him that he just drew us together. He was our love child. Our own Drew who was our beginning and would always be the center of our love. Of course his real name is Andrew, but from day one, to me and George, he was Drew.

So just how do you suppose *he* feels now after I fed him that sweet little number? Why did I have to make up such a good story? Why didn't I just tell him he got dropped off by some migrating stork on the way to Miami? How do you suppose he feels now that his father has taken off to make the center of *his* love a five-foot-eight-inch hussy with pink hair? Cotton candy torch, Lucille Duffy calls her.

Please pass the matches.

. . .

Now right here, I just have to be cut a little slack, because I can't speak generously about the woman who was teaching my child and kept calling my husband in for private conferences. I know George the First didn't have to attend; I know he didn't have to answer every one of her requests to see the principal, but it's just a part of their whole mess that along with him, I burn her, too.

Shoot! We all knew George the First was weak, a Man of the Flesh.

All the time I should have just warned every woman who saw him coming. Put a flaming letter across his chest.

(I might seem tough, but the truth is it took me almost six months just to call the kettle black.)

And so that's where all that left me: two years of a beginning major in art and, unfortunately—or fortunately, however you want to look at it—the ability to type. The only job I could get right after the divorce was as a clerk in the payroll office of the county dump, which was an hour's drive from my house and to Lucille Duffy's, where I could leave George the Second.

Let me tell you, none of that was fun.

George the First was, and still is, good about the child support. There was just not much of anything for any of us and nothing left for me.

Even if I could have gotten George to agree to send me back to school so I could finish my degree, he didn't have enough money to. It'd have been a lot of lawyers maneuvering and then finally seeing they were just pissing in the wind. (The kettle was always way too empty to ever pour.)

In my opinion, if a man can't afford two families, he ought to get out of the family business. What did he think he could do: put us on Visa?

That day I met Mark, Drew and I were driving back from the Highway Patrol Station. Drew had taken three tries to pass the driver's test. Third time's the charm, I told him. And he said, well, that's sure not true about George the Second—which, to me, didn't disprove that old saying in the least.

Even though my third child, George, is, I guess, the epitome of what gives meaning to the words *pistol, pill, live wire*—to me he was, is, and always will be, charming. And Drew was driving along just fine up Highway 40 to Lucille Duffy's so we could pick up George the Second on our way home.

We pulled up to Bill and Lucille's Handymart. That was easy for Drew. No one else was there. Plenty of room to park.

Lucille is big and wears her hair in tight curls all over her head, and during those first hard months after George moved out, I don't think I would have made it without her. She and Bill lived in an upstairs apartment over the Handymart. Along with gas and groceries and snacks and lottery tickets, they specialized in fishing gear. In the back, the yard was fenced in with a swing set and sandbox and picnic table where Lucille ran The Love 'em and Leave 'em Day Care.

Drew held the door open for me—he'd started doing that lately—and I passed beside the plant where Lucille filed away her losing lottery tickets. It was a Spanish bayonet, a dusty green thing with long spikelike leaves that had, on each one, a ticket spiked through the heart. It looked like some kind of strange creature, a symbol of comfort or despair—however you wanted to see it—for all losers.

Lucille came in from the back to meet us. That day she was

wearing a T-shirt that said PLEASE LORD LET ME SHOW YOU THAT WINNING THE LOTTERY WON'T SPOIL ME. And she grabbed Drew across the shoulders and pulled his head into her large bosom. (I myself had begun to wonder if Drew was not too old for that. I didn't want for me, or Lucille either, to get in the way of his budding sexuality. As though I knew anything about budding sexuality, seeing as how my own had budded up so long ago, then had gotten snipped while blooming—and was now compost.)

"Well, just look at this," Lucille said, smiling. "Driving up here good as Mario Andretti. Looking pretty as a pretty Italian, too." She ruffled his hair.

Drew turned pink under that beautiful skin of his. His eyes are gray like mine. George used to call mine Sea Wash, the name of a paint I used a lot. A paint he said made my watercolor skies look like captured raindrops. (Should have drowned him when I had a chance.) My whole life with George is now like a footnote. It creeps in in tiny little minutes in which I remember what he used to say, the way his hair curled around the back of his ears; the yellow flecks in the irises of his eyes that, with his head on a pillow, were enhanced like chain links of gold. Even as I looked at Drew, right then, the exact curl of George's hair was behind his ears. "He did great," I said. "Passed with flying colors."

Drew turned pink again and glanced at me. Well . . . flying colors is always relative.

Bill reached over the counter and handed Drew a key ring. It was plastic in the shape of a swordfish. "Here's a little something for your birthday," he said. "We got to take a day off soon and go fishing. What you say?"

Drew smiled, his head half tucked like a rising bean shoot. He was so uncomfortable in his new big body and in those occasional moments, which reminded us all that he was two seconds from taking charge of his own life, that he seemed to sneak looks at us like we were spectators on a beach. "It'd be great," he said. Eyes up, then down. "And thanks."

Bill grinned again and handed Drew an unopened Chap Stick. "Case you get to drive around in somebody's convertible," he said. Bill could never give anyone enough. As well as selling lottery tickets in the store, and buying them themselves, he and Lucille had also gotten into the cheering-up business. They were situated at the intersection of two highways, fifteen minutes from the middle of Palm Key, where they'd have more traffic. Bill had a sign in front of his cash register: WANTED: ONE GOOD WOMAN WHO CAN COOK AND CLEAN FISH. WITH A BOAT AND MOTOR, WHO CAN SEW AND FISH. PLEASE SEND PHOTO OF BOAT AND MOTOR.

Just then George the Second came in the back door, his voice high and fast like a soup pot set on high, boiling over. "Did Drew pass? Did you pass, Drew? You driving, Drew?"

Drew held up the car keys looped over his finger. I swear, the smile on his face could have rivaled a watermelon slice.

George the Second was four then, little scrawny, scraped knees. I could never get him clean. The insides of his ears looked like sweet potatoes. Both Lucille and I had just about given up. And I often dressed him in pinstriped overalls, like a tiny train engineer. I wanted him to look cute so he'd have a little protection. Because sometimes George could push just about anybody close to wanting to kill him. He was a walking contraceptive. Five minutes with him, and you might run out and get yourself fixed.

But given a choice, I'd still have five more just like him. (At least, after a good long rest.) Which, I guess, just proves for good how crazy I am.

"I want to sit up front with Drew," George was saying, opening the car door.

"Fine." I got in the back, wondering if the learner's permit said anything about me not being in the front. But then, being in the back would be like giving Drew even more of my total vote of confidence.

"Buckle up," I said.

The car was nothing fancy. A Ford sedan, sensible and not too fast. It was late Friday afternoon, and we had forgotten that the next day was the beginning of the Palm Key Shrimp Festival. Tourists from all over were on their way into the town, ready to fill up the hotels and get an early start on the booths of shrimp that would open the next day and fill up the main streets and the park. Shrimp pie. Shrimp salad. Fried shrimp. Boiled shrimp.

"Don't worry," I said to Drew, "you're doing just fine." His hands were tight on the wheel, and the side of his jaw was working. His ears had seemed to have outgrown his head—or his hair had been cut too short above them—those seemed to be already the ears of a man. I stared at the edge of his face, from what I could see from the backseat. I still couldn't quite believe he had started shaving. Once or twice a week, but still, shaving. The traffic was bumper to bumper on the one highway that leads into Palm Key.

"Go ahead," I said, "put on your lights." My voice was low and calm. It was only dusk, the sky gray fuzz, but I figured having the car lights on would help everybody to see us coming. And if I sounded like I was trying to get into *The Guinness Book of World Records* for being the sweetest backseat driver, ever, my feet were putting on the brake plenty on the floor right behind Drew.

I put my dark glasses in the pocket of my suit and switched

to regular ones. George pointed to three birds sitting on the wires between two telephone poles beside the road. "Why don't those birds get 'lectrocuted?"

"I'll tell you in a minute," I said. Then, "That's fine, Drew; just let him pass. If he's got the hots for shrimp that bad, let him go on around." Drew had us so close to the right side of the road, I was afraid we'd fall off. We were close to the bridges now, the wide expanse of water on either side with marsh grass sticking up like swirls of fur.

"So come on, Mom, why don't those birds get 'lectrocuted?" George was riding face forward, but he was turning sideways to throw his voice back to me, and his little index finger pointed out the window.

"I don't know exactly, George." It was never my style to not say that I didn't know something. And besides, speculation was my strength. "I guess it has something to do with insulation," I said.

"What's insulation?"

"A coating around something. Something that gives protection."

George turned his head so he could glance at me. "If I get 'sulation, can I sit on wires?" he asked.

"No, you're too heavy."

"How does the 'lectricity get in the toaster?"

"Through a wire."

"What does it look like?"

"You can't see it."

"Why can't you see it?"

"It's like one of those things you just can't see, George. Like air. Or God. Or a virus."

"Then why does it need wires?"

"I don't know. We'll have to look it up."

"You never look it up. You always say you're going to look it up."

"I will, George, I promise. Right after supper."

Drew laughed. "Why don't you tell him the same thing you told him about the TV?"

"What did I tell him about the TV?"

"You told him Socrates made it work. Old Socrates." He laughed again. The back of his neck was like a little tree, reaching up. He was trying so hard not to look nervous over the steering wheel.

"That's a thought," I said, which made George turn around in the seat and stare at me. Ever since he could talk, he'd driven me nearly to the end of myself with questions, and usually at the worst times. The year before I had written him a poem that, every once in a while, I'd recite, when my batteries were running low.

> You are three, George.
> And all day have queried me
> with the intensity of Socrates.
> And you know what happened to him.

The first time he'd answered: "I don't know Socrates. He live in Palm Key?"

Quickly and without thought, as though George was fifty years old and sitting at my right hand in Hell as my punishment, I had thrown back: "Keep it up, and you'll find out." Which meant that immediately afterward, I bought him two packages of Oreos out of a vending machine, along with three packages of gum, which, when they ended up stuck to the living-room rug, I cleaned up without a bit of complaint.

But now I was brought back to thinking about the road and to what Drew was about to do to us. I screamed: "Slow down, Drew! Slow down! You don't have to kiss his bumper!" Drew was gripping the wheel, his knuckles like clamps. "I don't want to look like a wuss," he said. "You're not a wuss," I said. "Yes, he is a wuss." George looked at Drew. "Pass him, Drew. Pass the old fart."

For three weeks, George had latched onto the word fart with the same sort of attachment he had given to his pacifier. I had, with great calm, explained to him that it was not a word adults liked hearing little children use. That didn't do it. I had, without calm, told him that if I heard him say it again, I would give him Time Out in his room and no cookies for a week. That didn't do it.

Every time I brought attention to his using it only seemed to make it more attractive to him. It was a word I had decided I was going to have to just wait out. And meanwhile keep him out of public as much as I could.

"Why do the license plates have different colors?" George pointed in front, then whirled around and pointed in back. "They're from different places," I said.

"Why are they from different places?"

"Because they have jobs there."

"Who got them the jobs?"

"Socrates."

"Socrates is an old fart," he said.

I sat in the back, watching the back of his head. Maybe I'd be a better person if I had plenty of money and understood electricity.

And for certain if I ever won the lottery, I'd have to give it all away to the Child Abuse Society.

Just before the main intersection in Palm Key, Drew turned right and headed to the First (and only) Palm Key Methodist Church. From a block away, we could see Mandy sitting on the top of the concrete steps. The car lights lit her up, and the church porch lights threw a circle behind her. Her little body in her new green Girl Scout uniform (she had just flown up from Brownies) looked so lonely that I had to swallow. Of all my children, Mandy is the most like me. She has George the First's blond hair and his nose. But her eagerness to please, her desire for a world where there is only peace, no pain, and for all eggs to be laid golden, without a whiff of rot, is—up and down and all over—me.

Behind her, Mrs. Farrigut, who was up for the Volunteer of the Year Award and had won it for the last five years, and who was now also the scout leader, stood guard over Mandy. I leaned out of the window, "Thanks for staying with her."

"No problem." Mrs. Farrigut patted Mandy on the back. "I just had to call and cancel a dental appointment and tell Fred to pick up some fast food and reschedule my Blood Drive meeting. But I wouldn't have left one of my girls here alone for anything in the world."

"Sorry," I said.

Mandy got in the back beside me and handed me a potholder woven out of fat tubes of yarn.

"Why're you so late?" She had an edge of complaint in her voice that I'd noticed when she started the sixth grade.

"It took a long time for Drew to get his permit."

"So, he bombed it."

"No."

Drew was pulling into the church parking lot to turn around. "What else would you call it?" he asked.

"I didn't know he bombed it." George the Second looked at Drew. "You didn't tell me you bombed it."

"He didn't," I said. "Except for a while. And it's not what you need to tell anybody, anyway."

"Yeah, I had to take it three times," Drew added. "A lot of people do," I said. "Your own father had to take it *five* times." Mandy and George turned to look at me, and Drew would have, but he was too busy pulling the car into a vacant place and backing out headed in a new direction.

"He did?" George asked. "Did he really?" Drew added. And then Mandy: "I didn't know that."

"Yeah, well, it's the truth. Ask him," I said. One of my favorite pastimes had become pinning a less-than-perfect past on George and then enjoying imagining him getting out of it in front of the kids.

Mandy leaned against me. I could feel the tiny little swellings of her breasts as she pressed against my arm. In the last few weeks, her body had begun to change, her breasts becoming about the size of infected mosquito bites. And they seemed as foreign to her as my own had become to George the First.

About a dozen cars were lined up at the stoplight at the main intersection in Palm Key. Drew put on his left blinker, so he could turn toward our house. There was no green arrow at this light. Palm Key would never get so busy or complicated to add that. It was just a plain old light, three colors, and half the time even turned off. But today there was too much traffic for it not to be on: too many tourists, bumper to bumper, coming toward us. "Go ahead, inch out," I said to Drew. I pointed. "That's right, just sit here under the light and, when you get a chance, turn."

But the line of traffic was so long, he didn't get to turn before the light changed.

"It's okay," I said. "Just put it in reverse and back out of the intersection. We'll be first in line when the light changes again."

"Wuss," George said. "Shut up, George," said Drew. His ears were red. "It's all right, Drew," I said, patting his shoulder. "We all have to remember that George is only four." "May not live to five," Mandy said.

I pointed as the light turned. None of us knew it, but Drew had left the gear in reverse. So when he put his foot down on the accelerator, we knocked the hell out of whoever was behind us. And ourselves. I sat up, grabbing my head, my neck still wobbling.

Smoke was oozing out of the hood of the car behind us. George was bracing himself against the dashboard. Drew looked sick. It was a good thing we'd all been wearing seat belts.

The car behind us was an old Mercedes, and in the streetlights overhead I could see that it was humped and rounded, probably more than twenty years old. Its grill was now mashed back into itself like the mouth of a fish.

"God, I'm sorry. I'm so sorry, Mom." Drew opened the car door to get out. "God, why did it have to be a Mercedes?"

I unbuckled myself, then checked George and Mandy to see if they were really all right.

"Boy, you sure hit the fart, Drew. I mean you really hit the fart!"

Drew was standing beside our car. Smoke was coming up out

of the one we'd hit, and we could hear the Palm Key fire siren. The station was only half a block away.

Mandy walked up to the man who was getting out of the Mercedes, and she stood beside him while he, too, stood looking at the front of his car. He was really tall. That was nearly all I thought about. And that we hadn't killed him. Or maimed him. In fact, he seemed fine. Long blond hair, a good way over his collar in back, and a mustache. And then I realized that I knew who he was. Last week his picture had been in the Palm Key paper. He was the new and only physician Palm Key had. The one the town council had recruited. And they'd had a pretty hard time getting some doctor to come to Palm Key, too.

I went over closer to him. "How bad do you think it is?" He looked down at me, then back at his car. "Oh, I don't think it's too serious. The smoke makes it look bad."

"I know you're upset." I was staring at the Mercedes. Mandy moved next to me and, even though I thought she'd outgrown this, she reached over and held a fistful of my skirt. "This is obviously a fine car," I said, my voice running on, fast. "Being so old, it's probably worth a lot—at least to you. It's probably real valuable and you love it. And, well, my son, Drew, he just got his learner's permit. I mean, *really* just got it—this afternoon."

"He failed the test two times," Mandy added.

"And I wonder," I went on, "do you think we could just not make too big a deal out of this? You know, it might really blow his confidence. I'd really appreciate it."

I was sounding great. But when I came to the last part of my speech, my voice cracked. I was telling myself: *You cry, sister, and you won't see another sunrise*. I switched glasses again, reaching in my pocket, and getting out the dark ones.

He stood there, listening to everything I said. Then he looked back at his car. We both did, just stood there and stared. In a few minutes, he walked toward it. "Why don't I see if it'll start?" He got in, and the firemen surrounded it.

"Aren't you afraid it'll blow up?" I followed him to the car as he opened the door. Mandy was practically riding my feet. I was ready, though, to run back at the first sound of a pop, throw my body across Mandy, Drew, and George the Second.

The firemen raised the hood and were looking down in it, holding fire extinguishers. Drew was hanging onto George by the hand, just standing there in the middle of the street like he was about to be hanged. The whole town seemed to be watching us. A fireman squirted something into the hood, and the car hissed and the smoke stopped. The new doctor was grinding the motor, and then it caught.

By then the editor of the *Palm Key Sentinel* was walking around us, taking photographs, using a lot of flashbulbs because it was pretty dark.

The new doctor leaned out of the car window and said to me, "I think it's going to be fine. But we ought to exchange names and phone numbers and who our insurance companies are. Your car doesn't look much better."

I turned around and saw that, as far as a trunk was concerned, my car had just been relieved of one. In fact, the whole back end was just about gone. Good, I thought. George the First had bought that car right before he moved out, and it'd been part of my settlement. I'd always even wondered if he'd driven that tart somewhere in it and they might have even . . . in it. And now it was just one less thing between me and him.

Then, just as though to add the final topping to publicly knocking the hell out of the new Palm Key doctor, George the Second got loose from Drew and circled the Mercedes. "Boy, we sure knocked this fart, didn't we? It's an old fart, too, in't it?"

I had to stand there and watch that: the Palm Key firemen and this new doctor, listening to my child call everything and everybody farts, right after my other son had caused the only wreck in Palm Key in three years.

When I got back in the car, I dug around in the bottom of my purse for loose change. It was clear: We were going to have to drive through some place for some fast food, quick. I was too shot to eat, much less to cook. But, as usual, George the Second wouldn't be.

And I probably don't need to add, I guess, that when I got home, I didn't really sleep much that night, or even for the next few weeks.

3.

Drew

I knew my mother hated her job at the county dump. She didn't piss and moan about it, but still, I knew. Sometimes I'd hear her cussing out her boss while she was putting stuff in the washing machine, thinking the sound of the water swishing and all that would cover up what she said. So I guess it really was a good thing that happened the day I was baby-sitting George, except that for a while, it sure looked like a tragedy in the making.

It was one of those school holidays—teacher conference day—which always made things hard for us. Because Dad was at the school, couldn't watch George or Mandy, and Mom had to be at The Dump. So between her and me, we worked it out. If I stayed home and watched George and Mandy, she'd save a little on day care. Mandy was too old for it anyway, but not old enough to stay home alone. So Mom would go to work, and we'd both forget that my teachers needed conferencing. "Your dad ought to take care of that, anyway," she said. It was my first year in high school; I'd only been in the ninth grade for nine weeks, so how bad could it be?

She taught me how to make grilled cheese sandwiches, balance it off with a can of pears and a sliced apple and a heated-up can of baked beans. That way Mandy and George, as well as me, would have one of the meals she believed in. She always said we had to have something raw, yellow or green; something white like potatoes or rice; and a lot of milk. My mother fixed meals with a color wheel, and she never gave in.

It was about two o'clock. I'd already cleaned up the kitchen after our lunch. And I'd just about had it taking care of Mandy and George. The summer before, when Dad had driven us down to a white-sand beach for a long weekend, Mandy had sat up in the hotel room while the rest of us went out for a swim. And when *Poltergeist* came on a cable channel, Mandy didn't do a damn thing about turning it off. (At home, Mom wouldn't let us have cable, so when we got in a hotel room, we went nuts.) So there Mandy sat, getting the wits scared out of her, so that ever since last summer, I'd had to escort her to the bathroom and just about everywhere else in the house where she had to go alone. (And neither of us wanted to tell Mom why either, so we snuck around in front of her when she was home.) Already that day I'd gone into the bathroom ahead of Mandy twice to check behind the john, in the cabinets, behind the shower curtain. And all the while, she had just stood in the doorway watching me, and when I complained that the poltergeist thing was not really real, she yelled at me: "It happened in a house, Drew, don't you understand! It could happen in a house like this."

"It was just a movie, Mandy."

"Yeah, but did you check in the hamper?"

And then I'd have to go through all the dirty clothes.

Now she and George had obviously seen that my patience was just about shot, and she had offered to take George to ride bikes out front, maybe walk the shoreline and hunt for stuff that had gotten washed up. I went out to sit on the porch, listen to my Walkman. The tide was out, making the shoreline look like the world was being sucked dry. The edge of the water was a long way away now on the other side of the road, and the oyster bars were sticking up like the scaly backs of some kinds of monsters. Palm trees dot the edge of our front lawn, their bark wrinkled like elephant skins, and their big leaves were rustling.

Beside me, our old car was parked in the drive, the crushed-in back now like the nose of a Pekingese. Mom had collected the money for it that the insurance company had given her, but she said she didn't want to fix the old, silly, ugly car—which I knew meant fix the car Dad had left her. Instead, whatever money the company gave her she put into a little foreign job, a lime green Toyota station wagon. It was already nearly ten years old, but Mr. Duffy said he'd work on it for her and help keep it running. He was a good mechanic. It'd had a FOR SALE sign on it parked out on the highway for three months. It was sort of okay. Not radical or anything I'd want for myself; Mom called it the Granny Apple. But most of all, it was hers, the first and only she'd ever bought.

That meant we were now a two-car family, except that the second one, which was really the first, was not exactly what I had in mind for myself. Didn't even have a back end. And riding around in the reminder of your first wreck sort of sucks.

I plugged in the earphones to my Walkman, mainly out of respect to the bird who lives in front of our house: an osprey, with a nest on a light pole. And the bird was up there, every once in a while getting up and stretching, pushing out her wings. She had been up there every time I'd looked to check on her over the last few days. Big as an eagle. Just not colored like one. Instead plain brown. And the nest looked like my room: big twigs and stuff woven all together, messy, but really real organized. That exact nest had made it through the last hurricane, while half the stuff on the street hadn't. So out of respect for her, I had my earplugs in and was deep into KISS 105 and didn't hear Mandy call me. She rode her bike up into the yard and stopped, then punched my knee. (The only part of Mandy that looks like me, as far as I can see, is her chin. It has a little dip in it, dimple, I guess, that makes it look like that's where the two halves of our faces come together. Otherwise, she's blond. Looks like Dad and George the Second.) I took the earplugs out of my ears. "Yeah, what?"

"George put a rock up his nose. Says he can't breathe."

"What in the hell did he do that for?"

"I don't know. George doesn't know. But it's not my fault."

I walked down the road, Mandy riding on ahead of me. I saw George sitting on this little sand beach a short way away, his trike mired in the sand. How bad could a rock be? Probably wasn't anything.

Mandy laid down her bike. "Show him, George."

George was wiggling his nose and snorting.

"Did you put something up there?" I knelt in the sand and tipped George's head back.

"Yeah."

"Why?"

"Don't know."

"What?"

"Rock."

"Why?"

"Don't know."

We sounded like two Indians in a Wild West movie. I mashed

down on his nose for a while, trying to work the skin like you would a hose. Nothing came out. I wasn't sure if I believed something really was up there. George has a wild imagination; makes up explanations for things all the time, sometimes even when he had the real answers, like when he believed barrettes held people up in water so they could swim. He'd insisted on wearing some of Mandy's barrettes the summer before when we'd taken him for swimming lessons, 'cause all the other kids in the class were girls and were swimming before him.

"Snort, George. Give it a big heave-ho."

He did.

Nothing came out.

"You sure something's up there?"

Suddenly his eyes puddled up. He really was scared.

"It's okay, George. We'll go call Mom. It'll be okay. You'll see." I picked him up.

I carried him back to the house. I didn't want to jerk him or move him. I wasn't sure exactly how far up the rock was, but I figured if I tilted him too far either way it might end up somewhere worse, like his brain.

"Mom." When I got her on the phone, I wasn't sure how to break the news.

"Yeah, Drew. What you need?"

"Oh, nothing. We had lunch. Didn't burn the grilled cheese. Didn't burn the house down either." I laughed. Then when she didn't: "That's a joke, Mom."

"Oh."

"No, I unplugged the electric frying pan, just like you told me. The beans were good. The apple was fresh, too, no bruises."

"Drew, why are you calling?"

"We got just one little problem."

"What's that?"

"George put a rock up his nose."

"Oh God!" She sucked in her breath. "It could go to his lung! It could kill him!"

"It could? I wasn't sure if it was really serious."

"It is. It's awful. I've got to come home. No, first take him to the clinic. To that new doctor. I'll call first, tell them you're on the way. I'll meet you there."

She hung up, and we flew into high gear. "Don't move your head, George," I said. "Don't sniff or do anything. Just hold yourself like a frozen person." I took him by the hand. The clinic was half a mile away, just up the road and one turn. Mandy rode the bike beside us. I put George on my back, piggyback. I had decided not to ride my own bike, because I might jostle him. This way I could put a lot of spring into my feet and keep him steady. I could also keep his mind off himself by playing like I was a pack mule and we were headed up Pike's Peak.

When I walked into the clinic, which is this little white building next to the bank, the whole waiting room was full of people. The clinic seemed to be drawing from all over; people weren't just from Palm Key. George was still on my back, and just like my mother said, the nurse, Mrs. MacHenry, was waiting for us. There just wasn't much of anything she could do. She said Dr. Haley wasn't there. I hadn't seen him since I'd knocked the front in on his Mercedes. Now he was up the highway at a nursing home giving flu shots, she said. She'd sent for him, and we'd just have to wait a little while. She set George down on a chair in the waiting room and gave him a sucker. "Breathe through your mouth, George," she said. "Every time you lick this sucker, breathe in, then out."

It was at least a comfort to turn George over to Mrs. MacHenry. She lived on the same street with us, in a stilt house with a boathouse on the canal that went behind all our houses. She had red hair about the color of a rusted yard chair and a mouth that wouldn't quite close because of her teeth. And to me, that made her look like any second she was about to scream. She was a good singer, though. She was asked to sing at all the weddings and the Shrimp Festival on the bandstand. She had this deep-throated country voice that, if it hadn't sounded so much like she had something caught in her throat, might have been good enough for making a record. My mother used to always call her a mess. "Oh, Betty, you're such a mess!" she'd say, which supposedly was a compliment.

My mother has all these funny sayings from having grown up in Alabama. (She's passed them on to me, too, and I'm not too sure I'm glad of that. Sometimes my friends, Northerners who've moved down here to get away from snow, can't understand what I'm saying, like when I tell them I'm fixin' to go fishing, and they say, "Why don't you just say go?" To me and my mom, it wouldn't be the same. There's a whole lot that goes into going somewhere, and, in that sense, fixin' makes sense.) One time soon after my dad moved out, Mrs. MacHenry paid me to baby-sit because, as she said, she was fixin' to drive my mother up the highway for some fun, which turned out to be The Flesh Paradise. They had male strippers there. Mom never did mention it. Only reason I ever knew that's where Mrs. MacHenry took her was that Mom'd insisted on leaving me a number where I could reach her. And then George threw up, and when I dialed the number, some deep-throated dude had answered, "Flesh Paradise." So I hung up. Told George Mom said it was just a two-hour virus, and he had only five more minutes before time was up. Which seemed to work, because George just sat down and watched "The Flintstones" on TV, ate a package of Cajun spiced potato chips, and fell asleep.

Now Mrs. MacHenry was coaching George on how to breathe. "Through your mouth, George. That's right. In. Out. Up. Down." And Mandy had picked up the movie star magazines and was sitting on the floor, reading them, or at least flipping through the pages.

Meanwhile, everybody in the waiting room was looking at George. It was as if any minute he could just keel over and die, like an old person barely hanging on. He sure was sucking that sucker like there was no tomorrow.

I didn't have a place to sit down, so I stood, leaning against the wall beside George. Then Mrs. Conner, my first grade teacher, came in. I hadn't seen her in a while. She didn't look good. She didn't look around, just walked straight up to Mrs. MacHenry's desk. "Is the doctor in?"

Since Mrs. MacHenry was standing with me, it was like Mrs. Conner was announcing the president or something. She just spoke her question out loud, and Mrs. MacHenry headed over.

Mrs. MacHenry's white uniform brushed against her hose, which sounded to me a little like a katydid. (In the Florida heat, women don't wear them often, but I've decided I really love the sound of stockings.) And all the while she was explaining: "Dr. Haley's up the highway, giving flu shots at a nursing home."

Mrs. Conner looked around. She'd always tried to come off as this sweet old lady, but she was the kind who'd give you pencils with no erasers and then make you stay in at recess for spitting on your paper and rubbing out mistakes. I could never understand why she had this thing about mistakes. She said we were supposed to not worry about them. But hell, even at six you know you make them, and want to fix them. In my book, that's normal.

"I have to see Dr. Haley today," she said, still looking around. "Do all these other people have appointments?"

Mrs. MacHenry sat down at her desk. "No. We do walk-ins. You just have to be willing to wait a while. Sometimes maybe even a long while."

Mrs. Conner leaned over closer, but there was no way an old first grade teacher could talk low. "Betty, I got this sore on my nose, you see, and I'm afraid it's cancer. I got to see him. I put a little of this medicine on it that I got from my sister. A little home remedy." She laughed. "But it hadn't gotten a bit better." She lifted up her Band-Aid."

I'd never heard that before—home remedy. It must have been the name of something an old person would use. But instead it sounded like something *we* ought to get—me, Mandy, George the Second, and especially Mom. Mrs. MacHenry looked at Mrs. Conner's nose. "Sure is some bump, Elaine. You better get it checked. I just don't know when exactly Dr. Haley'll get to you."

"So you think this is a bad bump, too?"

"Could be nothing. Could be a mosquito bite. Could be a passion hickey." She laughed, flashing her teeth. "Could be, I guess, something more serious like a skin cancer, or a wart. Why don't you just join in with the rest and wait."

"Guess I'll have to." Mrs. Conner looked around the waiting

room, then saw me. "Drew," she said, coming over. "Just look at you—all tall and nearly grown."

"Sort of." I grinned. I could never get over trying to get on her good side.

"And you're in your first year of high school?"

I grinned again. I knew she'd never thought I'd make it that far. And then it hit me: Mrs. Conner had this Band-Aid over her nose, and I could see this green medicine under it, oozing out. I guess it was her home remedy. And it smelled awful, all rotten and fishy. It made me think of something you'd get out of a swamp.

There was no place for either of us to sit down, so we were stuck standing beside each other. In a few minutes my mother came whizzing in, her face all red; and she'd been rushing like crazy, you could tell. She picked George up and set him on her lap and held his head real still against her.

Mrs. MacHenry came over, her white uniform crisp as a Ritz cracker. "I sent for Dr. Haley, Linda. He's on his way. I told him it was an emergency."

"God, thanks, Betty." Mom glanced up. Then, "Don't move, George." She clamped his head between her palms.

Mrs. Conner stepped closer. "Is he sick?"

"He's got a rock up his nose." My mother was petting George's cheek.

Mrs. MacHenry added: "Dr. Haley should be here any minute."

My mom was close to frantic. I could tell because she was stiff, trying to look good like she wasn't going to lose it and all, yet talking like her tongue had diarrhea. She does that when she gets nervous. It really bothers me to see her like that, and her voice climbing high: "I just wish I were closer; my job an hour away makes this so much harder. I worry, you know. Being that far. I need to get a job closer. Something that'll let me be here, near home. Something that'll . . ."

Mrs. MacHenry touched my mother's hand. "Let you raise your kids like you want to?" She laughed. "In Palm Key that means if you don't fish or oyster, then you got to stick to hairdressing, or punching a cash register, or waitressing till your feet are flat."

"Or teaching school." Mrs. Conner chimed in, leaning closer. Wow! Did she smell bad!

"Wasn't anything for me either," Mrs. MacHenry said, "till this clinic opened up. I've worn out the top layer of Highway 40 for over twenty years."

"You're gonna be fine, George." My mother was still rubbing his head.

Mrs. Conner bent down. "Bet you won't put anything up your nose after this." Then she reached out and touched his knee. He had on these cut-off overalls; he *did* look cute. Suddenly his nose crinkled up, and as Mrs. Conner got her own nose closer, George sneezed. The rock flew out of his nose and hit Mrs. Conner on the cheek, then fell to the floor between her shoes. "Lord-a-mercy!" she said.

Good shot, I thought.

My mother stood up. Mrs. Conner stepped back. My mother was still holding George, his feet dangling like wet clothes. And everybody was staring at the rock. The door opened, and Dr. Haley came in.

He walked straight over to my mom and George. "So, this the fellow with a little trouble?" He reached to take George out of my mother's arms. Boy, that guy was smooth.

My mother smiled. "I'm so sorry," she said. "I know you rushed back here." "It's okay," he said. "That's what I'm here for, to handle emergencies." "I just mean, it's not an emergency anymore." She looked down at the rug and pointed.

Dr. Haley stepped back, still holding George. He saw the rock my mother was pointing to, and then my mother added, "He just sneezed."

Dr. Haley looked at George. Then he laughed. "Well done," he said. He added that he ought to check George over just to make sure no damage was done.

As he carried George through the door to the other parts of the clinic, we all followed him. I don't know why. I guess we were morbid or so stuck together out of habit, we all just went with him. Mrs. MacHenry held open the examining room door, then came in, too.

Dr. Haley set George down on the treatment table and looked up his nose with a flashlight, while Mrs. MacHenry held his head. Boy, that guy was tall! Six-four, at least.

My mom was watching, but was still talking like her tongue was having a jerk-fit. I wished we could get her looked at next.

"I was just so worried it would go to his lung," she said. "I had to rush here; I just knew this wasn't something I should take lightly, but I'm so sorry we made you rush back."

"Not many people know something like that. How'd you know it could go to his lung?"

My mother looked at Dr. Haley, and for a minute she was quiet, her eyes squinted like she does when she's trying to think. Then she smiled and let loose, her words fast and hooked together. "I guess it's something I picked up when I was working for my uncle. I was fifteen, about Drew's age here—yes, just exactly Drew's age—and I had this thing about how I was going to be a doctor."

She smiled, then sort of laughed. "So my parents let me spend a summer with my uncle, working in his office. He was a pediatrician, and we had a lot of kids that summer with things up their noses." She laughed loud then. "I'd forgotten that."

He was watching her, holding that little flashlight thing and unscrewing it, and then he handed it to Mrs. MacHenry, and she put it away. George was now down to the end of his sucker.

"Did you go on to medical school?"

"No. My parents kept telling me it'd be best for me to be a nurse." She laughed again. "You know, that girl thing: We ought to be nurses, not doctors. Everything's changed now, thank God. But not then—and not to my parents."

Just then George started cutting up, wiggling around and wanting down from the examining table. "I want that rock," he said, heading for the waiting room.

Dr. Haley followed him; everybody was still there, and watching. We stood at the office door, watching, too, as Dr. Haley and just about everybody else in the waiting room got down on their hands and knees to help George find his rock. Then Dr. Haley came back into the examining room carrying George, with George holding the rock, and then Dr. Haley shut the door. "I have to listen to your chest, George," he said. "Make sure your lungs are clear. Won't take but a minute."

While my mother was taking off George's shirt, Mrs. MacHenry was handing Dr. Haley his stethoscope, and then before he put it in his ears, he said to my mom, "I've been wanting to hire a medical assistant or another nurse. We've gotten so busy. I had no idea this practice would be like this." Then he put the stethoscope tubes in his ears and put his head close to George's chest.

"Breathe deep, George," he said.

Mrs. MacHenry stood behind Dr. Haley mouthing: "Linda, if he offers you this job, take it." "Are you crazy?" Mom was shaking her head, her eyes wide, doing a no-go pantomime.

George was huffing and puffing in the background. "It's all right," Mrs. MacHenry whispered, "I'll cover for you. We don't need a R.N."

"But, Betty."

"Hell, I'm just an L.P.N. We don't need no genius. Just *do* it." She coughed, making a sound that covered part of her words, but since Dr. Haley had the stethoscope in his ears, me and Mandy were the only ones knowing what was going on, and maybe not even Mandy. She had this horrified look on her face, studying the reflex hammer on a little white table with a bunch of other things, probably trying to figure out which body parts all that stuff could be poked into.

My mother was breathing like George, coaching him. Then Dr. Haley pulled the things out of his ears and turned around. Both my mother and Mrs. MacHenry froze. "All clear," he said. "Must have been a lone rock."

My mother folded up George's shirt. She was mashing it up into this little square. "Thank God," she said. Then she smiled, adding, "and you." She had on this blue-and-white-striped suit, real neat. And her face was still flushed. She'd gotten into scarves in the last few months, and she had on a red one now draped over her shoulder. I don't know why, but she always dressed real fine to go to work at The Dump. "We've needed a doctor here for a long time," she said.

"So how about it?" He looked at her.

"How about what?"

Mrs. MacHenry was lifting George down off the treatment table, and she looked at my mom, her eyes glaring and rolling, with some blue stuff on her lids.

"You want the job?"

Dr. Haley was still looking at my mom; his mustache reminded me of the handlebars on a bike. I knew that in just a minute Mom was going to tell Dr. Haley the truth: that she'd gone to school to be an artist and didn't even finish that. *I* didn't even know she'd once had that nurse and doctor thing.

But instead she said, calm and quick, "Fine. Sounds wonderful. Give me two weeks."

She put on George's shirt, patted him on the back, made sure he had a close hold on his rock, thanked Dr. Haley again, and was standing in front of Mrs. MacHenry's desk by the time Mandy and I caught up. "I can't believe I did that," she was saying to Mrs. MacHenry.

"I can," Mrs. MacHenry laughed. "This is just the job you've needed all along. And don't worry. I'll help."

My mother reached over and touched Mrs. MacHenry's arm. "God, Betty. What would I do without you?"

Mrs. MacHenry grinned, "Not much. That's for sure." Her teeth parted her lips, reminding me a little of how my johnboat plows through the Gulf.

My mother laughed, "Betty, you're such a mess," she whispered, then added: "And by the way, send the bill to George the First." "Damn tootin'," Mrs. MacHenry said.

And we were out the door.

A second later, Mom stopped on the sidewalk, still holding George, looking stunned and just staring at the green Toyota parked at the curb. "Why did I do that? Am I losing my mind? What's wrong with me?"

Neither me nor Mandy nor George answered. Hell! What were we supposed to know? Besides, it wasn't our job. I didn't know what to say to women. Even if it was my mother who was asking, I didn't know what to say.

I watched her looking out across the street at nothing, her eyes glazed. "He didn't say he definitely wanted a nurse. He just said medical assistant. Didn't he say that first?" she glanced at us.

We were all nodding.

"Of course he did. I'm that. I can be a medical assistant. Betty's right. There's nothing wrong with that."

She pressed George close to her again. "I had to do it," she said. "I'll be here, close. I bet it even pays more. Anything would."

We were still standing, looking out into the street. Whenever Mom got stuck like that, we tried to just stay calm and wait it out. The sky was slate gray, almost dusk. The sun was hunkering down like an orange basketball, sweetly dunked and about to fall through the net of the Gulf. And then my mother opened the door to the Granny Apple and got in.

Mandy and George the Second got in the back, and I sat in front. "This is going to be fine. Really fine," she was saying.

She was still talking as she put the gear in D, and we blasted off onto the main road of Palm Key. We sped along the coast road and out to the airport. She was giving us a little spin, like we'd often done after those first few days when Dad moved out. "Let's get out of here for a while," she'd say, even sometimes late at night when we'd all be up watching movies. And we'd all get in the car, sometimes George asleep, and she'd drive and drive and drive. We'd skirt the Gulf, hugging the gray water and curling around it wherever it touched land. George would be asleep in my lap, the smell of his pajamas coming up over me, clean, sweet, and sour all at the same time—his head jostling in my lap like a warm melon.

And now we were driving out to the airport, which was just a big strip of pavement between marsh and ocean. Only little things could land, tiny private planes that came in on weekends like metal mosquitoes touching down. Sometimes the people flying them just taxied them up into the yards of their weekend houses and parked them. Which I guess said a lot about the kind of people who took a liking to Palm Key.

"Isn't this beautiful?" Mom parked beside the end of the runway. We looked out into the Gulf, where the sky at dusk reached the water in the same color.

The sun sat on the water for a long second, and we said goodbye to it as it slipped slowly down, then fell into the water and disappeared. The sky was now like gray cotton, thick and even, and swallowing the water, too.

Mom didn't start the motor, or even move. We just sat awhile, the windows rolled up so the little no-see-um bugs couldn't get in and eat us.

She was calmer now. Dressed up in the clothes she wore to work, she looked pretty fine—even though it's hard to be sure about how your mother looks. But she seemed to look businesslike, at least. And not bad for someone so old. And I could tell as she sat beside me that she was scared. Just practically about to lose it good after she'd taken a job she had no business taking. Except that the business was us.

I knew we were the reason she was staying in Palm Key. Same house. Same car, till only recently. Every day we get to see Dad. Even when she grounds us, she says that doesn't include Dad.

She'd do anything for us. Which, I guess, in the whole long run of things, is really probably the best of all things to know.

"Look." She pointed up into the sky out over the Gulf where a tiny plane was coming in, its lights like a net of stars. We sat there, watching, still, not saying a thing, following the path of the lights out over the water, and holding our breath at the mystery of how it could land in the dark.

We needed to see that.

4.
Linda

When the *Palm Key Sentinel* finally came out, Drew's wreck was on the front page. There was a picture of it, showing me standing beside the new doctor, both of us hanging our heads and staring at his Mercedes' grill, the engine smoking. Actually Mr. Clark, the Palm Key editor who took the picture, deserves a lot of credit. The smoke coming out of the car looks like a fine mist. And there in the corner is Drew holding George's hand, looking pitiful. The caption reads: *New doctor and new patient make a big hit. Related story on page four.* And then when you turned to page four, there was the write-up of George getting the rock stuck in his nose.

Guess there're worse reasons for getting famous.

Before I moved here, I'd never seen anything like a paper that had no big news, only everyday things and a running account of lives. Mr. Clark calls around every day and has two very busy ladies, spending a good part of every day phoning everybody to see what's new. Then he writes it up:

> Mr. Kapshaw's sister reports that he has been feeling

puny. But we saw him riding around in his truck, and he took his boat out last Wednesday. So he's sure hiding it well.

Mrs. Erlene Whittington slipped on an oyster bed and cut her foot. But two days later she made it back to the Dairy Dip. Says she gets along fine as long as she keeps her foot propped up on an ice cream vat.

Mr. Hughes had his children visit from Tampa for Sunday dinner. They had broiled flounder, green peas, grits, and hush puppies.

Mr. Tomas is also on the puny list with his arthritis cutting up. And we're sorry to hear that.

DeeDee Leeland's father passed. So sorry, DeeDee. We hope you'll call on us when you need anything. Betty MacHenry went over and fed DeeDee's cat, Lady Bird, while DeeDee was in Alabama at the funeral.

And we just found out, too, that Linda Marsh just found out that her husband George has been sticking it somewhere else. Wasn't anything to do, she said, but tell him to get out of their house and out of her life. After all, he was sticking it in the Palm Key fifth grade teacher, which, anybody would agree, was a definite conflict of interest.

That's, at least, the way I'd have written it up. Instead, Mr. Clark had put:

We just heard Linda Marsh and George Marsh are calling it quits. But George is staying on at the high school, where we've all come to count on him so much. Linda says she'll be looking for a job. Hopes to stay here. Y'all pass the word and help her out.

Of course, I didn't especially like having the end of my marriage appear in the paper like that. But at least it had been made to sound more matter-of-fact than like a funeral. And I was thankful for that. I think the worst thing you can do for somebody is to feel sorry for them. I didn't want sympathy, I wanted a job. I didn't want any "oh, you poor thing." I wanted a baby-sitter for George the Second. I didn't want kind whispers when I walked by. I wanted a ten-day cruise, a new car, my mortgage paid, and somebody to cut off George the First's dick and stick it up on the flagpole in front of City Hall.

(It took me three months just to get angry.)

Mark didn't come here until way after my dilemma appeared in the paper. So he wasn't offering me that job out of sympathy or anything else. He had a need, and I intended to fill it. And nobody needed to know that there was no nursing in my past. My past was my *own* business, and for all anybody need know, I was a full-fledged cousin to Florence Nightingale.

So when Mr. Clark called me, I told him what *he* needed to know. And the next week it appeared:

Our new medical assistant in Dr. Haley's clinic will be Linda Marsh. She starts next week. And we all think it's just fine. We didn't know Linda had all this ability in her past. But she says she's always been sitting on a lot. She also says she doesn't intend to give shots, so nobody need run away or treat her weird when they meet her on the street.

She just intends to generally help out and is real glad to be going to work in downtown Palm Key.

To Dr. Mark Haley that, too, would be sort of a formal announcement that I had my limits. He might as well read it before I got there. No way then would he take the job away from me; it'd already been splashed all over town. And the main thing I really was worried about was giving shots. I didn't know exactly what he had in mind for me to do. But I was dead-set on not killing anybody or getting sued. Never before had I been so cagey. I barely recognized myself.

I gave notice at The Dump and then drove to Gainesville to buy uniforms. I got these cute things: pantsuits, short skirts, foam-rubber shoes. It reminded me of the months when I was finding out about George.

•

Memories like old glue—dry, hard, still stuck: I am in the kitchen, fixing supper. He comes in the back door. Kisses me on the cheek like I am an old flounder. "Gonna leave the lumps in like you usually do?" He bends over my shoulder, looking at my white sauce. All those tiny little cuts, free-floating criticism—that kind of thing was new.

George is a good-looking man. Big shouldered, six feet, the features in his face even, no one thing too big or calling attention to itself, his hair with just a hint of salt since he turned thirty-eight. His eyes are hazel and have crinkles around them like he's laughed a lot. Guess he has. First with me. Then with Miss Teacher of the Year. (Hope they both laugh themselves into hernias.)

"Why chicken again?"

"It was on sale this week."

George the Second turns over his milk.

"That's all right, sport." His patience with his children is beyond generous. But with me: "I don't know why you insist on giving him milk in a glass. Why don't you give him a plastic one? Or a cup?"

In shock, I can not even defend myself. It is not so much what he says as the way he says it. His voice cold, businesslike. I am a clerk showing him bad goods. I am someone working for him who he wants to fire. I am someone sleeping with him who crowds the bed.

We made love like I was an old flounder, too. Flat, rolling along the bottom of the ocean, got to be spearfished quick, two eyes on one side. But from down there there was no light for me to see.

One day at a filling station I saw a sign: IF YOU THINK SEX IS A PAIN IN THE ASS, MAYBE YOU'RE DOING IT WRONG. And strange as that seems, it hit me: Maybe something really was wrong. Not just fatigue, boredom? Or three kids and fifteen years of getting worn out being on the same team?

"I don't know why you use this." He holds up the cream I bought for my coffee. "You're putting on weight. Your legs are flabby; won't be long before you have those dots in them like old ladies."

I went out and spent one hundred dollars on lingerie, charged it to him. Used his MasterCard. Well, they were all in his name. Wanted something beautiful next to my skin. I was sick of rough. Of ugly. I chose a chocolate-colored bra and matching hip huggers

My scalp began to tingle at odd times, as though I had taken too much cold medicine and was having a NyQuil high. But I didn't have a cold and had taken nothing.

It was not just the death of us that was wiring my body so strangely. *That* I could not yet quite totally believe anyway. It was something beyond that. I was being pushed to a place that was worse, a place I had never before visited and knew no rules for.

Several times, I tried: "Is something wrong, George?"

"No."

"Have I done something to upset you?"

"No."

Talking to him was pouring words into a drawer that he would not open.

I shopped for wine with twist-off caps. Anything more difficult to open was beyond anything I could deal with.

The sound of his voice, his irritation, criticism, awoke full-blown and growing in my mind each morning. I went through the grocery store in dark glasses with tears like standing pools beneath them. I hid my eyes from the children. I bought darker glasses, the lenses so dark and circular that I could be mistaken for someone blind. Yet it was just that I was beginning to see.

Over and over I tried: "Have I upset you, somehow?"

"No."

"What's bothering you, George?"

"Why? Why do you always think something is bothering me?"

He was surrounded by TV ball-game sounds, his mind stuck on scoreboards and yardage. He was so far away from me, he was an unknown person, a mislaid photograph that I was now hard pressed to recognize. The burst of irritation in his voice once so stung me that the next day, the words, the way in which he had said them, became a hard knot, growing, spreading so quickly that I drove out of town, spent the day in the first big store I came to: a china store, an outlet, a pretty place. George the Second was with me, and I put him in a shopping cart that I leaned against. There was nothing in the store I needed. Yet I kept moving through the aisles, waiting for something, looking for something that I had to have.

I walked up and down those aisles, picking up the discount plates, examining them, holding up the crystal, feeling the etching in the side of the glass with my fingers. Everything was overruns, seconds, discontinued designs. And beautiful. Yet that beauty, that thought, was something I only recognized in my mind. It was a flat thought: like the dishes need washing, the world is round, my name is Linda. George the Second was busy with a sucker I had bought for him.

For several hours without any thoughts, with only my senses being fed, I walked around the china store. The clerks looked at me. I went up one aisle, then another. I examined everything. I picked up pieces so delicate they were like pieces spun from glass hair. I rubbed my fingers against them, ducked my head so no one would see as I licked a crystal glass's rim so thin it could cut flesh. Near the last of the second hour, I could feel the heavy blackness lift a little. Suddenly I stopped and stood in the aisle of the checkout counter. This was why—now I knew—I was afraid to leave here, why I had to be somewhere, anywhere, where people would be around me to hold me in place: so the thoughts of suicide and my abandoned children would back away from me. I grabbed a handful of orange napkins at a dollar and a half apiece and checked out. They matched nothing I had.

So the closest I came to falling, and not getting out, was saved by my simple and honorable female habits: How could I kill myself in the afternoon and still be home to fix my children's supper?

Finally, The Night of Knowing. I had set the table with the orange napkins, which, after we ate, I threw in the washer. He and I both went into the living room. Drew had walked George the Second and Mandy downtown to a movie. I sat across from him. He was watching a game on TV—basketball, baseball; I didn't know. I wasn't registering much that was going on in the exterior world; I was broken, cracked, the seams no longer holding. Tears leaked down my face. He told me the season's history of this player, of that player. He asked me if I had bought any butter pecan ice cream. He did not look at me, and he did not see my tears. I brought the whole half-gallon carton of ice cream and set it down roughly on the coffee table in front of him. I opened the cardboard flaps and stuck a spoon in, then turned silently and walked into the bedroom.

"What is the meaning of this?" He stood in the doorway holding the ice cream. I looked at him. I knew my eyes were red; I blew my nose. "Oh my God," he said. "What's wrong now?"

The irony struck me: Fifteen years ago, or ten, or two, he would have quickly come into the room, knelt by the bed, and held me—so attuned to any hurt that I might have had, and the words that he would say would have been almost the same, only rearranged and in a soft, worried tone that, alone, would have soothed me: "God, Lin, what's wrong? Is it something I've done?"

But the words were said so differently now, at this time when no love or liking was left. I looked at him and told him, "Nothing about our marriage is working, George." He sat down. "I know."

"What should we do?"

"I don't know. But I feel the same way."

"Does that mean—are you saying we should separate?" I used the milder word—a test, like poking something with a sharp stick to see if it would move. And I, of course, expected him to say, God, no. "Is that what you want?" I prompted.

"Do you?"

Did I? Then I said, "I know only that I want something to change." It felt as though I was playing a board game, moving a stick man to a different square, seeing where he would move in response.

His eyes were on the wall, not on me. "Yes," he said. "I think we should."

Yes, he had said. Yes, this was where he was headed, where I was leading him, or pushing him.

The children came in. The front door slammed. He walked out of the room to go greet them.

Even though the words I had just spoken were mostly a way to get something said, even the most horrible said, they seemed to relieve me of so much that strangely I felt better, almost at peace. And then my body began to shake.

I was lying on the bed when Drew came in to tell me about the movie he had just seen. He told me the whole boring plot. George the Second came in, too, to give all the sound effects. Mandy sat on the foot of my bed, her hair mussed, a dot of chocolate on the left side of her mouth. I nodded unconsciously, smiling, looking at Drew, but not seeing anyone's face.

"What's wrong, Mom? Are you sick? Are you having a chill?"

It was three days later that I heard them on the phone: George and Miss Fifth Grade Teacher of the Year. All I had to do was listen. His voice light. He laughed. Then again. Then a lot. He was rubbing his cheek with his hand. Shifting his weight where he stood by our fridge. And it struck me. Clarity like crystal. He was in love with her. He loved *her.* That's why he was irritated, tired of, short, no longer amused with, angry at me: I, simply, was not her.

Is this true, George?

Didn't take him long to own up. Didn't take him long to pack up and move out either.

Didn't take me long to see, too, that by pushing me to mention the word "separate," which quickly moved to "divorce," relieved him. Watered down his guilt. He could always say I'd asked for it.

Black holes? Let me tell you about black holes. And not just the ones in space. But where I was headed. The place for which buying underwear was no cure.

I had been my mother's child. I had been my father's child. I had known what it was to be loved, cherished. And then passed to George, to be loved, cherished as his wife.

I had never known what it was like not to be.

Suddenly I was a song that no one was familiar with. Did not even hum. A painting no one saw. I was in a blackness and darkness that was more than death. My heart beat, but inside me nothing moved.

•

I reported for my first day at work at the clinic in a white pantsuit, a little crest on the pocket like I was ship shape.

"God, you look wonderful," Betty MacHenry said, taking me aside as soon as I walked in. "He's in his office, and before you meet with him I want to just show you a few things." She led me to the bathroom. We got in this one little space the size of a closet. Betty was giggling like we were teenagers trying to sneak into a movie, or hiding in the bathroom to light up a Kent. She rolled the blood pressure cuff onto my arm and pumped it up. She showed me how to read the dial, to put the stethoscope in my ears, the whole thing. Then she took if off and said, here, do it to me.

I pumped her up, read it wrong the first time, then got it right. "Good heavens, Betty, isn't that high?"

"Yeah. But I cut out all salt yesterday, and with you here, I'm gonna take a day off and go fishing."

She patted me on the back as we walked out of the bathroom.

Dr. Haley was walking out of his office into the waiting room. It was pretty embarrassing for us as he saw Betty and me coming out of the bathroom together, giggling like bimbos. "Thought we'd just go in there and clean it up a bit," Betty said, walking off to her desk, and calling back: "Don't leave the Lysol in there, Linda."

"Right," I yelled. Then "Morning" to him. And I smiled.

He had on a blue-and-white-striped shirt and a navy tie. Solid gray pants. Under his mustache his mouth moved. "Morning," he said back. Then laughed. "So, I read in the paper you don't intend to give shots?"

I glanced down nervously. Then the only thing I could think of to do was to laugh. "No. Well. You see . . ." And then there I went: carving a little of the truth out. "The other day when you hired me, you didn't ask me if I'd finished nursing school. The thing is, you see, I thought you were hiring a medical assistant, or a nurse's aide, something like that. I didn't get to the part in nursing school where you learn to give shots."

"Oh?"

"No. You see, I got married, and then I got pregnant, and I wasn't in school when they were going over the shots part." I smiled at my own joke, hoping he would. And he did—a movement under his mustache, so that the ends sort of wagged. What I said was a stretched-out detour, but still, aiming for the truth.

"I see."

"Yeah."

"Well."

He walked into his office, telling me to come, too, all the while talking: "I thought anyway, we'd use you to take histories and vital signs, and then do a little public health."

He handed me a pamphlet. "For the next few days, I'd like you to go to this CPR class. And then you can answer all these requests from around town, like teaching CPR at the high school and at the Rotary Club and to The Seamen's Association."

He was going to have me teach CPR at the high school? Maybe even to George!

"Sure," I said. I took the pamphlet from him. (It'd have been a pleasure to beat on George's chest. Or on hers.)

Dr. Haley smiled. I noticed in his hair there were little rusty red streaks, and on the sides a good bit of gray. He sat down behind his desk. "You've lived here long?"

"Yeah. Fifteen and a half years. Just drove down the coast and fell in love with it."

"Lucky," he said. I saw lines on either side of his mouth. They made him look tired. I saw that his eyes were a light color, mostly gray; and I noticed the tan mole in front of his right ear that reminded me of a thumbprint. The whole impression of him—hair, skin, eyes—was that if I were to paint him I would do it mostly in one color, just change the degrees of shading. Creams and wheat yellows, grays like water. But before we had time to talk about anything else—or for him to ask me questions about my nursing past (thank God)—Betty opened the door and stuck her head in. The waiting room was filling up with morning walk-ins, she said. "It's just about like somebody said we were giving out free lottery tickets," she added.

So all day long, I pumped up the blood pressure thing. Put checks beside measles, mumps; wrote in close relatives' names. Filled in the onset of menses and listed any operations in the proper squares. I committed only one big mistake when, probably because I was concentrating so hard on filling in the forms, I asked Mr. Tuttle when he had his onset of menses. And before I realized what I had done, he answered that to the best of his recollection it must have been last winter. I looked up from my clipboard, the sound of his deep voice making me realize what I had done. Even though I had been assigned to doing mostly public health, I didn't take it upon myself to straighten Mr. Tuttle out. I figured he was as entitled to have an onset of menses as the rest of us. "Any allergies?" I asked.

"Bumblebees," he said.

By the end of the day, I had learned more about the citizens of Palm Key and people living on the outskirts than I ever wanted to know. And I knew that about every bit of it, I was sworn to keep my mouth shut, which also meant that if that clinic job didn't work out, I wasn't suited for the *Palm Key Sentinel* either.

The next day I went to the county hospital to begin the CPR certification course. By the time I drove home that afternoon, I'd been given my own Annie doll, the CPR dummy that I would practice on and use for demonstrations. I put her in the backseat.

That night at home, I took her out and laid her on the living-room floor. For a while the kids were fascinated with her, then went back to watching TV. But every once in a while, I noticed them glancing over at me. For I was kneeling on the floor over Annie, shaking her rubber shoulders, and calling out: "Annie, Annie, are you okay?"—which was the beginning of the whole routine that I was learning. Eyes half closed, her skin hard plastic the color of bubble gum, her chest soft cloth where I pressed with the heels of my hands against her. I pushed and pushed and pushed, listening for air.

I know this might sound strange, but it really was sort of a thrill: pumping away on Annie, breathing into her, putting my mouth down on her plastic lips—learning to breathe life into someone who might be about to lose it. Practicing.

5.

Drew

It was the weekend, a Saturday. The Granny Apple wouldn't start, and Mr. Duffy had come out from the Handymart with a new battery. He'd leaned up under the hood for a long while, then, when he had gotten it started, knocked on the kitchen door. We were all inside eating Cream of Wheat with raisin toast and Mom's homemade applesauce. She wouldn't let us eat the kind you can buy at a store, because she was afraid they'd left pesticides in it. Mr. Duffy grinned as Mom offered him some. His hands were big as bear paws holding the jar that he walked out with.

Then Mom headed to the clinic to cover for Mrs. MacHenry, who was going out fishing. They were keeping the clinic open all day, a new schedule for every other Saturday.

George the Second and I went out onto the porch, to wait for Dad. Mandy was on a church retreat, out at a campground on the Suwannee River. She'd left the night before. Every once in a while, Mom makes us get deep into religion, says if we get a big taste of it now, we might not run off and join a cult later—which, overall, she says, would break her heart. I get the point, because then she might have to give up her own preaching, which she does often and late at night to me and Mandy. Says the one thing she most wants for us is that we never lose the ability to think for ourselves. But so far she hasn't let us get much practice. My mom can hold on to you tighter than a python.

George the Second and I watched Dad drive up in his new red Mustang, Anne Marie beside him. They were married now. I watched them walk across the front yard, their feet sliding on the sand between the tufts of grass. Our yard grows grass the way sweaters pile up fuzz.

"Hey sport!" Dad yelled as he reached out to swing George the Second onto his shoulder, because George was already climbing up on him. Anne Marie first smiled at George the First, then at George the Second. And then they were all looking at me. I wasn't going, I was saying. Didn't want to really go today. The agenda was the Dairy Dip and then a show. I wanted to watch the Dolphins on TV, I told them.

"Oh, yeah." Dad smiled. He had on a Redskins sweatshirt and jeans. "Supposed to be a good game." I was surprised he was missing it. He knows football the way I know fish. In high school he used to play. In fact, the old pictures of him in his uniform are what I mostly think of as what he looks like. The other ones, of him in a beard, don't seem right. And to tell you the truth, I know I'm breaking him up by not going out for the Palm Key Manatees. But with my grades I'd get kicked off before I got going good, and with my build, which might be tall like him but with Mom's bird bones instead, I'd get killed.

"I'm taping it," he said. "Want to come over later and see it?"

"Guess not. Have a lot of history. A report and all."

"Well, we'll bring you something," he said. "A fudge sundae, a Coke float."

He was always dying for me to do homework.

Anne Marie smiled at me. "Bye, Drew."

Frankly I didn't want to spend the afternoon with them because of her. I liked women and thinking about them and learning all about them. But I hated the way she licked ice cream. Her mouth down all over the top like she was going to smother it first. And in the movies she always held my father's hand, patting it and moving it around on her lap. She bore down on me, too, always talking about how cute my ears are. I know ears, and mine aren't especially cute. She's just hard up for something to say. Last week I made a list to remind myself of how I don't want to be when I get to be their age: Number one was not to ever have a beer belly and a fat butt. Number two was not to have a fishing boat that won't go over thirty or is not the sweetest piece of metal ever to hit water. And coming close was the promise to myself that I'll never settle my kids' fights without first making it clear which one is right and who is the real pain in the ass. And last, and maybe most important of all, is that I know I'll never get married to anybody who talks about ears. Or trade in one woman for another, especially when the second one is a certified ditz.

I watched Anne Marie and Dad and George walk back to the car, get in like a car commercial, the doors shutting crisp, heavy, not yet falling off or shutting crooked.

Then I went to lie on the couch and just hang out, watch a little TV—all by myself. During the night, a cold front had blown in off the Gulf. It probably wouldn't last but half a day. By afternoon we'd be peeling off clothes like the skins of ripe bananas. And the sky was so blue, it hurt. The sheepshead were biting. I was dying to go out and fish, too. But I'd been so busy babysitting George the Second while Mom carted her CPR dummy all with lots of lace. I was my own new bride, trying to find in me the part that was once lovable, that once set him on fire, the part that still could. And all the while charging it to him.

The hint that we were dying was like an odor, a chemical leaking out into the air, surrounding me as I breathed. The chocolate panties were slit up the side. I bought purple ones and pink ones, too, and lacy push-up bras—all matching. I'd never matched tops with bottoms before, ever. Wearing them I felt better—yes, I could take care of myself, protect and provide for my most private parts. And I was doing fine until about thirty minutes after I had on the chocolate hip huggers, when they began to ride up while shopping in the grocery store. I had to slip behind a display of frozen hams to pull them down.

But that night I was brave. I trotted across the bedroom floor, flaunting chocolate. George was propped up in bed behind a magazine. I dropped a tube of toothpaste to make him look up. At the sound, he glanced at me. Then away. Then back to *The American Educator.* I knew then, we were gone. No appetite for even chocolate.

First big clue: He no longer laughed at my jokes. I laughed alone, a big belly-driven whoop that he only stared at. Soon I, too, was drowning in silence. Hard, sticky silence. It pulled on my skin. Took out all my color. He was gone a lot. Meetings. He was working late.

My throat began to not let things go down it easily. It even began to make odd noises, like only air being squeezed can make—a *kathump* sound. So then I wondered if I had the beginnings of a weird throat disease. Would I lose my voice and not ever be able to say what already I was too afraid to speak?

over everywhere, that I hadn't had a chance to work on my boat motor, make sure it wouldn't quit.

I was glancing out the window at old Ms. Osprey poking around and rearranging herself in her nest—a regular June Cleaver, too—when the phone rang.

"Drew?" It was Mandy, and her voice sounded all out of breath and high.

"Yeah?"

"You got to call Mom."

"Why?"

"Quick."

"What's wrong?"

"I can't breathe."

"What?"

"I'm allergic to my sweater. Can't catch my breath."

"Mandy, it's a long way out there. Why don't you just sit down and wait a minute? See if it doesn't quit."

"I've done that! I'm swelling up, Drew. Call Mom."

"Listen, Mandy, I've never heard of anybody being allergic to their sweater. Just take it off, or sit down and think about something else."

"Call Mom, Drew. I'm telling you to call Mom."

"Mom's busy. I can't just call up down at the clinic and tell her she has to drive up there and get you because you're allergic to your sweater. You want her to get fired?"

"Then you come get me. Come get me, Drew. If you don't come get me, I'm going to die."

"Mandy."

"Drew." And then she let out a gagging sound.

"You're at the Suwannee Bend Campground?"

"Umhumm." And then she gagged again.

"Hang on, Mandy. We'll be there soon as we can."

I hung up the phone and picked it up again to call Mom. Then put it down again. I didn't know what was wrong with Mandy, but I knew what would be wrong with Mom if I called her and told her about this. She'd freak out, totally: first about Mandy and then about having to leave her job. She'd had to pull out three days in her first two weeks, because George had had a virus and couldn't go to day care. And, too, I knew she wouldn't exactly be crazy about having to barrel into the clinic with Mandy because she was allergic to her sweater, right after George had had to be rushed in with his rock, not to mention that Dr. Haley's Mercedes was still wearing its smashed nose, courtesy of me.

So I could either go alone and break the law; or get someone to ride with me, someone old. I ran down the street to Mr. Clark's. He had the only driveway with a car in it. Everybody else was either out fishing or shopping. But in his front yard, I changed my mind. I thought about him being the newspaper editor, and I didn't want Mandy's sweater written up. In fact, as I stood there in Mr. Clark's front yard looking at the boat rope he had wrapped around a pole at the edge of his driveway as a decoration, I felt ashamed. About as embarrassed as if I'd thrown up at the public boat ramp. It'd been bad enough having my father leave home to live with my sister's teacher, and me have a wreck with the new doctor right in the beginning of the Shrimp Festival. But also now my mom was blowing into this dummy's mouth all over town at whatever club meeting asked her to come: the P.T.A. and the Women's Club. The Elks and Mooses. I even had to watch her do it in the high school gym when they called a schoolwide assembly. It wasn't something you could be real proud of: seeing your mom bending over, blowing through some other woman's lips, even if the lips belonged to a dummy. I'm not the only one in my school without much of anything but sex on their minds—and while my mom was down on top of Annie, there was all this snickering and carrying on in the background in the bleachers.

Now I just turned around, sprinted home, got the keys to the Pekingese Ford. I'd decided I was going to do it, solo. My main problem would be getting out of Palm Key, where the roads are narrow and anybody could look in, see me driving alone, know I was breaking the law. I didn't want to get arrested or have my driving written up in the paper again. And so I ran into the house, got that CPR Annie. (Maybe all my family's craziness was catching.)

I carried her out of the house and to the car, first making sure nobody was around. Annie didn't have much of a backbone, just lay across my arms like a dead cat. This whole thing, I knew, could look like a murder, like a kidnap, or like I had a drunk date.

But only Ms. Osprey, up there on her pole, was watching, thank God. And I strapped Annie into the front seat. Then got in to see how we looked together.

Eyelids half closed like she was on drugs. Hair yellow as egg yolk. No bottom—just cut slap off below the waist—and with no boobs to speak of.

But there was something about her face that looked like she was mature and knew what she was doing. Even at a distance, anybody would think she was my certified driver.

It'd be just my luck, though, if there was a roadblock somewhere along the way looking for some serial murderer or drug dealer.

We came to *the* stoplight. It was red, and I had to just sit there. In the Pekingese Ford, everybody would know who I was right away. I might as well smile and talk to Annie like I was having my first hot date. For all anybody knew, I could be headed out to the cemetery with an older woman.

I drove toward the highway between the marshes. The water was sitting on the earth like a glass plate. And the air smelled so good, I rolled down the window, even hung my elbow out. The salt air was so fresh, I wanted to bite it. Everywhere the palm trees were moving their leaves like wings.

Just on the other side of town, I passed the Dairy Dip. Saw my dad's car, and him and Anne Marie and George the Second sitting at a picnic table, eating. I was not too worried about them looking up and seeing me. Dad and Anne Marie always had their eyes stuck on each other's like their eyeballs had been dipped into Krazy Glue.

The road out to the Suwannee was long and empty. At night it's hard to drive through here, so many deer. You have to have a deer whistle on the front of your car to scare them off, so you won't hit them and maybe even kill yourself. But it was early afternoon now, and I made a turn toward where I knew Mandy was.

I parked a long way away in the parking lot. From that distance, anybody could think Annie in the car was just someone who'd come with me, even my mom. I walked up to the main cabin, opened the door.

"Drew!" Mandy yelled, jumping on me the minute I walked in.

Mrs. Farrigut was sitting against the wall. The last time she'd been waiting with Mandy, she'd had on her Girl Scout uniform, which had made her look something like a big green tomato. Today she had on loose blue jeans and a sweatshirt that said PALM KEY, THE PLACE WHERE YOU CAN DO NOTHING. She stood up and walked over to me. "I don't think this is anything serious. But I don't know much about allergies." "I don't either," I said.

"Bet that new doctor does," she said. "Dr. Haley. I hear he can do wonders. How's your mother like working for him?" She handed me Mandy's red sweater, sealed in a Ziploc bag.

"Fine."

"Well, I'm just real glad he offered her the job. That was sure nice, wasn't it?"

"Really was," I said, smiling. This was one of the first real adult conversations I'd ever had, what with it seeming like I was being treated like an equal, with my opinion being asked right out for and all. And having to come up with stupid answers and pretending like I cared about them was pretty stressful, too. Then I could feel Mrs. Farrigut looking at me real close, and it made me feel like I was in a lineup and she was choosing me. "I guess your mother's there right now," she said. "I read in the paper they were keeping the clinic open today for flu shots."

"Well, no," I said. And then I started talking about as smooth as I could get. "As a matter of fact, she's sitting out in the car. I only have a driver's permit, so she has to be with me. And Dr. Haley gave her a few minutes off—that's why we're in a big hurry. We're going to drive Mandy straight to the clinic, get her looked at 'n' all. Mom was just too tired to come in, told me to just run in and get Mandy." I smiled again.

Mandy shot me a look of pure terror. Now the last thing I wanted her to do was to suddenly get well just so she could stay at camp. Then Mrs. Farrigut would probably want to go out to the car and talk to Mom. "Let's get a move on," I said to Mandy and halfway winked so maybe she'd know I was shooting a bunch of bull about going to the clinic. But part of me was so pissed at her for breaking up my afternoon that I wanted her to suffer.

Mrs. Farrigut patted Mandy on the back. "Hope you feel better," she said as we went out the door and down the cabin steps.

Having that adult conversation had stressed me out even more by having to lie my ass off through most of it. And now as I watched Mandy walking beside me, I knew that probably I hadn't been the only one shooting a bunch of bull, either. The only difference was, Mandy just didn't know she'd been doing it. Because the whole time I'd been talking to Mrs. Farrigut, Mandy had been scratching all up and down her arms and, every once in a while, dipping down to run her fingernails over her knee. But now she was just walking like normal and she was looking up at me and whispering, her voice with just as much panic in it as when she had called me at home, but now for a different reason: "I don't have to go to the clinic, do I, Drew? I just need to get home. Take a bath or something." I looked down at her and she was looking pretty pitiful.

I didn't answer her right off, though. She needed to sweat it out for a while. And then I just said that grown-up thing that, when I was little, used to really piss the hell out of me: "We'll see." Usually Mandy wore two ponytails that sprang out over the tops of her ears—a hairdo that Mom called Dog Ears. Mom had explained to me—as though I ever wanted to know—that pigtails were braids, and two ponytails on the sides of a girl's head looked like cocker spaniel ears and so that's why she called them what she did. Today, Mandy's dog ears were clipped with two yellow round balls, happy faces on each of them, that Mom had gotten for her at the grocery store. And the ends of her dog ears were bouncing against the sides of her neck as she ran on ahead of me to the car. I walked like somebody twenty or thirty, the car keys slung over my second finger, and I could see that Annie was slumped over a little in the car now. I was also aware of Mrs. Farrigut still standing on the cabin porch behind us, watching, and then I could hear her: "Your mother *does* look tired," she called out after me. "She must be really working hard."

"Yeah," I sang back. "She's really been digging in."

"Mandy stopped beside the car, staring in the window. "Why's Annie here? Where's Mom?"

"Still at the clinic. You know I can't drive without someone in the car."

She looked at me. "You mean you brought Annie and not Mom?"

I nodded.

And then Mandy accused me of the truth: "You mean you were just lying to Mrs. Farrigut?"

"That's one way of putting it." I opened the car door on the driver's side.

Mandy unbuckled Annie, pushed the dummy over, and sat down in Annie's place, so that now Annie was shoulder to shoulder between us. "This is cool, Drew," Mandy said. "Really cool." I backed up slowly and we both waved to Mrs. Farrigut, then I picked up Annie's arm and made out like she was waving, too. The fact that Annie was a blond and Mom was a brunette, didn't faze Mrs. Farrigut. At this distance, it might just seem that Mom had turned white-headed overnight. She had enough reasons to.

Mandy looked at Annie. "We can just drive anywhere like this—can't we, Drew? Even up to Canada."

I aimed the car back up the dirt road to the highway. Annie

was not much taller than Mandy, but she had an old look to her face, a wide solidness that I'd noticed on women at the checkout counters in grocery stores, or behind typewriters in offices, like they'd handled a lot. But then Annie had been beaten on and breathed into all over town, and then some. So maybe once she had looked better.

"Let's go to Canada, Drew. Don't you want to go to Canada?"

Mandy was staring out the front window now, looking happy, her mouth doing a little twist at one side, those happy faces riding tight at the top of her dog ears. She didn't seem allergic to anything. She didn't seem to have a bit of trouble breathing. I could still see the little closed-up hole in her ear, left from a few months before when I had gone with her to get the jeweler downtown to pierce her ears.

I knew she didn't want to go to Canada. Halfway anywhere she would have screamed and had me turn back. She had yet to even leave home to spend the night out with a friend. And if we had headed up to Canada, I would still have had to escort her to every bathroom on the way and to every one up there. She had Canada on her mind only because she had been doing a geography unit on it.

I glanced over at her as I pulled out onto the highway. She had buckled herself in just like Mom had always taught us to. It was a reflex now.

The day she and I got our ears pierced together had been the summer before, when I'd been doing a lot of baby-sitting for Mom while she got started at The Dump. It was right before the weekend when Dad had decided to take us to Disney World, drive down for the day with all of us and with Anne Marie. They weren't married then.

I had decided I'd try out a Rod Stewart haircut, something I'd had on my mind to do for some time. Got Mr. Tellis the barber to give me the cut, only he didn't know he was doing it. I just told him I wanted it the same length just about all over, then when I got home, combed it all straight out, and moussed it hard to hold it because my hair's sort of curly. Then went to the drugstore and bought spray-on color. Seemed like what I was doing was catching, just kept rolling along, getting more and more fun and bigger.

When I decided to get a gold stud put in my ear, Mandy talked me into taking her downtown to the jewelry store, too. Actually it's an art gallery for jewelry, a real with-it place, and a guy there who calls himself Red Herring—wears a ponytail—makes silver earrings and other stuff and pierces ears. I knew he wouldn't mind fixing me and Mandy up; in fact all the time he was fitting us with his earrings, he kept saying, "Cool. Really fine. I'm telling you, y'all going to be *tough*." And he put two pink earrings on Mandy, made out of shells. George the Second had walked downtown with us. We'd had no place to leave him anyway. And even though he didn't want to get a hole put in his ear—screamed the whole time Mandy got punched—he got dead-set on getting a temporary tattoo put on his arm. Red Herring was more than happy to oblige with that. He put the tattoo decal on George real carefully, smoothed it out—an eagle with a rose in his claws, and we went home. Then George asked me and Mandy to give him a new haircut, which we were more than happy to oblige him with, too. In the bathroom we trimmed the sides and front, then left him a tail down the back of his neck, like a little sweaty handle that I sprayed red. In a way we matched, or at least looked like we belonged together, all in jeans—except for George who had on his railroad overalls—and with some part of our hair sprayed red.

When Mom walked in from The Dump, she stopped in the living room where we were all sitting in front of the TV, and she sucked in her breath. She said low, a little bit like she had something stuck in her throat: "My God. My babies!"

It took only about a few hours of stony quiet for the first effect to wear off of her, during which we all stared at the TV, and she kept throwing out these spicy little questions during commercials, like: "Is there anything you all want to talk about?" "Are any of you worried about next week when I go to court and the divorce is made final?" "Are any of you having nightmares?"

To which we all just shook our heads and kept staring at the tube.

Then by the next day, even Mom had seemed to catch the mood and was up early, cooking us Belgian waffles, and singing "Don't Worry, Be Happy."

She gave us each an extra ten dollars for spending money. So when Dad walked in to pick us up to take us to Disney World, Mom smiled at him, dangling a pancake spatula in one hand: "The children are all ready for you, George."

You'd think he'd be real strict, being the Palm Key principal and all. He'd had a good bit of child psychology and interpersonal communication or something like that—went to night school when I was little, I still remember. I've always wondered if he passed. And there he must have learned that the best thing he could ever do in just about any trouble at school was to let it blow over. When you're the size he is, all you have to do is walk down the hall and practically everything blows over. Sometimes the idea of making trouble doesn't even get up. The only stand I ever remember him taking was when he stopped suspending people. Found out they were all out fishing in their boats and liked that better than school anyway. So now he just gives detention. Makes kids stay after and clean the bathrooms.

In a school where there're only about fifteen seniors every year, how tough do you have to be, anyway?

That day Mandy, George, and I got in the convertible with Anne Marie in front, staring at us. Dad got behind the wheel. "A little self-expression going on," he said, pulling away from the edge of our front yard and heading out for I-75.

The top down on the car put some final touches on our hair. And George was sitting between me and Mandy squirming like a gigged toad. Then about fifteen minutes from Disney World, he yelled: "I got to pee."

"Just a few more miles and we're there!" Dad had to yell because of the top being down and the traffic whizzing by. "Can you wait?"

"No."

George was hanging over the back of the front seat.

"I could stand to stop, too," Anne Marie said, rolling her hand over her hair that was blown nearly as wild as ours.

Dad pulled over to a glass building, a souvenir shop. We all got out and walked in. We went into the bathroom, one at a time, then had to wait as, one at a time, we all came out. And that gave us plenty of time to look over the loot in the store.

Mom's ten dollars was burning through the pocket of George the Second's overalls, and before I knew it, he was checking out with a bag of Malt Balls—the little round chocolate candies we called Moth Balls—and a slingshot packed in cellophane.

"Aw, God, George," I said. "You're not going to have any money for when we get there."

"Dad'll give me some more."

"Well, don't let him see you've got this stuff then."

George knew what I was talking about. One of the first things we understood after Dad moved out was that if he was giving money to Mom to use on us, when we went out with him, he didn't believe in giving it to us twice. If we had none at all with us, that was a different thing. But he always preferred using hers.

George stuffed the slingshot and Malt Balls into his pockets.

Then Anne Marie came out of the women's room, and Dad came out of the men's room, and we all got back into the car.

When we went through the Disney World ticket gates, the people working there looked hard at us. I don't think we were exactly what they liked to see walking around the Magic Kingdom. And Anne Marie was pretty embarrassed at us, too. Suggested to Dad that he buy us Mickey Mouse ears, which I knew meant she thought part of our hair would be hidden and held down if he just got us the hats. But the only one of us who agreed to that was George, and his little red tail trailed out anyway from under his black Mickey ears like a sunburned worm dangling down his neck.

We sure had an awesome time, though. Anne Marie got stuck with Mandy at the top of the Dumbo ride when it broke down, and they had to sit up there for a good fifteen minutes while it got fixed. Both of their heads were sticking out of Dumbo, baking in the sun. But Mandy kept waving at us, just practically loving her extra long ride. And then we went into The Pirates of the Caribbean to cool off.

When George saw we were going to get into boats, he grabbed all the barrettes out of Mandy's hair and put them on himself. I guess he figured it was the only life preserver he could get. Anne Marie was sitting so close to Dad, squashed all up against him and holding his hand, that the rest of us couldn't even get close.

We spent all afternoon walking around together and riding everything that George wasn't afraid of. Dad insisted we stick together—which I knew meant he was trying to mash us into a new family with Anne Marie. But all it meant was that we had to do a lot of stuff that was way too young for me.

Then in the middle of the afternoon he suggested we climb The Swiss Family Treehouse, a giant thing with little rooms all up in it, definitely George's speed.

Anne Marie was leading. She has this cheery voice and rushing way—all arms and legs waving and skirt flying—like she's gotten stuck in Cheerleader World. Climbing in the hot sun seemed as much fun to her as going to a yard sale. She was acting like a bigger kid than any of us. And making me sick. She was flirting with Dad. In one more week she'd have him for good, all on paper and everything. If only he wanted to, he could push her out of the tree that we were halfway up now. I knew that if he had any sense, he would. We all needed him a whole lot more than she did. Anybody could see that.

"Last one to the top is a rotten egg," she yelled, trotting up the wooden steps, showing her legs, swishing her skirt. I looked behind me; we were all panting. George wasn't on the step or even the platform under me. I stopped, looked past the other people coming up. I thought he'd probably stopped to sit down. But then I saw him, the stripes of his overalls like a blown piece of paper that had landed way out on the end of a branch. God! We should have been watching him. Dad had forgotten George was so little. Anne Marie required so much herself. And I should have been the one taking up the slack, watching George. But there he was, out there on the end of the limb unwrapping his Malt Balls.

"Dad!" My voice cracked. I called again. Below us the staff had seen George, too. About six guys in uniforms were pointing up, two of them bringing a net and unwinding it.

My dad stopped on the step a good way above me and looked back, then yelled: "George! My God."

Anne Marie turned around, saw George the Second, too. "Oh, for God's sake, Little George!"

Now there was a whole group of people on the ground, looking up; and everybody in the tree was standing, frozen, looking at George the Second, too, with a low whispering and gasping like leaking balloons.

Dad was heading out onto the limb. "Sit tight, George."

George had his slingshot unwrapped and had switched off sucking his Malt Balls to shooting them. He was aiming at the tree's fake leaves, sitting in the fork of two limbs. If he ever looked down or realized where he was, I thought he'd panic, at least I would have. But George seemed to be having a ball, was probably just playing out his fantasy of being in The Swiss Family Robinson.

There's no rhyme or reason to George, though. He's all reflex. Mandy's barrettes were still in his hair, and he was firing off Malt Balls like he was in the final scene of *Star Wars,* killing off the evil empire. Then as my father crawled close, whack, one landed right on his cheek. George looked up, seemed to see the chocolate stain on Dad's face, and at that, more than at realizing where he was, he let out a howl. He jumped toward Dad, grabbed his neck, his shrieks like an attacked bird, while below us, everybody clapped. Then Dad carried George down.

It was practically like a celebration down there. Everybody

looking at George and patting his head and saying "whew." I thought for a minute they were going to take our picture and put us in a Disney parade. Then they wanted to know how George had gotten out on the limb in the first place, so they could board up the spot where he had gotten loose.

Of course, none of us could tell them that.

Lying in bed that night, the day over, I remember watching the shadows of palm tree leaves coming through the window onto my bedroom wall, and how the moonlight turned the way they moved into wings. I thought over the whole day. Thought about George, how funny and terrifying and fine it had all been. We had gotten home right after dark. And then my dad had driven off with Anne Marie, leaving a space even bigger than the size of him.

There were many nights like that, when lying in my bed, the only one awake, I could hear Mandy breathe in her slow, spaced rhythm of deep sleep; and George in the short, lap-dog hiccup of his; and my mom. And I just lay there, listening to the sounds of them as they breathed, and to the sounds from the marshes, and of cars on the road out front, and the wind coming in off the Gulf, moving through the yard, rustling the palm leaves. I knew that I was the only one who could do anything if someone came in or something happened: a murderer, or a fire, or a gas leak. It was up to me.

I glanced over now at Mandy. We were almost home from the Suwannee. She was still gazing out of the front car window. Months ago she had taken the earrings out of her ears, let the holes close up.

"So what's the deal about the camp?" I asked. "You didn't like it?"

She turned and looked at me. "Where was Dad going to take us today?"

"The Dairy Dip. The show."

"Is it over?"

I slowed down real slow so I could look close at Mandy. Her skin wasn't broken out anywhere. And she didn't have any more trouble breathing than I did. She wasn't allergic to anything, at least not anything you could touch or fold up into a Ziploc bag. Maybe it was only the way we were living—the big space we didn't know how to fill—that was making it hard for her to breathe. I pulled into the driveway, home, and put up Annie. I left Mom a note: *Mandy called, said she was a little sick. Dad went out and got her. We're all downtown at the movie.*

So by the time Mandy and I walked down there, there was only twenty minutes left of the show. But it was still time enough for her to wiggle into the row and sit on Dad's lap. And I found an empty seat for me—just on the other side of him, right beside George.

6.
Linda

I liked the feel of all those nurse's uniforms against my skin. Smooth, sanitized, white, looking germ-free. They reminded me of nuns. I'd always wanted to go to a Catholic school, wear a uniform, mainly because I was raised Presbyterian and imagined that Catholics had a terrific sex life. (The church talked about it so much you knew everybody except priests and nuns must definitely be having one.) And now I was like a nun, or as close to being one as I might ever get. Chaste as a marble Mary.

I woke up watching the ceiling drip a line of disconnected dots onto the edge of my bedspread: 6:00 A.M., and the light in the room fuzzy. My mind, for a second, too, tacked to the world of sleep like a Band-Aid I didn't want to pull off. For a while I just stared at the drip, reminded of a coffee commercial, a close-up of percolating. Drip. Drop. The liquid even stained the bedspread brown.

I lay there calmly imagining myself climbing up onto a ladder and hacking the hole out bigger. Becoming my own tornado. The roof falling in, then the whole house. Whoosh! Gone as if swallowed by a sinkhole. I'd collect the insurance. And move on. Then I was out of bed, sane as a traffic light, organizing everything.

There in the phone book, on the last page in a little square next to an advertisement for a dentist who said he specialized in cowards, was a blurb for Rex the Right Roofer. He was listed as being in the next county, but still, the closest roofer to me.

I put a turkey roaster on the end of my bed to catch the drip, got the kids up, made their breakfasts, and then called the number for Rex. Just as I half expected, he had his answering machine on, and the message didn't exactly thrill me. But since I was desperate, I left my own message to call me as soon as possible, or, better yet, just come on out and look at my roof. Then I gave the number for the clinic. I told him it was an emergency.

I got the kids in school, George the Second out to Lucille's day care, driving with my nose two inches from the dash since the windshield wipers on the Granny Apple didn't work but once every minute. Still, I was at the clinic in time to change all the linens there, sterilize the day's instruments, and empty the garbage cans.

Dr. Haley was making rounds at the county hospital, where he'd sent three patients that week. He and Betty both got to the clinic an hour after me. At ten o'clock, when I hadn't heard from Rex, I called him again. The answering machine was still on, same message, everything: "Hey, this is Rex the Right Roofer for You. I do all kinds of roofs, both high and low. Right now I am out doing one high, so just leave me your message after the beep and I'll beep you back." Then he started singing, which I assumed was a joke about adding his own waiting music. At least his voice was a joke—deep, scratchy, and monotone: "If I had a hammer, I'd hammer in the morning. I'd hammer in the evening. All over this land . . ." Luckily he was cut off by the beep. He couldn't carry a tune any better than George the Second, who already was as obviously tone-deaf as George the First. And I left my own message: "This is Linda Marsh again. I'm desperate. I've got to get somebody to look at my roof today. If you can't do it, at least call me back and tell me you can't. Thanks." And then I left the clinic number again.

An hour later I asked Betty if I could take an early lunch hour, so I could go home and empty the turkey roaster. "Sure, sweets," she said. "Take all the time you need."

Before I left, I put one more message on Rex the Roofer's machine: "If you are alive and anywhere that you can hear this, I am headed home to empty the pot that is catching the rain that is coming through the roof that I have called you to fix. So either get in touch with me or get out of the Yellow Pages." Then I added "please" and my name and hung up.

As I was going out the door, Dr. Haley came out of his office to look at the appointment book. "I have a little emergency at home," I said. "Be back quick, though. Just a little hole in my roof." I laughed. Last thing I wanted to do was look like a flaky employee—at least any more than I already did. Or crisis prone. Between Drew and George the Second, we'd already played the introduction to that.

He looked at me, then at the window. "Sure, fine," he said. When he was around Betty and me, he had started acting a little awkward. She and I had done so much whispering and giggling, hunched together like teenyboppers as she had filled me in with whatever nursing stuff I needed at the moment, that he stood back, even looked a little shy. "Better get it fixed quick, though." He looked from the window to me again. The rain had washed off the dust on the waiting-room glass.

When I got home, no truck was in the drive. No one had been there either. No signs of anybody's truck tires sinking down and leaving little rivers of rain in the sand of my drive. I opened the door and headed straight for the turkey roaster. I knew I was in danger, being in the house alone. In danger that it would talk to me. In danger that I would meet myself turning one of the corners into one of the rooms. See myself there with George. See us dissolving. See myself with my fingers wrapped around the bed linens in sleep, hanging on for dear life.

Dear life. The turkey roaster was full and spilling over, the bed soaked already, and the floor wet. The sheets were a milky brown. There were little pinhole dots on all the kids' rooms ceilings now. The top of my house was a tea strainer with the sky coming through. I ran to the kitchen for all the pots I owned. I set them around.

I sat down in a rocking chair in the corner of my bedroom, knowing it was not the room I should wait in, but drawn somehow, like maybe stopping on the side of the road after an accident to gawk at the victim. I listened to the drip of the water hitting the metal of the pans.

I stared at the bed. A queen-sized antique, a four-poster like pioneers might use. When George moved out, I stayed in it a lot, sick. Actually it was just that the bed and I had made a pact: It wouldn't leave me if I wouldn't leave it; we were going to ride this out together. Sleep as our glue. The hardest thing was telling my mother. For a while, I just didn't. For two weeks I told her, and Daddy, too, whenever they called, that George was out at a meeting, or in the next town at the hardware store, or out fishing. And all that while, the kids and I just crawled up on the bed and rode out the late afternoons and nights together. I would get Drew and Mandy off to school in the mornings, then George the Second and I would come home, get in the white foam of the sheets, play Candy Land and read Dr. Seuss until it was time for Mandy and Drew to come home in the afternoons. Then they, too, would take up with us on our raft: propped against pillows, balancing a checkerboard on the waves of sheets, or doing homework on the mound of a blanket. Popsicle sticks burrowed down in the linen folds, and potato chips took root at the foot. The laundry climbed out of the basket in the bathroom and headed toward the ceiling. The dishes played rabbit, multiplying and just sitting around.

When my parents kept calling and I couldn't keep George out shopping or fishing anymore, I told them. He had moved out, I said. The marriage gone. Kaput. The Fat Lady had sung.

Couldn't say it any other way or my soul would leak.

And then I told my mother that I, myself, was a little under the weather.

"Well, I'm going to be down there on the next bus," she said. "Leave everything to me. I'll take over till you get your strength back."

Strength back. She leaned in the bedroom door, saw me there wadded into the sheets. "Why didn't you tell me about this soon as it happened? Why didn't you send the children to me? You know, I don't think Little George has brushed his teeth in a month. I just gave him some Kool-Aid and it stuck to the scum on his teeth like it was a dental test. And Drew hasn't had his hair cut in so long he looks like a commode brush. Why didn't you tell me? Just call up and tell me?"

I sat propped up on pillows, marveling at how she could make such lively descriptions and realizing both Drew and I had inherited some of her tendency for that. My lips were closed, and my eyes were barely open. I didn't even know how to defend myself. What to say.

"You know, you look a little yellow to me, Linda. Have you been to the doctor, got your blood checked? You don't have to be alarmed. People don't die from it. Not these days. Yep, I really do think you have hepatitis. I sure do. I bet you've been eating oysters. Must of got a bad one. Yep, I sure do think that's what's wrong. I'm going to call and get an appointment this afternoon. Who do you go to? You mean there's no doctor within fifty miles of here? You have to drive all that way with the flu or an ear infection? I can't believe that. I don't know why you and George settled here in the first place. It's like a place at the end of the earth where people come to drop out. Why! I've never seen so many forty-year-old hippies in my life. That's probably got a lot to do with why this didn't last. Nothing happens here. It's so little, nothing *can* happen. Men get bored, you know, Linda. It's up to us, their women, to keep them interested."

I didn't keep him interested. I let myself go. Didn't buy new clothes, just got jeans and T-shirts from the beach-wear shops. Didn't even buy tank tops to let a little skin show. Mama had always told me—I had even grown up hearing her friends talking about it all the time—that a married woman can't just get fat and happy and let herself go.

Let myself go.

Gone. So I lost. Lost him. Lost us. Lost me.

We packed George the Second into my car; Mandy and Drew were at school, and Drew would look after Mandy until we were back. My mother drove the fifty miles to Gainesville to the university hospital. They were going to work me up. We started in the women's clinic. My mother thought that was always the place to start: work from the bottom up, rule out every female part that might be on the blink. And anyway, she said that if it was hepatitis, they could pick it up there as well as anywhere else.

I didn't argue with Mama the M.D. George and I sat in the women's clinic side by side as if we were the same age, with Mama in charge.

She leaned over and whispered: "You couldn't be pregnant, could you?"

Fat chance. The way George was spearfishing, and then finally just not even taking his boat out? And fat chance too that I'd be the one chosen for an Immaculate Conception. But "no," I said, no feistiness with words even left in me, no ability to laugh at my mind's own jokes either.

George the Second was rearranging the magazine rack. All around us were pregnant women, sitting in their chairs, their feet flat on the floor, their legs unable to be crossed. Mama leaned close. "Are you sure?"

"Um humm."

"Well, how can you be so sure? That's how you and George started out, you know. That might be all that's wrong now. Maybe he doesn't want any more children. Maybe he doesn't want to have to support any more. Lord knows, he can't."

"I'm not, Mama. I've got hepatitis, like you say. Must have eaten a bad oyster. That's all."

Mama is short and round, her hair close to her head in a fashionable cut. The color is a light shade of gray, almost white. And that day she wore earrings and a pin on her jacket collar to match, silver.

"Well, let's not brood on the fact of how this all started out," she said. "That won't help anything. If the marriage started out on a bad foot, that doesn't have a thing to do with how it ended up, necessarily. Right?"

"Right."

"You aren't thinking about that now, are you?"

Well, no. At least not before she mentioned it. Or was brought up to think like her: that girls who let guys try on the goods before buying end up on the bargain table, being pulled on and looked over and then finally just happy to be taken home by anyone. Yes, Mama, with you here it was easy to see. Feel your thoughts and opinions, rooted in the thoughts and opinions of your own mother and hers before her, growing in me as seedlings blown here through time. Me. Me. It was me only who drove George away. Boring and plain and no fun. Too easy to have in the first place. Too easy to leave.

"Ms. Marsh." The nurse's voice called out in the room.

"That's you." My mother poked me.

"I know." I stood up, thinking how it was a signal of these times that the nurse pronounced all the names she called with Ms., protecting everyone's marital state and the size of their bellies, even though it may have been only my mother who cared. And then had made me care and opened old wounds like taking cans of stuff you hate off the back shelf of a cabinet that you thought you'd never use.

I was tested from one end to the other and liquid parts sent to labs with the results to be called to me in a few days. Meanwhile,

Mama ran up and down the hospital halls with George the Second, who built tents out of magazines, jumped into vacant wheelchairs, feverishly worked the drink machines, and went through trash cans.

We drove back, too pooped to say much, except George, who was singing in the backseat:

> The first marine found a bean.
> The second marine cooked the bean.
> The third marine ate the bean
> and blew a hole in the submarine.
> Hinky, Dinky, Parley Vous.

When Mama was going into the house, and George the Second was on his way down the drive on his bike, wobbling on its training wheels, she stopped and looked at me: "You know, Linda. I don't think you ought to worry about Little George. They can do wonders with these children these days."

I had just enough mother bear left in me to wake up and take note. "What are you talking about? Who says I'm worrying about George?"

"Well, you must be." Mama looked close at me, her blue eyes almost twitching, she was so intent on what she was telling me. "He's hyperactive—that's clear as the nose on my face. And they can fix that, these days. They have medicines they can give these children. I think when we go back with you, we'll see about that. The pediatric clinic was just down the hall. I saw the sign."

"Mama, George is not hyperactive. He's four."

"Well, he's the livest wire I've ever known."

"You've just forgotten four, Mama. It's been a while since you've been around anybody four."

She glanced at me, her mouth still and her eyes considering what I had said, which was, after all, one of the few things I *had* said. "Well, if I were you, I'd have him looked at the next time you go."

She went into the kitchen. She was wearing spike heels. She wrapped an apron around her waist, one she had ironed the day before. On the front it said, YOU'RE GONNA LIKE WHAT I WHIP UP. She fixed tarragon chicken, wild rice, creamed carrots, and cherry pie. Even made her own crusts. If I had made pies, George wouldn't have left me. If I had made jokes, or at least funny ones, he would have lived to just hear the next one. To be close. Wouldn't have been able, ever, to get enough. Leaving wouldn't have crossed his mind.

If I had been Mama, he wouldn't have even thought once.

•

It was Lucille Duffy who saved me. Peeping in the door, her hair tightly curled with a new perm, a T-shirt on that said CALL ME WHEN THE SURF'S UP. "Hey." Her voice was soft, not a whisper, but soft. "I heard you were ailing. Mr. Clark told me when you didn't show up at the meeting last night."

She meant the town committee for running the spring art show, one of the biggest money-makers for the town; it brings in tourists and artists for two days.

I sat up and stared.

"I guess you know," she said, "this means you will make it in the paper this Friday on The Puny List." She laughed.

I tried to send out a laugh, too, an echo of hers, but the most I managed was a curve of my lips.

"I must have eaten a bad oyster," I said. "We think I've got hepatitis. The hospital's going to call in a few days with the test results." I got up out of bed and sat in the rocking chair. I hated to be seen in bed, seen low, seen like that.

Lucille came all the way into the room, glanced back to see where my mother was. On the way in she had given George the Second a bottle of bubbles and Mama was out in the yard, supervising his blowing. We could hear her through the windows: "Out this way, George. No, don't blow them on the hibiscus. That's right. This way. No! Not on that bush either!"

Lucille leaned close and whispered, "If you ask me, the only bad oyster you've eaten was named George."

I looked at her. I liked hearing George's name said in someone else's voice. But I was not sure if I especially liked hearing her demean him.

"You can't sit here and blame yourself. That cotton candy torch was after him from day one. All she had to do was trot it by with the hem a little up."

I looked wide-eyed and surprised.

"Hell, honey, wadn't George the kind who couldn't stay away from it except in solitary confinement?"

I was not used to that. I could not seem to clear my ears of that. I was not used to talking about George in all his nakedness. "I don't know. How do you know all this? I didn't think he was that bad."

"Shoot, I believe George would have even come after me if he didn't know I could out Indian-wrestle him any time I want. I saw it in his eyes. But then I showed him this."

She rolled up her T-shirt sleeve and flexed her biceps. Lucille *is* built like a linebacker. "Now didn't he just know I'd give him one of these straight in the old kisser?" She whipped her fist around, cranking it, like a propeller.

"And wouldn't you like to? And then didn't he know that I'd step back and give him one of these?" She kicked out, her calf muscle taut with her toe pointed. "And now don't you want me to? Huh? I hire out. I'm cheap. I got a special on this week: two for the price of one. Which means you could lay her out, too."

I sat back and smiled.

"How much?" I said. I was thinking that I could probably really get into this. Felt a little good, in fact, thinking a new way, thinking outward, thinking mean about him.

"I'll trade you," she said, standing up straight, but still flexing her muscles, cutting up, making strong-woman stances, hiking her shorts so the thigh muscle showed. "You send George the Second to my day care and I'll lay out George the First for you and put a hex on her so her hair will fall out."

I laughed.

"She's not going to look good bald, now you and me both know that."

I laughed again. It *was* fun.

"Linda." Lucille was suddenly serious, her eyes meeting mine, all the muscle-shining stances gone: "You didn't deserve this. You and I both know you didn't do anything to bring this on."

"I didn't?"

"No. Everybody in this town knows you were dedicated to your children, to him, helping him get everything done that he's signed up for. Which meant you were the one holding down the fort, keeping the troops fed, so he's out riding around, scouting the territory. You did everything fine. Even *he* knows that."

"He does?"

"Darn tootin'. Knows he's gonna burn in hell, too. And right now wouldn't you like to buy him a one-way ticket? Go ahead. Get mad. Chew on your anger. Get your strength back."

I smiled, and this time I could feel myself saying yes, knowing that what I heard was what I needed to say for myself. With one quick word, "thanks," I agreed to send George the Second to her day care as soon as I got the job I knew I would have to get if any of the ends were to be met.

And so it was that Lucille pointed the way for me, showed me the anger that I had to look for each day as I woke up, to chew on, ride on, point out the door into a world that I knew would never, for me, be still again. I was on a rolling ball that could move all too quickly in a sudden turn, unsettling my feet. It was up to me, alone, to balance.

And it was not nice or pretty or safe either. But I was through with nice and pretty and safe. The anger gave me back myself.

After a few days, the hospital called. Told me that I was anemic, that was all.

I went to the drugstore, got the right pills. And then I put Mama on the bus.

I sent her home with a list naming all the people who had gotten married because they had to, starting with Shakespeare.

Then I made another one for myself—listing all the people whose approval my selfhood would never again rest upon. I started with George the First, and then moved on to the approval of any other man. And then I included Mama.

Now while I was remembering all this, outside my bedroom window, when I looked up, was a man—just standing there, looking in at me. My whole body rose off the rocking chair in a reflex, and I could hear my breath sucking in. I was in overdrive. My heart beating double-time.

"You called me?" His voice was low, and he yelled it sort of loud.

"I did?" I couldn't imagine calling *him*. Big and dark. A day's growth of beard. Blue workshirt and jeans. A face round as a clock, his nose red. We were talking through the window. And he was smiling. "I'm Rex." When I still looked dumb, he added: "Rex the roofer."

"Oh. Oh, yeah."

"And you're desperate?" He grinned.

"For a roofer, yes." I went around to the front door, to let him in.

He stood in my bedroom with me, both of us looking up, studying the ceiling. And then in the same way that people often talk about their cars—as if they are them—he said about my roof: "Your bottom layer's give out."

"So what does that mean?"

"Means you can't put shingles on till the tar paper's tore off."

"Oh."

"Yeah. You got to start all over. Wasn't done right in the first place. That's clear enough to see. Who built this house?"

"I don't know. My husband paid attention to all that."

"Well, what does he say? He want to see if these shingles still on warranty?"

"I don't know. I guess so. Only I doubt it. The house is pretty old."

"Well, I guess I can put you a new roof on for about a thousand dollars."

I gasped.

"Best I can do. You want to see if you get a lower bid?"

"I think I'll have to. I'll have to talk to my husband. Or rather my ex-husband. See if he'll help with this."

"Oh. He don't live here no more?"

"No."

"Just you?"

"I have three kids."

He looked at me. I felt his eyes. "Eight ninety-nine, that's firm. Half now, the rest on completion. Can start tomorrow."

"I'll let you know."

He turned around. I escorted him out the door, and drove back to the clinic.

Betty looked up as I walked in. "Get it all settled?"

"Not quite."

Dr. Haley was eating a bag lunch at his desk as I walked through to the treatment rooms to get them ready for the afternoon. "Did you get it straightened out?" he asked, too.

"It's a big hole," I said. "Bigger than I thought. But I met with a roofer, and at least he can start soon."

"Too bad it had to happen on a day like this."

"Yeah."

He was holding up an apple, getting ready to bite into it. The cuff of his shirt had so much starch in it, it encircled his wrist like a rim. "But the rain's supposed to stop this afternoon. Shouldn't last much longer." He bit down, and the apple cracked.

I turned into the treatment room. "I hope."

I felt him watch me as I went in to change the linens for the afternoon, set out new equipment. The rain beat the roof of the clinic. I was tempted to sit down in private for a minute, to take my own blood pressure, see how I was doing.

7.
Drew

My family was driving me nuts, totally out of my tree. Mandy was still having all these allergy attacks, getting so she couldn't breathe because of something she was wearing, she said. Mom had taken her in to see Dr. Haley, and he had put her on some kind of medicine and had given her this little inhaler that she walked around with. Could stick it in her mouth at any given minute and breathe like Darth Vader. Meanwhile, Mom was sending all sorts of Mandy's stuff down to the Salvation Army: pink sweaters, her yellow house shoes, a skirt with red dots on it that Anne Marie had bought for her, so ugly it would have made me stop breathing, too.

And George had taken up with his Halloween costume like he had with the word *fart*. Wouldn't take it off come hell or high water. He was walking around in the rabbit suit every day now. I was hoping Mandy would get allergic to it. But even worse than his rabbit suit was that he'd started carrying a purse. Got one of the old ones that Mom had given to Mandy, and he had filled it up with stuff that was usually in Mom's: Life Savers, loose change, old notes, a set of keys. I kept telling him it just didn't go together—a rabbit and a purse? But as usual with George, making sense didn't mean anything.

I thought sure Dad would talk him out of the purse when we all went out to dinner on the nights Dad stopped by. But instead, Dad just tolerated George in his rabbit suit and the purse, wasn't bothered by any of it. I heard him whisper to Anne Marie that George was just working out his emotions about women and men, and it'd blow over. (Now, I don't know what in the hell that meant, but it seemed to me the little bit of psychology my dad got before he became principal ruined him.) Of course, he didn't have to live with George now. Didn't have to spend more than a couple of hours a week with a sexually confused rabbit. It was me who had to appear most often with George in public. It was up to me.

Sunday afternoon I decided I'd take George the Second out fishing in my boat—just me and him. Which means that when you take George out to fish, only George can fish. He can't control where he throws his line, and he can't sit down for longer than two minutes, so the whole time you have to be keeping him from hooking you with his gear or turning the boat over. Taking George out fishing means total sacrifice. You can't afford to expect to do one fun thing yourself or you will have to kill him first. So I told him I'd take him. "You will?" he said.

"Yeah. If you give me your purse."

"*You* want it?"

"No. I just want you to give it to me."

I figured I could bury it under the garbage if he'd just give it up for a while. He stood in the boathouse behind our house, looking down at my boat tied there and waiting, then at his purse. A mullet jumped out of the water in the marsh, practically flew two feet before diving back in. The tide had just turned and was coming back into the marsh now, covering up the oyster bars. It was lapping against my boat where it was tied at the dock. A pelican skied across the water, then floated. George took a step to get into my boat, and I grabbed him. "Un uh," I said. "Got to hand over the purse first."

He stared at it for a moment, then at my boat. I'd packed it with a cooler full of drinks and candy bars, and, on purpose, I'd left the lid up as a bribe. When George put the purse in my hand, I ran inside to slip it in the trash can. And the phone rang.

"Is Drew there?"

"This is me."

"Well, this is Heather."

"Heather?"

"Yeah. Heather."

"Yeah?"

Her laugh was like glass bells, or like, when the table is set for Thanksgiving, you pop the edge of your water glass with your thumbnail. "What you doing?" she asked.

"Nothing."

"Me too."

There was a minute when only breathing was happening. My breath and hers, our noses and mouths not even an inch from the part of the phone you talk into.

"I was thinking about going to the four o'clock show," she said. "Wanna meet me there?"

I thought of how she sat in study hall in front of me, long honey hair that curled up in the humidity, and the way she chewed the side of her lip when she was bored, which was almost always.

"Sure. I guess."

"Okay."

She laughed again, then told me all about how her and Lindsey Collier went to the mall in Gainesville the day before and to the Record Bar and The Pizza House. Generally I hate shopping, but she sure made it sound good.

I wasn't clear on what you were supposed to do when you met a girl at the show, but I was willing to try it.

When I got back to the boat house, George was sitting in my boat, barrettes on the head of the rabbit suit, eating a Milky Way.

"What we going after, Drew? Huh? What's hittin' today?"

"Whiting. Mostly what's here this time of year."

"Catfish, too?"

"Yeah, there's always catfish."

"They're my favorite."

George was fascinated with the whiskers on catfish. His own, on his bunny suit, were made out of broom straws. Mom had sewed him the suit the week before Halloween, had gotten a pattern at a sewing place and made it out of some kind of white fuzzy material. On Halloween the weather had been so hot, George had sweated himself wet in it, but now with the cooler weather he could sit in the damn suit all day.

We putted out into the channel in the marsh. I know where the deep-water channel is, like I know the way my hair parts. It's just something I have: this feeling that I can know the Gulf as well as I can know me. When the tide goes out, and the bottom of the marsh and the wide flats rise up out of the water in the Gulf for miles, it's like I can look at them and see them and they never leave me. I know where the channels are and where the rises of sandbars are and where the riptides will form when the tide brings all the water back. It's easy for me. Out here I don't run aground, or get in trouble. I am always warning others, telling them where they're likely to have their props caught. I am safe out here, as long as I respect the weather and the tides.

We moved on out to where the marsh meets the Gulf. I glanced back at our house. The roof was half torn off, and tar paper was flapping. The roofer Mom had hired was slower than a one-legged crab—only showing up with his roofing crew every few days, saying he was having to work her in. The house was such a mess, Mom couldn't do her usual Sunday afternoon housecleaning. She'd gone with Mrs. MacHenry and Mandy to the mall in the next town to a discount grocery. No doubt we'd be eating forty pounds of chicken all month, because if you bought thirty you could get ten more free.

We were out by the town pier now, just about right under it, because it was still low tide and the pier has high piling, made for big boats. And I let George bait the trout rig we were using. Our bait was shrimp, and I took my fish knife and cut a little off, so it would last longer. George can go through a supply of bait quick, because he throws his line around so much, and a lot gets slung off. And as he threw it out now, off the front of my boat, he missed my nose by about an inch.

"Un uh, George," I coached him. "Don't reel it in yet. You got to let it sit awhile."

"I wanna reel it."

"I don't care if you do want to reel it. You got to wait. You got to be patient to catch a fish."

"I wanna catch a shark."

A pelican sat on the pier over us, watching, hoping when we finished we might throw him a little of our unused bait. The pelicans always chase all the boats coming in, begging for leftovers.

And then as I looked up at the pelican I saw Dr. Haley sitting on the pier eating a donut, his legs hanging over the side, and a mangy-looking dog scampering around him, begging for some of his donut. "Hi," he said down at us.

"Hi," I said back up. I wasn't thrilled about being seen with George fishing in his rabbit suit, but I didn't let on.

"Catching anything?"

"Not yet. We just started."

He flipped the dog half a donut, and the dog came and lay down close beside him. You could tell the dog hadn't had a good meal in a long while. His ribs were showing through his long black fur, and his mouth was watering. His eyes looked so pitiful, I was tempted to give him one of our candy bars, but dogs don't tend to like chocolate, and I know it's not good for them.

"I guess you grew up here, fishing." Dr. Haley was looking at me.

"Yeah. I've been going since I was two. Didn't get my own boat, though, till four years ago."

"I don't think I went more than about two times when I was growing up," he said.

"Yeah?" I couldn't even imagine it.

"Yeah. I played basketball and ran track and then I went off to boarding school. I just never did water sports."

And then we both saw George's line grow tight. George yelled. "Got one. Drew, I got one!" He was pulling on it, and his rod was bent. "Go on," I said. "Set the hook." I reached over to hold onto George's hands so I could help with the timing.

"This is something. Something big, Drew. A shark, I bet," George said, reeling in now.

"That's right. Play him a little," I said.

"Bet it's a hammerhead," George said. "You suppose it's a hammerhead, Drew? A great big old hammerhead?"

"Yeah, Jaws," I said, unable to not tease him. George was kind of cute, fighting the invisible fish in his bunny suit, and trying, like me, to imagine what any minute would break through the surface and tail-dance across the water like a prize from God.

And then it did: this little old whiting about eight inches long. But to George it was as fine a catch as a deep-water tarpon, and it was on his line and giving him a good fight for both their sizes.

"Nice fish," Dr. Haley said, leaning over, watching us pull it up into the boat. The pelican stretched its neck out too, little yellow pointed feathers on its head like a ski cap. "No way, José!" I said, pulling the whiting away from the bird as it swooped out over us and dived down.

The dog beside Dr. Haley sat up and barked.

"Congratulations, George," Dr. Haley said. "That's a good-looking fish."

George grinned. And then, maybe because he was getting a little hot, he slipped the head part of the costume off, just let it ride back on the top of his shoulders like a hood. But he reached around, undid the barrettes, and stuck them in his own hair.

I saw Dr. Haley watching. "Thinks they hold him up in the water," I said. Dr. Haley nodded as though to him that made all the sense in the world. And neither of us said anything else. I knew I couldn't explain George even if I wanted to, and Dr. Haley was nice enough not to ask me to.

George was now petting the side of his fish, looking down at it on top of the ice I'd brought in my second cooler in case we caught anything. "Now how exactly did you do that, George?" Dr. Haley asked, "What bait did you use? And what kind of a rod is that?"

George filled him in with everything, even the brand name of the plug we had on the line. He was catching onto the love of fishing just like I had. Then George looked up at Dr. Haley on the pier and asked: "Wanna come with us? When I catch my next one, I'll teach you."

"I don't know," he said. "Doesn't look like your boat'll hold three."

"It's okay. George is little, anyhow," I added.

I figured that the least I could do was to offer him a boat ride after mashing in the front of his car.

He walked back to where the pier met the street and walked around onto a small sand beach, took off his shoes, and waded out to us to where I putted in to meet him. The stray dog followed him down to the water and then stopped.

We headed out a little farther into the Gulf. Now I had two of them who didn't know a thing about how to fish or even rig up their gear, and it was all I could do to keep them from getting tangled up with each other. Dr. Haley was so tall he folded into my boat like a pocketknife, all knees and elbows, and he was so busy trying to do everything just right. I was messing with him and George for a long while, and then it hit me: Heather. I looked at my watch. I was an hour late. The movie would be half over. Quickly I pulled up the anchor and said I had forgotten to run an important errand, and to hang on. And then I sped the boat back to the town pier, while George and Dr. Haley sat together in the bow, their hair whipped back as I opened up the motor all the way.

I threw out the anchor, asked Dr. Haley if he'd take over with George for a minute, and then I waded to the beach. I went as fast as I could, without splashing too much up on me, but still, the bottom of my pants got pretty wet. That stray dog was still there, waiting, and it followed me toward the movie, then took off after a stray cat. There are so many cats in Palm Key, skulking around in the bushes and sitting around the old salts' boats when they come in every day with their catch.

There wasn't anything else for me to do: I paid my three dollars and went in. The whole place was as dark as the inside of a witch's brassiere, and it took me a good three walks up and down the aisle before I spotted Heather sitting with Mary McVane and Crystal Roberts and Tommy Larkin, their feet stuck up on the backs of the seats in front of them. I sat down in the row behind them. "Heather." I whispered it.

She turned around and looked at me. When she realized it was me sitting there in the dark, I could see her eyes about like two bottom coals on a grill. "What happened to you?"

"Look, Heather," I said. "Something's come up. I can't make it."

"Well, that's obvious. I stood out front and waited twenty minutes. I missed the whole previews."

"I would have called you, but I wasn't near a phone."

"That's a pitiful little excuse."

"It's the truth."

"There's phones all over this town, Mr. Smarty. There's a pay phone in every Quick Stop and on every corner."

I was getting ready to tell her about having to take George fishing, all except the purse part—I could always blame babysitting George on the fact that my mom was working—and then I was going to get into having to take along Dr. Haley because he'd invited himself and you just couldn't say no to the town doctor—I mean, it was up to all of us to be nice to him so he wouldn't leave and not be here to take care of everybody. And by the time I finished with all of that, no doubt, she'd feel guilty as hell and would be apologizing all over herself to me, and then she'd come back and sit by me before I got up to leave again. "It was beyond my control," I started, which I thought sounded sort of suave and mature.

But she cut me off and glared at me. "Oh yeah, like you had to get a heart transplant?"

Mary McVane and Crystal Roberts laughed when she said that, their heads getting slung back because their laughs were about like exploding damn torpedoes. And then Mary grabbed her nose. There was a scene on the screen now of a car crash, and it lit up the audience a little, and we could all see each other pretty good. "What's that I smell?" Mary said.

"Oh God," Crystal joined in. "Someone's died." She grabbed her nose, too.

Heather looked around, and then she grabbed her nose and gagged.

Tommy turned around, looked at me, and I grabbed my nose, too. And we all sat there talking through our noses and pretending to watch the movie.

"Has it gone?" Crystal looked at Mary, still pinching her nose, and Mary took her hand off her nose and sniffed. "No. Oh God!" she said, loud; and they both cut up laughing and still pinching their noses, and then Mary and Crystal got up and ran out—to the rest room, I supposed.

But then I looked down at my feet. I had forgotten I was still barefoot after wading out of the Gulf, and then as I reached down to unroll my cuffs, I felt pieces of bait stuck up all over my pants, and I realized it was me we were all smelling.

I held my nose and pretended to gag like I was an inch from death and was probably going to need the CPR that my mother had taught all over town.

"A dead cat musta crawled in here," I said, my voice as nasal as if I was doing a medicine commercial for a head cold.

"Well, I'm going to complain to the management," Heather said with the same head cold, and got up.

I watched her walk out, and then I said, "I got to go, too." I snuck into the back row and sat there, because I didn't want to take a chance on bumping into Heather out in the lobby where she could see me barefoot and decorated with shrimp guts and might get another whiff.

When she came back with the usher with a flashlight to shine up under all the seats to look for the dead cat, I got up, skulked up the aisle and snuck out.

I was embarrassed and nearly sick to death about the whole afternoon. It was pretty depressing, going back to the boat with Dr. Haley and George in it. I kept thinking about Heather and how she'd looked pretty cute holding her nose and walking up and down the aisle with the usher, and now I'd fried my future with her. And maybe even with Mary McVane and Crystal Roberts. And there just weren't that many girls in Palm Key in the first place. I also knew now, too, that it wasn't just my family who could drive me nuts; I could do it to myself.

I walked up toward the sand beach near the pier. My boat was bucking on the high tide and a little wind, and George and Dr. Haley were bouncing up and down. It wasn't really a bad sea, but Dr. Haley was green. Some people are like that, no stomach for being on water at all. He was still fishing like hell, though. It was obvious he wasn't going to cry uncle, come hell or high water. And high water was here.

"Where'd you have to go, Drew? Huh? Why'd you leave us sitting here?"

As I walked out and climbed into the boat, I noticed that George had parts of bait stuck all over in his rabbit fur, too.

"I forgot to turn off the broiler on the toaster," I lied.

"That was really dumb, Drew. Really dumb."

"Yeah."

Dr. Haley was quietly fishing off the bow. "You catch anything?" I asked him. "Two," he said, and lifted the cooler lid to show me. His lips under his mustache were white, and the skin around his eyes was about the color of peas.

"You ready to head in?" I started the motor.

"No." George stood up and held onto the side of the boat with one hand and his rod with the other.

"We can do a little bit in the marsh, then," I said. "At least get out of this wind."

We puttered around to in back of the house. Mom was there taking clothes off the line because our dryer was broken. She waved. And then she stopped and looked again, and when she finally realized it was Dr. Haley in the boat with us, she waved again, sort of wild, like a football referee.

We came in close to our boat house, and I put the anchor out. The water was calmer here. George sat down, and I baited him another line, making sure the bait wouldn't fall off. He had him a few keepers now, and he kept saying that, about as proud of knowing what a real fisherman would call them. "We got us some keepers, Drew," he kept saying. "Don't we have some keepers?"

"Yeah, sure do," I said, just sitting back and getting a kick out of watching him now.

For a good long while we sat, watching the sun set on the other side of the torn-out roof of our house. It lit up the sky like a horn blasting notes, showering pink and gold all out over the water.

Mom came down and sat on the dock. "Catch anything?"

George yelled back: "Four keepers."

And then Dr. Haley, like he was a kid, too, and imitating George, called to her: "Two little keepers."

She laughed.

The sound was short, her voice looping in a surprised sort of sound, not a high-sounding laugh or light like Heather's, or Crystal Roberts's, or Mary McVane's, but deep and steady and nice, real nice. All around us, mullet were jumping, playing a tune in the water. And then down a palm tree right by the dock, I saw a baby raccoon scoot. I pointed. "Shhh," George said, as he saw the baby, too. It came out from under the big, weathered leaves, and by the time it touched ground, another one—same size, same tannish gray color—came down, too. We all looked in silence. My mother was sitting cross-legged on the dock, holding herself so still she didn't look alive, except that she was smiling, just practically tickled to death, you could tell. She must have seen the first one just as I had. And Dr. Haley was not moving either. But smiling. The size of him so still and quiet, he was like giant wood, solid in my boat. Even George was keeping himself quiet.

By the time the second raccoon hit bottom, a third scooted backward to the ground to join the others. Then all three together started walking—so slow they touched, as if hitched together and pulling some invisible wagon. Their gait was sticky slow, their backs arched like cats, their tails hanging low, and their feet moving in a pacing stride—both feet on each side moving together—so that the three of them were like a rocking ship. They tiptoed that way onto the weedy beach beside the boathouse and disappeared in the sea oats—for sure to fish and crab all night.

Just as we thought the show was all over, and we were about to move, one more came down out of the hiding of the wide palm leaf. It walked alone across the beach. And then, just as the light was about to leave the sky, a fifth and final baby raccoon toe-danced down the palm-tree trunk, just like the others. Seeing all that seemed both strange and wonderful, 'cause it reminded me once again that I wasn't so smart—if I ever thought I was—because all that life had been there all the time, so near us, and we hadn't known it. And now we'd gotten to watch it come out and show itself—to us only—and it was right this second in the marsh grass near us, hidden again. But still with us: all that life.

When the mosquitoes started to bite, I took the boat in and tied it up at the dock.

Mom stood up, looking at Dr. Haley. "I was just about to put some chicken on the grill for supper. You're welcome to stay."

I watched her looking flustered, having her boss there in her yard like that. Maybe no one else would think she looked bent out of shape, but I knew all the parts Mom could play, or at least I'd seen a lot of them: June Cleaver, Carol Burnett, Bill Cosby, Rambo. I watched her offering him stuff, just to be nice, so he wouldn't think she was caught off guard or not capable of throwing a five-course-meal party at the drop of a hat. She was practically naming everything in the fridge he could have right that second: lemonade, iced tea, wine, smoked oysters, nacho dip. He stood quiet, looking sicker and sicker as she went on with her list. I knew he had no stomach for anything, much less supper, but he sure as hell wasn't about to mention that. I watched him and my mother tiptoeing around each other's feelings and the truth, about like I had that afternoon in the show with Heather. But Heather wasn't my boss, or work for me, or anything at all that you could put a finger on and call something.

"Thanks, but I better get home," he said. "Maybe another time." He took his fish out of my cooler. "Here, George," he said, handing him the whiting. "Put these with yours, and you can have them for supper sometime."

George took them, grinning. "Hey, right. You can come over for a fish fry. He can, can't he, Mom? You know how to fry these, don't you? Yeah, she knows how to fry these good."

George thanked him, and then Dr. Haley thanked me, and he and Mom said, "See you tomorrow," and he walked up the road to his house, about a quarter of a mile away.

As I was pulling my boat up onto the beach, I looked up and saw that stray dog come out of the woods near the corner and trot up the road after Dr. Haley.

"Mom," I said as she was going into our house with the laundry basket. "We've got a real problem. I mean a real *bad* one."

She stopped dead in her tracks, the laundry basket in her arms like a stiff body, and gave me that wide-eyed look she can get sometimes when she thinks we really are about to go under.

"George has shrimp guts all in his fur, and he's gonna smell to high heaven by morning. We got to do something."

She looked relieved, like George's rabbit suit was the least we had to worry about. "I can wash it tonight while he's asleep," she said, which was a terrible way, I thought, to handle a really serious problem.

8.
Linda

On Sunday nights, when I was fighting to keep the lights sorted out from the darks in the wash, a week's worth of groceries stocked in the pantry, and a week's worth of sandwiches made and frozen for the kid's lunches, my mother called. "Did I catch you at a bad time?"

There was no good time, but I didn't want to be that honest. "No. No. I was just fixing supper."

"What are you having?"

"Broiled chicken, wild rice with apple seasoning and grapes, green beans with tomato relish, and homemade cherry pie." I only lied about the pie part. It was cherry; it just wasn't mine. It was Mrs. Smith's.

"Em. Sounds good. I might be interested in that rice recipe. Can you send it?"

Mama always equated your mental health with what you were able to put on the table. It probably harked back to the time when Mrs. Johnson, who lived across the street from us in Montgomery, served hot dogs for fifteen days in a row and then went berserk and had to be taken out in an ambulance. We learned that the hot dogs were the tip-off from Mimi Johnson, her daughter and my friend, who used to come over to our house after supper and brag about what she'd had.

"You still like your new job?"

"Yeah."

"Now, what is it exactly that you do?"

"Mostly receptionist stuff. I just help keep the clinic running, that's about it."

"Are there any unmarried doctors there? You might keep your eye out, Linda. You know, George isn't going to be able to send all those children to college and keep up that woman he's married. And she's young enough to have babies, too, isn't she?"

"I guess." Anne Marie's womb was not exactly my favorite subject. I didn't like it any better than I liked my mother telling me to keep my eye out for some man to support me. The last thing I wanted was a man, and next to hell would be being married to one. I didn't feel like taking the time to explain that to Mama, or her other wrong idea: that a clinic doctor in Palm Key was going to be living like a Rockefeller. The town council had enticed one to come here only after they had gotten a federal grant to ensure a salary. Most people in Palm Key had no insurance, and the clinic did little more than break even. But the reeducation of Mama would poop me out, so I concentrated instead on reading the back of the rice box with the phone crimped under my chin.

"Well, what if that woman *does* have babies? Have you thought about that? George might just stop all your child support right there, and you'll have to get him arrested. Have you thought about that?"

Sure, I'd thought about having George arrested for all sorts of things. But I only said, "Oh gosh, I'm sorry, Mama. I've got a load in the washer and the tilt alarm just went off." I reached across the kitchen and turned on one of George's battery-run trucks and held the phone receiver over it, so it would sound like the washer alarm. "I'll talk to you next week." I hung up, smoothing over the good-bye with a promise to send her my rice recipe.

The early days in December were clear, the light and air crisp, the afternoons warm enough to sit outside without a sweater. A few days before Christmas, I bought the biggest tree I'd ever had—I wanted a tree bigger than George the First would ever have put up. Stuffed the Granny Apple with all three kids and drove down to the tree lot that Bill Duffy had set up outside his Handymart.

Bill helped us pick it out, threw George the Second up onto his shoulders so he could check out the top of each tree, Bill's cheeks polished red with Lucille's blush, wearing a Santa cap and a flannel shirt like a woodsman from Minnesota, while sweating in the Florida heat. He roped the chosen tree onto the roof of the Granny Apple so half of it hung out over the front and half out over the back. And while Bill finished tying it down, he told us a joke, jollying all of us up for Christmas: "Why'd the chicken cross the road?" George the Second grinned, looked up at him: "Oh, I know that one."

Bill gave him a slanted look, his eyes nearly disappearing into the fat of his cheeks, his gray hair under his Santa cap like sprigs of marsh grass: "Bet you don't."

George yelled: "To get to the other side!"

Mandy yelled, too, her face loose with joy for once: "To prove he wasn't a chicken!"

"Nope." Bill shook his head, a solid tough look on his face, a bell jingling on the end of his cap. "To show an armadillo it could be done," he announced, watching us.

At any time of any day, probably half the roads in Florida have a dead armadillo on them.

Drew twisted his mouth, a grin licking the side of it. "Aw."

I let Drew drive us and the tree home, all of us watching the green branches moving over the windows in front and back. And all the while, Drew drove as if hauling a newly broken leg that couldn't take any bumps.

Slow. Slow. So slow, I could actually see what I almost never took the time to look at: the exact way the late day's light was almost absorbed into the water of the Gulf in front of us, the sky and water harmonizing in just the same way, so that they each seemed to be giving up at the same time as the night claimed them. It made me think of the way I used to put water on paper when I prepared to paint, bleeding the whiteness of the paper away. And I remembered now, too, how for hours I would squint into the sky and the landscape, a way to blur the details so as to release the essence of what was there, to discover the shadows, to uncover what was important—a trick to allow me to see the essential lines. In all my paintings I was always searching to create the effect of real light. In school, when I was learning to use oils, my favorite word had been an Italian term *chiaroscuro*—chair-o-scuro, o-scuro (I even liked to chant it). It was seeing things in relation to their shadows. It held the idea that by including the shadow that an object cast, the object itself could be truly seen. The arrangement of light and dark, the effect of it, was what I longed to master. Soon after George the Second was born, I stopped painting altogether. Gave up trying to keep him out of the paint or hurrying to finish something while he napped, which was never long enough to even get started well. The December light in front of me now was spreading out where, there on the horizon in the distance were the trails of smoke from the twin towers of a nuclear power plant way down on the coast. I realized it no longer seemed so strange as when I had first seen the towers and the smoke and learned what it was. Now I accepted it as if it were the smokestacks of a ship, just steaming along, not going anywhere, always there whenever I cared to look. Except that now with every view of it, I had a habit of feeling nervous, a scar of a frequent worry.

We turned onto our road, and I saw too, as I often failed to, the tangling vines and palm trees that huddled over every house or trailer on our street—on all the streets—as if the earth were waiting to reclaim the small circle that had been cut out in it. We were all campers. In single homes, campsites, squatting for just a little while, borrowers.

Being a passenger, with Drew in charge, was releasing me for all sorts of observation.

After we pulled into the driveway, the kids and I stuffed and poked the chosen tree through the front door, stood it up, spent a whole hour screwing it into its "easy-to-assemble" stand. Then stood back. It touched the ceiling in the corner of the living room. A ceiling that Drew said now looked like a colander for draining spaghetti. Rex the Roofer hadn't been back in three weeks, and every time I'd called him he'd only said I'd been on his mind. I was ready to fire him, but I couldn't find him. I had no one to finish up the roof anyway. And I'd already paid him the money that was required up front.

Every night just before supper, the kids and I bowed our heads:

"Lord, thanks for these peas and carrots, chicken and rice, and please don't let it rain till Rex the Roofer gets done." Then we moved on into: "Gracious Father, accept our thanks for this lasagna. And if You see Rex the Roofer, tell him we'd like to set his underwear on fire. Or, if You want to, just go ahead and do it Yourself." And George the Second started adding: "Yeah, like that burning bush You did."

The night we got the tree, the kids and I baked a green glaze onto papier mâché stars so the color would stick, then tied them onto our tree, and stayed up—all four of us—till midnight popping enough popcorn to go around that obese tree until George the Second totally pooped out—went to sleep on the floor under it. Mandy tied a ribbon around his neck, and Drew made a card to stick to his chest: "For Mom. 'Cause nobody else asked for this."

Luckily George the Second couldn't read and was too sleepy to have even tried when we carried him off to bed.

Then came the real hard part: because the tree was still too naked, at least for Christmas, looked like a wrestler in bikini tights. I hadn't wanted to get out the old ornaments, untangle fifteen years of lights, see probably half of them burned out. I wanted to start over. All new ornaments, everything different, everything all mine, so that the past wouldn't slip in like an oil leak for me to lose my footing on. I wanted to get rid of everything that would make me come loose, could freeze a minute and set tears in it.

But keeping the past out of the living room that night was no more possible than my parading around in a two-piece bathing suit, flaunting a middle with no stretch marks. I knew, too, I had to make some kind of arrangement with the past. My children needed it as much as I needed to get over it. It was—for them—a lifeline, something to hold on to. While for me, my life with George would always be a footnote in the days of my week.

How could I not see him in Drew's ears along with the color of my hair on Drew's head? And the hazel eyes of Mandy, twins to his, only hers now scared—she had seen more than any of us. Her teacher and her dad had been hiding feelings under professional skins, which had been probably as strange as watching two peacocks sashaying full tail feathers around each other. (It was Mandy I was most worried about, afraid that she no longer knew how to be a child, how to see the world as only an eleven-year-old should see it—with possibilities and brightness and promise. She seemed to have trouble going anywhere in the house alone.) And obviously the last bit of life in George's and my marriage was there in George the Second, full-blown and played at the highest pitch as though to be heard as a memorial.

After Mandy and George the Second were too tired to stay up with us, Drew and I finished the tree: blended the ornaments of all the Christmases past with the popcorn strings and the papier mâché stars that were us, now.

Then the strangest thing was when I woke up on Christmas day, the sun not even up yet, but hearing the kids tearing at the paper on their presents and the sounds of them finding the toys I had hidden around the living room. And I realized I had recipes coming out the yin-yang: rosemary butter for the turkey, cornbread dressing to be made from scratch—had to hurry and start the cornbread baking in the big iron skillet so it would have time to cool before I crumbled it up along with some day-old biscuits and stuck it all together with eggs and broth—peach pickle that I'd put up last summer, creamed onions that I must not let clump up, and giblet gravy (oh God, please let the gravy thicken right). And then I remembered: I wouldn't have to do any of that, or worry about or sweat over or complain about any of that. George was to have the children for a whole week, starting now. He would come for them at ten o'clock.

He came. They went.

Veni, vidi, vici—like my eighth grade Latin.

And so there I was, banging around in the house alone. Picking up wrapping paper and toys with no kids to play with them, heating up turkey noodle soup for myself, and keeping "Rudolph the Red Nosed Reindeer" playing on the turntable so this would seem like the cheeriest house on the street (just in case anybody was driving by and wondering).

I called Mama and Dad and wished them a Merry Christmas. I told them I was going out to dinner with some of my friends, that the kids were with George.

"That's so sad," my mother said.

"No, it's not sad. It's the way it is," I said back.

By midnight I was sipping a brandy alone on the porch, had shot Rudolph, and hung him up over the mantle.

The day after Christmas I was so glad to go to work, I felt sick. Never thought I'd be so happy over a job where it was mostly my duty to label body liquids and change sheets. Though, I found myself—really found myself—coming face to face with the girl who had once thought of becoming a doctor herself, who had found the thought of pushing away sickness and pain as rich in feeling as anything that could be done on this earth. Found myself picking up a lot of the lingo, feeding a coming-awake, once-buried interest in how things worked: blood and temperature, kidneys and hearts.

Hearts. My own. Waking up, too. It was like looking at an old photograph of myself: braces, dog-eared hair, wide untested eyes, not yet thinking it was only boys who became physicians.

I was becoming in harmony with someone I had not visited in a long while. And that day after Christmas, Dr. Haley, Betty, and I were a little bit more busy than usual, what with kids playing with new toys and sucking on them and passing them on with a couple of hundred germs at least. And people overeating and getting indigestion and thinking they were having heart attacks.

About noon little Jimmy Wampler was riding his new bike up and down Second Street with Kelly O'Neil and decided he needed some air in his tires. Pulled into the Mobil and went to do it himself. Pulled the air hose up to his bike, blew it up so big it popped and the bike frame hit him in the head, at the bridge of his nose. Blood everywhere, and Mr. Turner, who owns the Mobil, slid him quick onto a towel in the backseat of his car and drove him to us.

Jimmy was knocked for a loop, to say the least. Groggy and not able to even remember his name. I helped with him for a little while. And then it was my job to try to get in touch with his mother, while Betty and Dr. Haley kept working on Jimmy.

Adele Wampler didn't have a phone. She had seven kids and lived in a trailer a half mile from town. I started calling all the neighbors close to her. Couldn't find anybody home.

I could see Dr. Haley in the first treatment room, still bending over Jimmy, shining a light into his eyes, asking him questions. Then Dr. Haley told me to call for the county ambulance to drive Jimmy to the county hospital for a CAT scan. He and Betty put a pressure dressing over Jimmy's nose, and in about ten minutes, the ambulance driver and his helper slid Jimmy onto a stretcher and headed off, siren wailing.

I was shaking by then, having trouble even dialing the phone, still trying to find his mother. The blood and seriousness of it all had been the most in this job I'd had to deal with so far. I didn't have—after all—what it took for this. I was too fragile myself to have to deal with someone maybe dying. And then Kelly O'Neil walked through the door of the office with Adele Wampler. Adele's face was as pale as paper. She was the biggest woman in Palm Key by far, a good six feet and nearly as wide. She looked at me. "Kelly here says she and Jimmy were up town and Jimmy got hurt."

I nodded. I told her to follow me into Dr. Haley's office, and when I did, he walked out of the examining room and came close to her. He reached out and took Adele's hand—his habit with patients when he had to say something not exactly easy to hear. And he was holding her hand, just a few inches taller than she was, so they were looking almost eye to eye, his voice low and calm as he told her what everybody else knew: how Jimmy was putting air in his bike tire and it exploded, and the bike frame hit him in the forehead. He told her he thought Jimmy would be just fine, but that it was likely he had a ruptured artery under the bone, and, if so, a blood clot could be pushing on the brain. Jimmy had had to be sent immediately to the county hospital; even twenty or thirty minutes without treatment could have been too long. "You see," he said softly to Adele, "I couldn't wait to talk to you."

Adele looked closely at Dr. Haley's eyes. "My baby, Jimmy?"

"Yes."

Dr. Haley was still holding her hand, his shirt stained with Jimmy's blood.

And while Adele talked, she moved her eyes from his face to the stain on his shirt. "Got hit in the head?"

"Yes."

She kept staring at the blood stain on his shirt, then back at his face. "In a ambulance? On his way now?"

"Yes."

And then Adele Wampler took one more look at his shirt, pulled her hand out of his, reached out her arms, let out one long, hair-raising cry of "Oh! My Lord!" and fainted against him. For a second, he held her, but his legs were slipping, and then he fell back onto the floor with Adele covering him. Her arms were splayed out across him and the floor. She covered almost every inch of him. "Mrs. Wampler?" He was speaking just at her ear.

There was no answer.

I leaned close. "Adele?"

Betty went to get some ice and some ammonia for Adele to smell. And I sat down on the floor beside Dr. Haley, ready to try to help roll Adele off of him.

Through the top of Adele's hair, he glanced at me. "You have to put something soft on the floor, first. We can't take the chance of banging her head."

"Right." I hurried to get a pillow from the treatment room. When I came back, it struck me: the awfulness and seriousness and hilarity of Dr. Haley and Adele Wampler taking up nearly the whole floor space of his office.

"Okay," he said. "If you can just move her arms." He looked at me, gazing through Adele's bangs again, blowing her hair away from his mouth. Then, neither of us could help it: The sounds of both our voices played around each other's—first his laugh, then mine in echo. Then both together. Then both quiet and still as we tried not to. Out of respect to Adele, we wanted to keep our faces straight and our mouths shut. I mean, it wasn't something we'd want for ourselves: somebody laughing their heads off at us if we were out cold.

But as soon as we were quiet, the laughs would come again. It was as bad as being a kid getting tickled in church.

Adele wasn't dead or seriously hurt, we knew that. We could see her breathing. And Dr. Haley was holding his hand against her neck, taking her pulse. Then we stopped looking at each other altogether, because it was the only way that we could stop laughing and remain dignified.

I reached across his chest, which was Adele's back and positioned her arms close to her sides so we could roll her off him.

"All right: one, two, three," Dr. Haley said.

Adele eased back onto the pillow on the floor where I had put it, and Betty brought the ammonia.

Before Adele even opened her eyes, she asked: "Where's Jimmy?"

Dr. Haley told her: "We'll get someone to drive you to him."

He helped Adele sit up. We supported her back. "What happened?" she asked.

"You fainted for a minute." Dr. Haley was kneeling beside her. "I want you to sit here now and rest a minute."

While we sat with Adele, Betty called the fire station for a volunteer, and Mr. Lewis came to drive Adele to be with Jimmy.

Dr. Haley explained how she'd probably have to sign some papers if Jimmy had to have surgery, but that she shouldn't try to worry too much because he would drive down there and oversee the treatment himself, as soon as he found out what exactly the situation was.

Adele walked out, still dazed, and I turned to look at Dr. Haley, who was walking into the examining room to see the next patient, who had been waiting all this time. "Mark," I said, then realized his first name came so easily. We'd been working together for all these weeks, and it just hadn't been necessary to call him anything—we were just there together—me watching for what he might need next, second-guessing him, trying to stay a half-step ahead of what he was doing. And now, he turned back to look at me, "Yeah?"

"Maybe you ought to change your shirt." I pointed to the stain of Jimmy's blood.

He looked down. "Oh yeah." We were already off schedule now by several hours. He didn't have another shirt there, and he didn't know where I kept the surgical greens, so I went to get him some, and he was standing there with his shirt already off and I handed him the new one, and he slipped it on, and then we stopped and looked at each other. We were both embarrassed and turned quickly away.

I hurried into the examining room where he wouldn't be—the one where Jimmy had been—to clean up.

That afternoon late, it started to rain. I asked to leave work a little early. I called from the office first and left a message on Rex the Roofer's answering machine. I told him this was it—absolute D day—and if he didn't finish my roofing job, I was going to take him to court. (The kids were dying for me to be on "The People's Court," anyway. The fact that it was held in California didn't hold a bit of water with them.)

But when I got home, Rex was there. He had his crew up on my roof—all two of them—nailing down shingles. Inside my house, all the pots I had set out were playing a tune as the rain leaked through the ceiling into them. If it had to happen, at least it was a good time; the children would be at George's for six more days, and I'd have plenty of time to clean up.

I turned around from wiping up a new leak in George the Second's room to see Rex standing there, right behind me, watching me. "I'm just sick about how long this job's taken," I said, ignoring the fact that he'd come in unannounced, or uninvited. I was startled. But I didn't want to pick a fight right then about anything but the roof. "You didn't tell me you wouldn't finish it right away."

"Sorry," he said. He had on jeans and a blue work shirt, and he hadn't shaved in a few days. Guess he thought it was that new Miami Vice sexy look. He was grinning. "It just slipped my mind how desperate you were."

"So how much longer?"

"A day. Two."

I went into my bedroom to reposition the pots. He came in behind me. When I leaned over, he put his hands around my waist. "Bet you get lonely here. No husband anymore."

At first my body wouldn't move, and I could barely think. I was frozen, appalled that he would do that, not quite believing it yet. And then I straightened up, looked at him. He moved his hands away, but quickly reached out and put both hands on my shoulders.

"You're here to fix my roof," I said. "And not one thing else." I sounded a little flustered, but I was getting the point across, at least. "Well, I know," he said. "But I figured you might be interested in a special I had this week." "Back off," I said, reminding myself of a gunslinger in *High Noon.*

He touched my cheek. "I like women who talk mean." I stepped back. "I don't care what you like," I said. "Aw, come on." He reached out again, his hand near my face.

"You need to cool off," I said, and with good aim tipped over the turkey roaster I was holding, throwing the rainwater out. It splashed against the front of him, wetting his clothes and his feet. "Oh rats!" I said, as I looked down and realized the mess I was going to have to clean up. The carpet would take days to dry out. And "Shit," he said, at the same time, only louder and shaking his hands, dripping, looking down at himself. His pants looked like he'd lost control and wet himself. And to me, that's exactly what had happened.

"Leave," I said. "And get your men off my roof. I don't want you to forget anything here you have to come back for."

"Hellcat," he said, then took one of his business cards out of his back pocket and put it in the pocket of my blouse, leaving his fingers there for a second, rubbing against my breast. "For when you change your mind," he said, grinning at me, then walked out.

I moved out behind him, bolted the front door that now I saw he'd left open all that time. And I pushed a chair in front of it. I moved the garbage can in front of the back door and bolted it. At least the holes in the roof weren't big enough for him—or anybody like him—to come through.

I sat in the rocking chair in my bedroom, sipping a brandy, waiting for my nerves to settle. I just kept watching the rain come through the ceiling—cussing one minute, crying the next, and, in between, rocking like a crazy person.

Then behind me and through the house, the frogs began to sing. Apparently a bunch of them had come into the house, slipping through the door that Rex the Repulsive Roofer had left open. And during the rain they had hopped into some of the pots I had sitting around. Nothing better to do, I figured, than just bellow along with them: me and the frogs, like backups for some lead singer who never showed up.

When the phone rang, it took me a minute to hear it over myself.

"Linda?"

"Yes?"

Mark's voice was calm, professional, as usual. "The hospital just called. They've started operating on Jimmy Wampler. I thought I'd go down there, and I wondered if you'd want to go be with Mrs. Wampler until we know how Jimmy is."

"Sure. That'd be fine."

I was hoping my own voice didn't show any stress or anything that'd tip him off that I was two seconds past berserk. Medical people are supposed to be able to handle any emergency. Stay calm. Show no emotion. Be totally terrific in a crisis.

"I'll be over to pick you up in a few minutes," he said.

"Fine."

Didn't know what to wear—nurse's outfit or plain stuff. Wanted to look professional for him; but, for Adele, like just who I was, a friend. An ordinary everyday P.T.A. mother like her.

Didn't much matter. Half my clothes in my closet were wet. I put on green checkered pants, sort of nice and dressy and put the hair dryer on the back of them. Then I heard his car out front, the old Mercedes chugging like crazy. I didn't want him to see the house like this. But my pants still weren't dry, and I shot the hair dryer up to high and bent over closer to it. Then I heard him knock. Now I had to open the door and the whole bit, which I'd forgotten I'd have to do: shove the chair away from the door, unbolt it, open it. And when I did, the bullfrog's chorus came out in the background.

"Hey," I said, leaning on the door frame, and on the other side of the screen door he stood, looking in at me. Looking nice: dark pants, white shirt, tie.

Totally discreet—or just shocked past remarking: "Ready?" he asked.

"Yeah." I pulled the door closed, quick.

"Still haven't gotten your roof fixed?" He looked up. Tar paper showing like burned meat. "Got a little problem with that."

"Bad day for that problem."

"Yeah."

On the drive to the county hospital, we just listened to the radio, barely saying anything, Jimmy Wampler on both our minds.

At the hospital, Mark spent almost all his time with the other doctors, and I sat with Adele in the family's waiting room. She and I talked about the P.T.A. and Jimmy's head. The Shrimp Festival and the school carnival and Jimmy's head. Christmas and bikes and Jimmy's head.

It was night when Mark and one other doctor came out to tell us that Jimmy was out of surgery and in the Recovery Room, and Adele could see him in a little while. He was going to be fine, as far as everyone knew. They'd let out the blood clot, and Jimmy was missing some hair, but that was all.

Mark and I both looked quickly at Adele. We saw her raising her hands, reaching for him, and as she put one arm on his shoulder in a hug, I grabbed the other one, stood on tiptoe so I could support her other side, and she hugged me, too. We backed her up and set her on the couch.

"Can I stay with him?" she asked. She looked at me. I looked at Mark. "It can be arranged, can't it?" I asked.

He nodded.

"I want to be with him when he wakes up." Adele was looking at me, saying it to me as though I was the one in charge and could arrange anything. "I wouldn't be doing nobody any good at home." Her face was wet and hot with worry.

"Who's looking after your other children?" I asked.

"I called Lucille. Asked her if she could take them in the day care till my sister would drive over and get them."

"Good." I touched her arm in a signal that everything would be fine.

"Yeah." Adele grinned, her face gaining color. "That Lucille's good as gold when you need her."

"And better." I went down the hall to get Adele a Diet Coke.

"I can't thank you enough, Dr. Haley," she was saying when I got back.

"Ready to go?" Mark looked at me. I nodded.

We walked down the hall toward the elevator. But before we left, we went into the Recovery Room, walked to the edge of his bed and looked at him, then put on masks and all surgical greens so we wouldn't pass anything harmful on to Jimmy. I'd never been in a room like this. I was treading water way over my head. But I knew I wouldn't be called on. Too many other people, good, smart people, and ready. Mark read Jimmy's chart. He talked to the nurses there. I stared at Jimmy, his head wound in bandages like a beehive. His eyes were swollen shut, a red drain was coming out of the side of his head, but he was responding to almost everything the nurses were asking: his name, and to move his arm, then his leg. I watched. My stomach was turning and squeezed in on itself, and my throat closed as the tiny line of what was life and what was not lay drawn across Jimmy's face and across my own as I felt our hearts beat in a similar rhythm. I had never come so close to watching life leave, and with the presence of it now easing itself more strongly into Jimmy's face, erasing the line that he had come so close to crossing, it was as though I, too, had crossed over into a place I had not fully known. I could not comprehend either one—life or death—not really. I knew only the fact of them. But I had now been there when they had shown themselves. And I could feel the presence of my own life as intensely as watching the certainty of his, coming back. Knew it as what I never again wanted to lose. As what I had to now change, coddle and move, prod to where I could fully be alive.

"Ready?" Mark went out the door, holding it open for me.

We got in his car, which was still only half fixed. The antique grill was proving to be hard to find. And the front of the car had this big gaping hole, sort of like a missing tooth. The rain was almost stopped now—the windshield wipers going back and forth only once in awhile. We were again listening to the radio on the way back, occasionally mentioning the Shrimp Festival and Jimmy's head. The sky at Palm Key, the restaurants, and fresh fish and what had happened that day. As my own house came into sight, its tar-paper roof and the feel of my own heart beating inside me mixed with some music playing on the radio, a Mozart concerto like sound being squeezed. It was so sweet with longing that the sensation of feeling my own life and how I wanted to change it, came out onto my face. I looked down.

I wiped the water out of my eyes before it fell. I blew my nose. I passed it off as a little sinus trouble. I even said I had something wrong with my contacts.

But I wasn't wearing contacts. I even had on my glasses. And then, when I couldn't pass off my evident feelings as anything else, I told him it was my roof.

We sat in his parked car in my driveway, looking at the tar paper and the half-nailed shingles and the rain and the frogs on the walkway. He didn't say anything. I didn't either. It was strange how we could be still and quiet and not want to leave the stillness and quietness. And then I told him that I didn't have a chance of getting the roof fixed any time soon either, because I'd fired the roofer.

He looked at me. Until then, he'd tried not to. I mean, I was sort of like Adele blacking out and knocking him to the floor and pinning him there. We were trying to preserve our dignity by not looking at each other. And then he said, as I forgot to hide my eyes: "You know, just last week I started renovating my house. I have a great carpenter. I'll tell him to come over."

"You do?"

He nodded. I raised my hand toward my own house again. "I'd invite you in—for some coffee or something. But I have all these frogs in there."

He tried not to look surprised. Then as what I had said struck me, I laughed.

I led him in through the front door and we sidestepped the pots that were sitting around, a frog in or near just about every one. He followed me into the kitchen where the kids' Christmas breakfast was still sitting out like I was preserving it for their baby books: George the Second's Chocolate and Marshmallow Loops, which I let him have only on Christmas. Mandy's barrettes beside her box of Pop Tarts, and Drew's cup of hot chocolate.

"Sorry," I said, making a clean spot for him to sit down. "My kids left on Christmas Day. Their dad gets them on the holidays. And all this is sort of a signal to me that I can take a break from cleaning up after them." I laughed. "Want some Pop Tarts?" He nodded no, smiling.

"Coffee, then?"

He grinned. "How's that whiting I left here?"

"Frozen."

"Are they good cooked?"

"Yeah. Especially broiled, a little Spanish sauce over the top." I took two cups out of the cabinet. "But you and George will have to catch a few more before I have enough for a good dinner." I glanced at him.

He was watching me.

I sat down while the coffee perked. And then after a few minutes, we went out into the living room. We sat looking at that huge Christmas tree wearing its mixed bag of finery and were serenaded by my house frogs while we sipped the last of my brandy.

It was as if we had a pact without ever having signed it: no past, no life before this, no time ever but *now*—not for either one of us. Then, just as quickly as he had come inside, he said he had to go, had to meet someone.

The abruptness of his leaving bothered me. It made me wonder what I'd done.

After I let him out the door, I watched him walk across the yard to his car. Then I barricaded myself in—or the world out.

9.
Drew

All that winter women just kept killing me.

As for Heather? I was nothing less than cold busted with her. Ever since that day in the show, she would barely talk to me. At school in the hall would only nod, flip her hair like a horse might aim its tail at a fly. I left a few messages on her answering machine: *Yo, Heather. It's me, Drew. If you get a chance, give me a call. If you don't, I'll call back.*

Yo Heather, it's me, Drew again . . .

Yo Heather . . .

Thought about going to court and changing my name to Drew Again.

And as for my mother? She was driving me just about totally out of my tree. (Wonder if they ever had to put June Cleaver on tranquilizers.)

Mom's nerves weren't totally frazzled, though, until a man got shot up on the highway by someone who forced his car off the road and robbed him. The man lived, but it had happened so close to us that everybody came a little unglued. There were letters in the newspaper about it. About how no place seemed safe anymore. Not even Palm Key.

We got the roof fixed, finally. A carpenter showed up right after Christmas. Finished up the roof in one day. Dr. Haley stopped by to watch awhile—he and my mother talking out in the yard, then having coffee on the porch in the late afternoon while the roofer finished up. Mom filed a complaint at the Better Business Bureau about Rex the Roofer. Said he didn't follow through on his contracts. Didn't respect his customers either. We tried to get her to take him onto "The People's Court." But she said he'd done half the job, which was only what she'd paid him for up front, so she didn't really have anything she could sue him about except for being a piss-poor human being (course she didn't use those words with me, but still I knew what she meant). Smearing his name seemed to give her some pleasure, though.

And soon after Christmas, George gave up his rabbit suit. It wasn't one trick that did it, he just lost interest. And Mandy stopped losing her breath so much. The inhaler just sat by her bed like a semiretired tool, like a second-string quarterback. And she could even go to the bathroom alone, every once in a while.

But that Christmas week when me and Mandy and George were still staying with Dad, I kept checking in at home. Wanted to spend some time there in case Heather returned my call. Dr. Haley came over a few times that week. Then Mom told him one day that if we didn't go ahead and thaw out the fish that he and George had caught, and cook them, they'd have freezer burn so bad they wouldn't be worth having. Dr. Haley said he didn't have time to go fishing to catch any more (which I knew was a deadass lie to cover up for the fact that he'd just as soon go out in my boat again as have all his teeth filled without Novocain). Mom was sweet about it, though, said she'd just go to the fish market and get something fresh to round out the dinner. So the night when we all got back home (Dad returned us a little early because Anne Marie was dying to go to Miami and spend her Christmas cash, and we were just dying not to go with her), we all got in the kitchen: George dipping his fish in milk to cut the fishy taste; and Mandy squeezing lemon on them, then rolling them in white cornmeal, then handing them to me so I could fry up some while Mom and Dr. Haley made Spanish sauce to go on the ones they were going to broil. (George wouldn't eat broiled fish yet. Mom was going slow on forcing him to watch his cholesterol count. Was going to work him into it, gradually, she said. Which, with George, was the only way she could go, anyway.)

That night I noticed Mom and Dr. Haley getting pretty tight. They sat on the porch like two crabs on the beach finding out they liked the same patch of sun, the same marsh-grass hideout, digging holes side by side, watching out for each other.

The stray dog that had taken a liking to Dr. Haley that day on the town pier had also taken up living with him. He'd lie on our front porch beside Dr. Haley's feet while he was there, or chase around after George when he was on his bike. Dr. Haley said the dog was fine, except that he couldn't seem to break him of chasing cars, or bikes, or joggers, which drove everybody crazy: that frenzy of running and barking after anything that moved, which is probably why somebody drove into Palm Key and dumped the dog in the first place.

My mother brought cheese slices out onto the porch and fed them to the dog while Dr. Haley was there. Dr. Haley just kept calling the dog What's-his-name, and then we all just shortened that to Whatsy. And it stuck.

At night, after Dr. Haley and Whatsy left, Mom would bolt the door, put a chair up under the door knob and then go to the back door and move a table across it. So there we'd be, barricaded into the house for the night like in a fort.

Fort Marsh: That was us.

New Year's Eve Dr. Haley came over and sat on the porch with Mom for about an hour, then said he had to go. I think Mom sort of hoped he'd stay late and ring in the new year with her, or whatever people old as them were supposed to do on New Year's Eve. I knew, at least, that Mom was dead-set on ringing out the old, since it was about as good for remembering as an ingrown toenail.

But that New Year's Eve, as far as ringing in the new year with Dr. Haley, she was cold busted, too. And that worried me. She had this sort of hang-dog look, like maybe she'd counted on him coming over.

Instead she put on her old red robe, her fuzzy shoes that are striped like a tiger, and read Uncle Remus stories to Mandy and George, with Br'er Rabbit accent, the whole works. Mrs. Cleaver herself couldn't have done better. After she had gotten them warmed up with Uncle Remus, she moved on into Shakespeare, out loud, and rolling, looking up first at Mandy, then at George, and even me, while I was still there. I was headed over to a friend's house to play a couple of hours of video games.

Lately, Mom had gotten this thing about reading Shakespeare to us, said he was an old buddy of hers—ha—and furthermore would be good for us. She'd gotten on this grammar kick, mainly because George had started playing with Teddy Lambert and his little sister, Sissy, and had picked up all these new ways of saying things. Mainly just Cracker talk, but it drove Mom nuts. When Teddy and Sissy were over playing on Saturday afternoons or before dinner when Mom got home from work, she'd take apple juice and graham crackers on a tray out to them so they wouldn't sneak junk before dinner, and Sissy would look up at her as she lowered the tray, and ask: "Ain't you got no Coke?"

Then when Mom offered Teddy celery stuffed with peanut butter, one of her hold-em-off-till-dinner-good-for-you snacks, Teddy picked up the celery and twirled it close to his face: "I ain't never seen nothing like 'at."

And then pretty soon, George was doing the same, his language going downhill so fast I knew my mother was about to have a cow.

She heard George say one night, "I ain't never seen nothing like that old fart," and that did it: Out came the Bible and Mother Goose, Uncle Remus, whose Br'er Rabbit grammar was explained to be what was used only in a story and nowhere else, and then Shakespeare.

Good old Shakespeare. Mom did everything but totally act out the parts. Her voice low for Hamlet and then rising up for his girlfriend's, and it'd hit several strides in the middle so she usually went to bed hoarse. But if it hadn't been for Mom acting things out, we wouldn't have had a chance at knowing what in the hell was going on. (Shakespeare was a hard dude to follow.)

Then one late afternoon she told Teddy and Sissy and George that she'd give them a dime each, if for ten minutes none of them would say a double negative or an *ain't*. Then, of course, she went into all this detail about what exactly a double negative was, and as for *ain't*, Teddy quickly piped up: "Oh, we don't say *ain't*, 'cause we know it ain't right." He was game for the dime though.

Mom looked at her watch and said, "All right. Go." She'd put them at the kitchen table with some Play-Doh and cookie cutters while she cooked dinner and timed their *ain'ts*. After ten minutes, she had to give them all a dime, because they *had* followed her rules, even though none of them had said anything, just kept totally mute for the whole ten minutes.

Now on New Year's Eve, Mom was into *The Tempest*, her cheeks puffed out for the storm's sound effects, which was keeping George's interest. As I was going out the door, headed to my friend's, I heard her tell George he could act out the part of the dethroned king, Prospero, who had ordered the tempest.

"I don't want to be no king. I want to be the storm."

"You don't mean you don't want to be no king, you mean you don't want to be *the* king."

"Yeah. That's what I said."

"Well, if you don't say any *ain'ts* or *he don'ts*, then you can be the storm."

"Storms don't talk anyway," George said and blew air out of his puffed-up cheeks and ran around the room waving his arms and twirling like a tornado.

"Okay, go," Mom said to George and also to Mandy, who was reading the part of Ariel, and Mom started reading the part of Prospero herself, "When first I raised the tempest. Say, my spirit . . ." She looked up at Mandy. Mom's chin was tucked like some old dude with a turkey waddle, "How fares the king and's followers?"

Before I closed the door behind me, I heard Mandy's voice high like a flute, "Just as you left them; all prisoners, sir, In the lime-grove." Mandy was studying the words so hard that she was bent over the page like a goose-neck lamp: "They cannot budge till your release."

I closed the door, Mandy's voice fading behind it. But for a full solid second my sister's voice was stuck echoing in my head—pretty damn close to being not only about those dudes Shakespeare was writing about but also what I thought was our whole damn situation, too: Waiting out a storm. Prisoners. Huddled down in Fort Marsh. In the lime grove.

I walked across the front yard. George swooped past the window, his arms out, twirling. I looked back at our house, the shadows of Mom and George and Mandy against the curtains, and then back at the road where I was going. Our giant Christmas tree was now lying beside the driveway for the garbage man. Depressing as hell. I mean there's not one thing more depressing to me than that: a Christmas tree lying out as garbage when only hours before it was the God-almighty in the living room.

At my friend's house I played a couple of thousand video games, left a few more hundred messages on Heather's machine, then went on back to sit with Mom till it was one.

We watched the new year get rung in on TV, then were on our way to bed, when she went into George's room to check on him, and then into Mandy's to check on her.

I could hear Mandy and George breathing in sleep even way out in the hall, like tiny trains steaming along, Little Toots climbing hills. And then I heard Mom let out a cry that was not quite a scream but more like brakes squeaking. I went in there to see what was wrong.

She was standing over Mandy's bed, holding one of her dog ears in her hand, Mandy asleep like she was drugged, just moving a little after Mom's squeak.

She turned around and looked at me, her hand cradling the dog ear in the dark, lit only by Mandy's Donald Duck nightlight, her voice like radio static, a whisper that was tight; "Oh God, Drew, look at this." She pulled her hand down Mandy's dog ear and a handful of hair came out tangled around her fingers. She had polished her nails in a new bright pink, for the new year, I supposed. I couldn't remember ever seeing my mother's nails done like that. But whatever new things she was trying out, wound around them now was Mandy's hair no longer attached to her head. "Do you know what this means?" she said.

I shook my head. But it didn't matter; she was not looking at me, and it was too dark to see me anyway. "The power plant's leaking. Look at this. Mandy's hair's falling out. Oh God, Drew, she must have radiation sickness. We must be the first ones to see this. To know this. Oh, God. Drew, do you know what this means?" She glanced at me and must have remembered that I was her son, her child, too, and she grabbed my hair and pulled it, and I grabbed her hand where she was grabbing me.

"Geez, that hurts!" I yelled, but my voice was held down to radio static, too. Neither of us wanted to wake Mandy up, especially if she was dying and needed her rest.

Then Mom was running on at the mouth, and I couldn't stop her. "I shouldn't even be telling you this. You're still just a child yourself. You shouldn't have to have my worries. I shouldn't be scaring you like this. But God, Drew, do you know what this means? If Mandy doesn't have radiation sickness, then it's leukemia."

If you ask me, Mom had gotten so much into that medicine thing since working at the clinic, she knew too much for all our own good. Always pushing on our bumps and scrapes, studying the color of our eyelids and fingernails. And now Mandy's dog ear had let loose new things.

For a little while, the sound of her voice and all that she knew convinced me. Mandy was going to die, and then maybe all of us; and I could not understand that or accept that. I reached out and picked up Mandy's other dog ear where it was lying on her pillow attached to her sleeping head. A handful of hair came out onto my fingers, too. And then I felt the heavy wiggle of a rubber band in my palm and looked at it in the faint light as it lay like a tiny worm stretching across my skin.

I held it up. It had been cut; and I looked down on the floor and found the other one that had been holding together Mandy's other dog ear, and I picked it up, too. I held up both rubber bands and showed Mom.

"She just cut 'em out herself," I said. "And missed."

When Mom realized that that was, indeed, the truth, and that Mandy was not dying, and we were not next in line, she reached over and grabbed me as tight as the rubber bands had held Mandy's hair. "Oh, Lord, Drew. Thank God. We're fine. We're all fine!"

She was laughing, and Mandy was sleeping, and I was being squeezed to a pulp in a mother-hungry hug.

But damn did I feel smart! I mean, it was a drag, and tiring too, digging my mother out of holes, but I was sort of swelled up with it and not as sleepy as I had been.

I closed my eyes on the last day of that year with the certain knowledge that I could do a lot of things well, and not the least of them was living well; in fact, getting it done pretty good. I was outright hot at taking care of not only myself but someone else, too.

Believe me, that wasn't a little thing to know when it seemed pretty certain on that last night of that year that I was pretty close to flunking my whole first half of my first year of high school.

• • •

We hadn't been asleep any longer than an hour after the radiation scare, when the phone rang. Mom must have drunk a lot of brandy getting over Mandy's dog ear, or maybe to celebrate the new year, because she didn't wake up at first. I made my way into the kitchen and picked up the phone there. After all, it could have been Heather returning my call, even though it was 2:00 A.M. "Hello?"

Then I heard my mother's voice on the phone in her bedroom, "Hello?"

It certainly wasn't Heather. Instead some dude with a deep ugly voice said quick and even: "I'm jackin' off."

On the other end, my mother's voice was sleepy but polite. "Jack who?"

"Jackin' off," he said again, obviously delighted.

"I'm sorry, I don't know any Jack," she said. I could hear her yawning.

"Mom, for Christ's sake," I said into my end of the phone, "it's an obscene phone call!"

"Drew, is that you?"

"Yeah."

"And I'm jackin' off."

"Hang up, Mom," I said.

"Aw, don't do that," Jack said.

"Drew," my mother said, "where are you?"

"In the kitchen."

"And I'm jackin' off," Jack said again.

"Who is that?" my mother demanded.

"Don't you get it, Mom?" I screamed. "It's an obscene phone call!"

"It is?"

"Yeah," Jack and I said together. And I slammed the phone down.

In a few seconds I picked it up again to see if, by some stupid chance, my mother or Jack was still holding on. There was breathing, but I wasn't sure whose it was. "Mom?" I said, low.

"Drew?"

"Yeah." Then I thought I might as well: "Jack, are you still on here, too?"

There was no answer, only my mother's breathing. Then, "Lord, Drew," she said. "That's never happened to me before. Are you still in the kitchen?"

"Umhumm."

"Well, come to bed. You're way too young to have heard that."

I passed her in the hall, me on my way into my room and her in her robe and tiger feet on her way out into the living room to sit a while longer and probably drink some more brandy, to calm down again.

•

Fort Marsh continued on like that full blast: barricaded doors every night, me and Mom hearing each other's sleep-broken breathing as we waked up to listen for anything that was not anything. I don't think it was so much that we were watching and listening for something to get us as much as that we were waking up with a sense that something was missing. Waking up to listen for something to return. Something to release us.

10.
Linda

Mark took a few days off from the clinic, and Betty and I did our best to run it ourselves—at least listening to complaints and making appointments. First thing I did to start off my new year was to get an unlisted phone number. When George moved out, I took his name next to mine out of the phone book—and, dumb me, didn't know that listing myself as just Linda Marsh was an invitation for all sorts of creeps to call. Sometimes I wondered if that dirty voice on the end of the line on New Year's Eve had been Rex the Roofer. Didn't sound like him, but with both that creepy call and Rex's sneaking into my bedroom happening so close together (and me smearing his name all over town, which would definitely tick him off) made me realize I had to do something to bring back my sense of ease.

I wasn't about to go out and get me a gun. Mean as I sometimes felt, I knew I might shoot somebody who didn't need it.

But the idea of a dog didn't just jump out at me all at once either. I'd missed Lolly ever since he died. Having Mark come over and sit out on the porch with me, his dog Whatsy hanging around, made me think about Lolly and how much I missed him.

Mark didn't know a thing about how to take care of that dog or handle him. Wore shoes with dents all in the leather the shape of Whatsy's teeth. Just talking about the dog got the idea of dogs on my mind, I guess. And too, Mandy had this thing about animals, loved anything with four legs. I thought a dog would be good for her, if not for all of us, and we talked about it at supper, about what kind we wanted and all that.

George the Second was game for a big one, so he could ride it. And Mandy talked about it all the time: "When we going to get it, Mom? We going to keep it in the house? Can I name it?"

Drew didn't care at all what we got, as long as it would do the job. I don't think he liked the feeling, either, of sleeping in the house now that George the First was definitely gone. So I set down the rules when I finally decided what they were. First, we'd get a dog at the humane society, because that'd be the cheapest, not to mention that we'd be taking some poor critter off of Death Row. And two, it had to be some kind of dog that would make a good watchdog. I didn't want something to feed that would just lie around. And then I made the additional rule that Mandy would get to pick it out and name it. Thought maybe we'd break through the quiet circle she'd barricaded herself into, thought I'd brush her life with a little joy, encourage her to be a kid again.

I told the kids we'd go that next Saturday to Death Row. And by Wednesday Mandy had settled on a name for whatever dog she picked out. I told Mark that day at work that when he came over now with Whatsy, they'd have more to visit than just me.

He glanced up from his desk where he was sitting writing a letter or something, his shoes sticking out from under it, the tassels on his loafers chewed off. He smiled. "So you finally decided?"

"Yeah. I figured I might as well. It'll be nice having a dog around again. And Mandy's set on naming it Rambo." I laughed.

"Nice name." He laughed a little, too, his laugh like a cold engine, a motor trying to start, a chuckle turning over and over that I found myself sometimes hungry for. I would try to remember jokes that Bill Duffy would tell me when I picked up George the Second from Lucille's day care, so when Mark came over to sit on the porch, I could tell them to him. It was funny and strange and wonderful, because I found myself saving parts of my day in hopes that by telling them to Mark I would get to see and hear him laugh.

I looked at him now, and he looked at me for a long second, then I slipped into the linen room. I could still see him when I reached way back onto the towel shelf, and before I knew it, I had stacked my arms up with towels until I had to press against them with my chin. Why was it that I had become so hungry for the look and sound of him? Did I just have a strong, unnatural appetite for the sight and sound of anything that was male, since I no longer lived in intimacy with that? (Horny, Drew would call it.) Or was it that I was just finding more to look at and think about than my own life, and what was wrong with it?

The angle of his elbow there now against his desk was sharp with the bones under the skin moving as he wrote, his head bent in concentration. The length of his nose leaning over what he was writing made a line through the center of the room. Every day I took note of the small tan mole on the side of his right jaw that he had so carefully shaved around, the skin seemingly scraped in a circle to avoid it. Was it him, or was I just responding to the part of him that I found within myself—how we seemed to desire to avoid the past, how we spent such constant wild energy in whittling every day to stand alone, to live it as it came, to remain awake in the present only?

Whenever he and I sat on my porch looking out into the Gulf, we let our gazes lie quietly on the water and spoke of nothing that we had not shared here, at the office, or within the last few minutes, or that we would tomorrow. I knew almost nothing about him, and yet everything, since we passed time here together caring for other people's needs. I respected his mystery and his quietness that seemed to be a signal that there would be no questions asked aloud between us. There would be only ourselves and the moment to deal with. Like now: When turning in the linen room, I saw him moving his hand in small tight circles across the paper, not yet letting his pen make a mark or touch down. It was that telling fact, like with George the First, who never tolerated any clutter; and now Mark, who wrote in the air, practicing, editing, honing whatever it was he wanted to say before he touched anything that would leave a permanent mark.

I walked out of the linen room and into the treatment room where I would straighten everything up. "Rambo, huh?" he said behind me, laughing again.

Then the clinic door opened, and I heard Drew's voice. He was talking to Betty MacHenry; I was just naturally tuned into the sound of his voice, coming from anywhere, and I threw down the towels I was carrying and rushed to where I heard him. "Sliced it on a Swiss Army knife," he was saying. "It's not too bad, but it seems deep, and I thought it might need stitches." I thought he meant himself, and then I saw Mandy standing beside him, her hand wrapped in a blue towel, stained in deep red streaks. Her face was pinched, and she was sucking her bottom lip. I went to her, unwrapped the towel, and took a look for myself. Across the fatty base of her thumb was a deep but small cut, and from what I knew it *did* need stitches if it was going to heal properly.

"She was whittling on this board. She was going to make a sign for our dog. Beware or something, I don't know." Drew looked at me. He had on a red sweater, and he was sweating.

"It was going to say, SLOW—DOG CROSSING," Mandy said. "And I was going to put it at the edge of the yard by the road." She looked at me.

"Let's go get this fixed," I said, and led her toward Mark's office. "You can go on home, Drew. I'll bring Mandy with me."

After Mark looked at the cut in Mandy's hand, he said that he, too, thought it needed a few quick stitches, and I took her into a treatment room. I made her sit up on the treatment table, and her legs, which she had just started shaving—getting long and bony now, too—hung off, her blue Keds and purple socks dangling. But when Mandy saw the needle with the Xylocaine in it, to put her thumb to sleep, it was as if she became four years old; and all the months, or rather years, of being good and acting her age flew out the window—and out of her mouth. Suddenly I knew where George the Second had come from: he was only Mandy in disguise. "Hell, no!" she screamed. "Get that shitty thing away from me!" I didn't know she knew words like that, or, anyway, how to use them so easily. She bolted off the treatment table and into the back hall. And then Mark and I heard a door slam. He and I looked at each other. He put the Xylocaine down, and we both went to hunt for Mandy. It appeared that she'd barricaded herself into the linen room, because I'd just left that door open, and it was now shut solid, and when I pushed against it, it wouldn't give. "Mandy," I said, "are you in there?"

"What if I am?"

"What do you have across the door?"

"A carton of stuff, so what?"

"Honey, Mark is just going to put your thumb to sleep so he can stitch it up."

"I don't want any stitches. It never was my idea to get any son of a bitch stitches."

"It's a bad cut, Mandy. If we don't stitch it up, it might get badly infected before it can heal."

"I don't give a shit."

"But if it gets infected it could turn green and you might lose it."

"That's stupid. How can I lose it?"

"It'll get gangrene and rot half off and then the whole thing will have to be cut off and you won't have a thumb at all." (I wasn't about to paint a pretty picture.)

"I don't care. It's a son of a bitch thumb. I've never liked this thumb."

"Open the door, Mandy!"

"Hell no!"

I was standing at the door, talking through it and getting nowhere, and wondering if my children embarrassing me would ever stop (I knew that from their view I embarrassed them plenty, but it was getting to be an uneven trade, as far as being in the clinic was concerned). I was hoping Mark would know my child was cussing only because of the stress. And then I noticed that at some point, he had left me there alone, and I didn't know where he was. I heard Mandy talking again, on the other side of the door, but I hadn't asked her anything. "No. I don't want to," she was saying. "I don't care what you say. I'm not opening the door, and I'm not coming out, and I'm not having any shitty stitches!"

I was really embarrassed, for apparently she was talking to Mark now. I left the door to the linen room and went outside through the back door of the clinic and saw him standing in the garbage-can cubbyhole, where the only window in the linen room looked out. He was wedged between two galvanized trash cans, and three cats were skulking around his legs, looking over the garbage. He didn't see me walking toward him through the alley. He was leaning up close to the window, his hands on the frame. Then he put his lips against the glass and pressed his whole face into it. I could hear Mandy starting to laugh. Then he said, "If you let me put stitches in your thumb, I'll give you a box of money and a cat."

I couldn't believe what I was hearing, and then what I was seeing. Apparently, Mandy took him up on the deal, because the window started being opened from the inside, and Mark was helping wedge it up from the outside, and then he reached down and took the cat who was rubbing up against his legs, while the other two started picking around the fallen garbage again, and he handed this cat through the window into Mandy's arms. "What about the money?" I heard her saying.

"Soon as I get the first stitch in."

I turned around, walking back into the clinic and stood in the hall, ready to watch the rest of this, half wanting to kill him for giving my daughter a cat without even so much as asking me, and right after I'd promised her a dog!—and, at the same time, half falling in love with this man who would have enough imagination, if not enough child still left in him, to strike such a deal.

I stood mum while he came back in the clinic and stood beside me, and then we both watched the linen-room door handle turn slowly and finally open. "Voilà," Mark said, as Mandy came walking out, a skinny yellow cat in her arms, the towel around her thumb pressed against its front legs.

In a few minutes Mandy had the first stitches in, and Mark had emptied a Band-Aid box and then shook the loose change from his pockets into it, and the cat was sitting on the edge of the treatment table eating the leftovers from Mark's lunch.

"I can't believe you gave my daughter a cat," I said, when Mandy was finished and aiming out the clinic door with Mustard, which was the name she'd given to the pitiful-looking half-starved thing. Her Band-Aid box of money was sticking out of her pocket.

"And such an ugly one," I added. "Couldn't you have at least picked out a better-looking cat?"

"That's the only one that volunteered," he said. "Besides, everybody needs a cat. It'll go with your dog." He grinned.

Three days later, Mandy and I walked up and down the aisles between the wire cages. I couldn't go back on my promises. I let her study each dog for a long time before having to decide on the one for us. Drew and George the Second walked behind us, giving suggestions, pointing toward different cages. The attendant there was trying to help, too. Told us which one had the breeding, or part of the breeding to make a good watchdog. He was a tall, skinny, young man with a face that was so narrow, it seemed squeezed. He looked at me and said: "No sense going with anything with no terrier, bulldog, shepherd, dobie, or rottweiler in it." He reached his hand through the spaces in a cage and patted the head of a small dog with a mean look.

"We had in mind something sort of medium sized," I said. "And by any chance do you have anything already housebroken? Maybe even fixed?"

He led us down the aisle to the cage from which a tall black dog with brown feet looked out. "Mighty fine," he said. "A real bitch of a dog."

'It's a girl, then?" I asked.

"Yeah. But they said it was fixed. Some folks brought it in that was movin'. Couldn't take it with 'em, they said. Had lived out in the woods in a trailer, best watchdog around, they said. Now if you're looking for safety, then you're sure enough standing here and looking at it."

"What do you think?" I asked Mandy.

She stuck her finger through a space in the cage. The dog licked it. "I had in mind a boy dog," she said.

"Get it," George the Second said. "Go on and get this one. It's the biggest here."

Drew put his hand up to the cage, and the dog growled.

"I don't know about this," I said. I put my hand up, too. The dog showed its teeth, looked at me with round, dark eyes that reminded me faintly of my grandmother. Then it took its cold wet nose and touched my hand.

Mandy was in front of me, her dog ears fastened in yellow smiley faces, her jeans half the size of mine, the bandage on her thumb like a small mummy, since she'd drawn a face on one side of it. She looked at me. "I guess we could name her Rambona."

She slept beside Mandy's bed. After a few tense hours with Mustard, Rambona settled down. As long as Mustard stayed high on the furniture, and Rambona stayed low on the floor, they were fine in the same room together. And right off, Rambona took us all on as her flock, or however she saw us. She guarded the yard with the fierceness of a roving bazooka. She was even protective of Mustard, ran other dogs off and sent them whining. Within three weeks she had treed Mr. Clark, ripped the skirt off of Drew's old first-grade teacher during her after-supper-work-off-the-fat walk, then pinned the electric-meter reader against the back of the house until he was throwing out Hail Marys and saying his own last rites, when Mandy found him. She was the main one who could control Rambona. (I had not bargained for this. My life wasn't supposed to whirl again off the peaceful track I was trying to get it to go on.)

Mark would sit on the porch with me in the evening, after work, after the clinic was closed. We would have a glass of wine and watch the sun sit on the water in front of us. Whatsy and Rambona played in the yard, best friends—mainly, I guess, because they were of a different sex. Whatsy was the only other dog Rambona would tolerate near us.

Mark and I mentioned the newspaper article that had appeared that week, next to the social news: an announcement that the narcotics division of the police force in Miami had sent out a feeler for dogs. Seemed they were looking for a few good citizens to volunteer their own dogs, if it was pretty evident their dogs were the kind that'd make good drug sniffers. "Any of you good citizens of Palm Key want to take the Miami police up on this offer?"—obviously a comment straight from Mr. Clark. He hadn't especially enjoyed being treed by Rambona when he took his garbage out.

Mark laughed. "Had five patients this week ready to nominate Rambona for Miami."

I looked at him to see if he was teasing. His gaze left the Gulf for a moment, and he looked at me. A smile was playing with the side of his mouth, his mustache hitched up on one side. His eyes lighted on my face for a long minute as if making a careful brush stroke. "You're kidding," I said.

"Nope. That's the truth. I think you and I have the worst two dogs in the history of Palm Key. And we're probably gonna get run out of town for it. I hear they're calling a town meeting about us."

"Aw, come on. Jed Taylor over at the Oyster House had a pit bull that ate Mr. Fallow's poodle."

"Yeah?"

"Yeah. And for a while Adele Wampler had a pet alligator that she tied up out front at night."

"I guess we got a little leeway then." He glanced at me again. I saw his mouth moving at the corner, the tip curling down.

"You're teasing me," I said. "There's no town meeting scheduled about us. You're just pulling my leg."

"Maybe a little," he said. "Nice leg, too," he bumped my knee with his own, looked out onto the water, then cut his eye at me and smiled, a slight curve of his mouth that, if I were to paint him, I would have most liked to capture.

It was the first man-woman thing he had said to me. I laughed out of nervousness, moved my leg away from him out of nervousness, then moved it back out of desire and the nervousness of that.

"Guess we ought to do something about the dogs," he said.

I drove Rambona to the vet, in the next county, for her rabies shot. I figured the least I could do for all the citizens of Palm Key was to make sure she was up on her rabies.

When I told the vet there that Rambona was quite a bit more

than I had bargained for, and mentioned her overaggressiveness, he looked at me, then at Rambona lying on the floor of the treatment room. "Well, you can always have her put to sleep." When he took a step to lean on the examining table which Rambona was too big even to be put on, Rambona growled.

I felt a sudden rush of sweat. The kids and I seemed to be the only people in the world that Rambona did not want to kill. The vet leaned back, the hem of his white clinical coat dipping sideways. "Or, we could put her on tranquilizers," he said to me.

I didn't especially like that idea either. What would it be like with Rambona doped up and lying around the house all day? I looked at her. Her eyes were focused on me like two circles of melted chocolate. Her devotion to me was touching, but scary.

"Neither of those really appeal to me," I said. When the vet looked at me, I smiled and added: "I guess they're not my style." To myself, I sounded like a bimbo, but I didn't care. What did this man, this vet, this doctor of little animals know what getting rid of Rambona might mean? Why, she was the dog Mandy picked out, that she was writing love letters to during English at school, that she fed in a ribbon-trimmed bowl. And even more than that, getting rid of her might echo inside of me too much like what George did to me. I had never been the kind to get rid of something when it turned out to be not exactly what I had in mind. And how could I turn my back on a dog with the eyes of my grandmother!

I looked at the vet again. No doubt he'd been hoping I'd choose putting Rambona on tranquilizers. She seemed to be a young dog and a pill a day for the rest of her life could mean a million dollars for him. I smiled, pitifully. "I guess I could get more insurance—and keep her tied up. But I really don't want her to bite anybody.

And I hate the thought of keeping her penned up—every second." I turned my head and smiled again, hoping the vet would look sympathetic in exchange.

He looked back at me, then at Rambona, and cleaned the end of his stethoscope with a cotton swab. "I guess there's one more thing you could consider then. But there's no guarantee it'll work. There's a young vet student near here who works with problem dogs." He gave me a card with a phone number on it.

•

When I called Mary Crumpet on the phone, she sounded like an older woman. She seemed like someone who weighed two hundred pounds and lifted weights in her garage while doing laundry. "What exactly is your dog's problem?" she asked.

Rambona was lying under my feet in the kitchen, watching George the Second eating a Pudding Pop. Rambona didn't like Pudding Pops, but she was watching for drips anyway.

"She's overly aggressive. Won't let anyone outside of the family pet her or even get close. I wanted a watchdog, but this one seems to take it too far. If anybody even tries to touch her, she growls and blows up."

Mary Crumpet didn't say anything, and I laughed. "Well, I don't mean blow up literally, of course. You know. I mean her hair stands on end—and she looks and sounds just awful. The trouble is, I'm afraid she might hurt someone."

"Sounds like a helluva watchdog."

"She is, but . . . I don't especially want a watchdog I have to watch." I laughed at my own joke, again. But Mary Crumpet was silent. I weighed not quite ten pounds more than Rambona and at least three hundred less than Mary Crumpet's voice.

"That's the whole trouble with people having dogs," she said. "They always expect them to be less trouble than they are, to do things that are absolutely impossible and unreasonable—for a dog. I'd say your dog's problem is you've confused her. She senses your fears. And she'll have to become more afraid of you than of the world."

"Me?"

"Yes, you."

I looked at my feet. Rambona's eyes were aimed lovingly on my sneakers. Every once in a while she glanced at George the Second, and, since she didn't lift her head, her eyebrows twitched as her eyes moved. Something about this wasn't going right. I was probably almost old enough to be this vet student's mother. I was a fully grown woman who cared for three children and worked at the clinic every day caring for even more, and I shouldn't have been feeling so cowed just because I had a dog I couldn't control. "I'm sorry," I said into the phone. "I just don't see myself as Rambona's problem. I see Rambona as *my* problem. And it just seems to me she ought to be able to tell—by instinct or something—who to bite."

Mary Crumpet didn't say anything, and I felt a haunting need to fill in the silence. "I mean *whom* to bite. Well, don't you think she could know if anybody in our family was in danger? And right now, I don't want to have to worry about her biting anybody." (Except Rex the Roofer, which for both me and Rambona would be a pleasure. But I didn't want to go into all that with Mary Crumpet.) I could hear her breathing on the phone. Maybe I'd been too hard on her. After all, I didn't want to be overbearing. My own Drew would be out in the world, trying to make it on his own, soon. I laughed. "Shouldn't Rambona at least wait to hear 'sic 'em' or something?"

Mary Crumpet cleared her throat. "Mrs. Marsh, I can't help you until you're ready to take control of your dog."

There was that terrible silence again. This was silly. I felt dumb and ridiculous. "What does that mean?"

"When you're ready, you can bring your dog to my classes. Tuesday night at the county fairgrounds, in the parking lot behind the livestock barn, seven o'clock. But I just want to warn you, Mrs. Marsh. It's never easy to rehabilitate a dog."

•

I mentioned to Mark at work that next Tuesday that I was taking Rambona to these special classes. "Good," he said, then looked at me and smiled. "Hope you pass."

I drove in the Granny Apple with the kids and Rambona in the back. Drew sat beside me. Rambona's training, we had all agreed, was to be a family affair, even though I was to be the main handler.

Rambona sat on the seat behind me as I drove. She wore a choke-chain collar. Mary Crumpet had mailed me a letter telling me to buy one, and she had also sent me a notice of her registration fee. After the cost of taking Rambona off of Death Row, giving her all her shots, heartworm pills every day, and the special medication for a skin rash she got on her right hip, she was now close to being a five-hundred-dollar dog.

I parked in the parking lot beside the livestock barn and took Rambona out of the backseat.

Mary Crumpet walked toward me. She was accompanied by a Doberman pinscher with his ears in a white-cloth training harness to make them stand up. She stuck out her hand for a shake. "I always bring one of my own dogs to class, to keep them sharp, and sometimes I use them for demonstrations," she said. Rambona growled. Mary Crumpet moved her hand back from the handshake in slow motion. "Reprimand her," she said to me. "Quickly."

"Don't do that, Rambona," I said.

"Oh! Mrs. Marsh." Mary Crumpet looked at me. "You have to be forceful!"

"Rambona," I said, "*please* don't do that."

Mary Crumpet was about five feet one and weighed less than I did. She had a wiry build, and her hair was wiry, and it ran over her head in a short bush the color of sand. She had a handful of freckles across her cheeks the size of pin pricks, and her eyes were the barrel gray of a shotgun. "Jerk on her collar. Let her know you mean it."

I gave the leash a jerk. Rambona coughed and sat down.

"That was more of a tug than a jerk. But we'll let it go this time."

Thank God, I thought as I walked to the rest of a group of owners and dogs in the parking lot as Mary Crumpet had told me to. "Go for it, Mom!" George the Second yelled, as Mandy and Drew lowered the tailgate of the Granny Apple to sit on. I heard them popping open soft drinks. And then I saw him: Mark, at the corner of the group of people who all had dogs, Whatsy sitting beside his chewed-on shoes. He looked at me, smiled, and said calmly, "Hey."

I took my place in the circle. "What are you doing here?" I

looked away, as though I didn't know him. Asking him that was a really stupid thing, for everybody knew he had the worst dog in Palm Key, next to mine. But I didn't want him to be here. I didn't want anyone I knew—and especially him—to watch me and criticize, except Mary Crumpet, who had already made it clear that that was exactly what she thought I was paying her for.

He leaned over as I parked Rambona by Whatsy: "Thought these classes sounded like a good idea. Just called this afternoon and they had a place for me. I mean us." He looked at Whatsy, who seemed miserable at having to be still.

Rambona was keeping up a low growl.

The lesson for the night was To Sit, and all of us quickly got to know each other through our dog's names and problems. A few minutes into the lesson, a Saint Bernard named Fluffy dragged his owner toward the livestock barn, and Mary Crumpet had to go after them. "This is a prime example," she said, walking toward Fluffy, who was pulling his owner closer to the barn door, "of some person buying a puppy and never thinking the cute thing would one day grow up. And so he is spoiled, pampered, undisciplined, and with no idea what his owner wants out of him except to be cute." Fluffy's owner was hanging her head, backed up to the barn now, where Fluffy's nearly two hundred pounds had pinned her as he began humping her leg. All of us there on the blacktop, in the circle with our dogs, politely looked the other way. Except Mark, who laughed beside me, a low laugh with a half-attempt to hide it. "You're going to get an F," I told him. It *was* funny, yes, but embarrassing, too—not only for what Fluffy was doing, but also because of what Mary Crumpet was doing to the woman who owned Fluffy. I felt as if I were Drew's age again, dressed out in ill-fitting gym shorts with socks that didn't match and a safety pin holding together my training bra, which didn't really have much to train.

Mary Crumpet dismissed Fluffy's owner with comments that meant she was a helpless dunce and took over his leash. We were all sneaking peeks, all except Mark, who just out and out turned and looked. Then Fluffy backed Mary Crumpet up to the barn door, and humped her leg, too. Finally she kicked him off, and with quick businesslike strides, went to her pickup, got a choke collar with spikes. In a few minutes, she walked Fluffy back to the circle of us with his eyes bulging, as if any movement of his head might pop them out. "Fluffy, sit!" Mary Crumpet said, mashing the back end of him down with the palm of her hand. He strained for a moment, but his eyes only bulged even more. And it seemed that the only way I could tolerate watching any of this was by thinking of Fluffy as Rex the Roofer. Then finally Fluffy gave in and sat down in his place in the circle.

That next day at work, Mark and I made a bet: Two more lessons, and Fluffy would drop out. One, Mark said.

And he was right.

He kidded me at work: Do your homework?

I hated him for having more time than I did. Even as a physician and with rounds to make and constant phone calls, he didn't have supper to fix for three hungry kids, or homework to help with, or tons of laundry every night. The only nights I could practice with Rambona, really practice, were when George the First came to take the kids out to dinner. I enjoyed watching Rambona show her teeth to Anne Marie. I loved having to call Rambona off of George the First when she pinned him every time before he took a step onto the porch. Yes, I was Rambona's forever. I loved this dog. How could I ever dope her up or drop her off? All I needed was a little more control. Just a little say-so on "whom" she backed up and terrified.

Mary Crumpet did not understand me, though. "Look," I said, when she chewed me out because Rambona would not sit instantly after I said, "Sit," "she's not a show dog. That's obvious. Just look at her. And I don't ever intend to go anywhere in public where she has to sit on a dime."

"It's the principle, Mrs. Marsh. When you say 'Sit,' she has to know you mean what you say."

"She does. She's just not quick. All I want is a little reasonable control, so I don't have to worry about her every minute. I don't need instant obedience. She just needs to do it."

"Mrs. Marsh, this is not a philosophy class. We're not here to discuss exactly how many minutes should elapse in the universe between when you say 'Sit' and the dog's haunches hit the ground."

Mark leaned toward me, whispered: "You're going to have to stay in. No recess. No juice and crackers."

Mary Crumpet walked away from me, then looked back. "Now let's see you do it again."

"Better hurry," Mark said. Under his thick bush of a mustache, he could get away with murder. Say things without Mary Crumpet knowing exactly where they were coming from.

"Geek," I said back to him. Then to Rambona a loud, "Sit."

She did it. Not swiftly, but did it.

Mary Crumpet gave me a half-sour look.

•

At home in the late evenings, Rambona and I would practice out by the Gulf under the streetlights. We would "sit" and "lie" and "heel," at our own speed and in our sweet time. We were a team together, not a pretty one, but we were proficient. And at the other end of the street, near his house, under another streetlight, I often saw Mark with Whatsy, whirling and heeling and sitting like crazy. Mark was the teacher's pet, the best in the class. And he always had been, you could tell—in fact, Mark would surely die if he weren't.

The night before the next lesson, I stayed a long time there, out on the pavement, the lap of water just on the other side of the tall grass where the Gulf was hidden in darkness. I looked down the street at Mark. He waved. I stopped in the circle of light from the pole over me, the one the osprey's nest was on. I waved back. Mark did quick, curlicue circles with Whatsy heeling like a magnet, like a dog aimed for Madison Square Garden—if only he'd had a breeding that could have been identified. Together they were better than they would ever need to be. Mark stopped, bowed toward me. And Whatsy sat beside Mark's left shoe. I laughed.

I laughed low, moaning sounds, and my shoulders shook in a hiccuping movement, up and down as if I had lost my breath. Without even knowing when it had happened, I discovered that my laughter had moved into sobs—same rhythm, just a different tune, as another sense of who we were flooded over me: clowns. Talking through our dogs. Two grown, lonely people moving in dance steps, close and barely touching, playing with what we were afraid to admit we felt.

"Lie down," I said with great authority.

Rambona let her stomach slowly down onto the pavement. But inside, I was not still.

11.
Drew

All that spring, those dog lessons beat staying home and worrying about my own. We were supposed to do homework in the car while we cheered Mom on, but watching her and Rambona try to follow that battle-ax of a teacher's instructions was more fun than reading *Great Expectations*. A three-and-a-half-inch-thick book? Come on, give me a break.

I felt sorry for Mom, though. I knew what she was going through. That night they had the Line Up and Pet Rambona class. It was funny, but the funniest thing was, we didn't laugh. Somehow, it became so serious. We just hated seeing Mom get chewed out. So on the big night when Rambona was going to have the whole class centered on her, we drove her through McDonald's and got her three Quarter Pounders minus lettuce and pickles, so maybe she'd be so full she wouldn't have biting anything else on her mind.

By then there were just eight dogs left in the class: three car chasers and two carpet wetters and two thoroughbred puppies in dog show training. And of course, Dr. Haley's stray dog, Whatsy, who now looked like a big black feather being blown right beside him all over the fairgrounds, about like a professional dog or something. I knew Mom hated like hell to be the hind tit of the class. It'd have burned me, too. Though I was pretty used to it.

That night when they had the Line up and Pet Rambona class, Mary Crumpet walked with her Doberman-of-the-week into the middle of the parking lot and told everybody to line up.

Rambona let out a groan and rested her stomach on the pavement. Mom mashed the rest of her all the way down. Then Mom smiled at Mary Crumpet, and Mary Crumpet walked over and stood in front of Rambona and said to the class, "Rambona, as we all know, is a fear biter, which often stems from not having been handled with affection between the eighth and ninth week after birth."

Hell, we didn't even have Rambona at her eighth and ninth week. It wasn't our fault she grew up and wanted to kill everybody.

But Mary Crumpet was looking straight at Mom. "And to handle a dog like this means the owner must be in total control. Now, I want you all to line up and pet Rambona."

Rambona set up a low growling interrupted by burps. The hair around her neck rose up slightly. But Rambona's body was too busy digesting for much else. Mom had to excuse her twice from the rest of the night's lessons to get her off the pavement and into the grass.

Mom was embarrassed, even though she laughed when she got back to the car. Dr. Haley always came over and leaned on the top of the Granny Apple while we all got back into it. Seemed like he'd rather be around us—or around Mom—than anywhere else. He had this thing for her, I could tell. He was leaving messages on her answering machine just about like I was still leaving on Heather's. (Mom got an answering machine right after that obscene phone call. Said it'd give her a little space. I don't think she realized that all she might be doing was recording them.)

Yo, this is Mark here. I was just going to walk over your way. I'll be down at Fisherman's Bend watching the sun set, if you want somebody to walk with.

The thing was, you see, the first time I realized Dr. Haley was sort of interested in her, I felt like I wasn't supposed to let that happen. In fact, I *didn't want* to let that happen. And then it hit me: My dad was married. Even though seeing Anne Marie made it hard to believe anybody would be married to her, over the months, it *did* sink in. At least, float around on top so long it covered up whatever else I was thinking whenever I thought about Mom and how she'd be alone now forever. In only a couple of years, I would be out on my own. Mandy was already pushing on Mom to buy her high heels, growing so fast it was like turning to the last pages of a comic where you can figure out the end. And lately George wouldn't let Mom hold him on her lap any longer than two seconds. I had recently started having this dream of my mom in her rocking chair in her bedroom, just moving back and forth on the runners, not going anywhere. And when I would come back, a grown man, married to Heather and rich and everything (it was a dream, so what the hell), she would only turn and look at me and ask me how did it feel being out in the world, going somewhere, not being alone? So I started leaving messages on Dr. Haley's machine: *This is Drew Marsh. Mom's not here right now. She's going to be late picking up George. If you call after eight, she'll probably be in.*

Of course, eight was too late for the sunset. There wasn't much else to watch or do in Palm Key, either. Instead, they would just sit out on the porch during those first few months when they were starting to get tight. It was all that January and February that they would spend time there, their hands tucked into the sleeves of their sweaters, Mom sometimes wearing a ball cap when it was windy. I could hear them talking about this patient or that, how to fix soft-shell crab, or maybe getting racing bikes, or the best places for camping, swapping the worst problems they'd ever had with cars.

Then they started going to the dog classes together, and that was a weekly thing for the next two months.

Just before the final exam, Mary Crumpet seemed dead-set on making an example out of Mom. Bugs circled the lights at the fairgrounds. Mary Crumpet ran her hand through her hair in the heat. It was the first really hot day we'd had, right at the end of April. She studied the class. They were down to four. "We'll go one at a time," she said, her eyes and voice—in fact, her whole body—like a dare.

Mom was supposed to tell Rambona to "sit" and "stay," then drop her leash and walk ten steps backward, then call Rambona who'd come running like Lassie and sit down in front of Mom. Then as Mom said "heel," Rambona was supposed to circle behind her and sit beside Mom's left foot. All of this was supposed to have been taught by using the choke collar with gusto, as Mary Crumpet called jerking the chain till it sounded like a zipper. I knew that all week Mom had been too busy to work much with Rambona, and she didn't like using the choke collar anyway, much less with gusto.

When they started, Rambona was cheery; in fact, she ran to Mom faster than any dog ran to any owner. But then Rambona did nothing but look up at Mom and pant.

"Mrs. Marsh!" Mary Crumpet came to stand in front of Mom, right beside Rambona. "You haven't done your homework, have you?"

"I did," Mom said. "It just seems this is a hard thing for Rambona."

"Mrs. Marsh. This can't be blamed on Rambona."

Dr. Haley was looking at Mom; he was looking sort of pissed, too. I mean there's only so much one person can take. And that Mary Crumpet had had it in for Mom from the beginning.

"By next Tuesday," she said to Mom, "you have to have twenty-three credits on the exam or you don't pass."

To hell with passing, I thought. I don't know why Mom hadn't dropped out weeks before. Except I knew she was trying to set a good example for us. She wasn't the dropping-out kind, anyway. She'd always played Monopoly to the end, till every damn hotel and railroad was bought and the bank closed.

"All right, Mrs. Marsh, let's see you try it again."

Mom looked up. She moved to where Mary Crumpet pointed. She told Rambona to stay. And when Rambona did, Mom looked up and smiled at Mary Crumpet. God, she had a look on her face like Karen Dupree does when she sucks up to Miss Calloway in algebra. Mom was even willing to lick boots. I never thought I'd see her go that low.

The next night at home, Mom went out to under the pole with the streetlight, and passed hot dog after hot dog behind her back, with the tip dangling a few inches from Rambona's nose, until Rambona got the idea and circled her.

The next night after that, Mom showed us: Told Rambona to "sit," then to "heel"; and we watched her, stunned, as Rambona whirled around Mom's back and sat down by her left heel. She salivated a little on Mom's feet as she walked around, but that wasn't anything compared to how she moved. She hadn't done anything that fast since she'd pinned Dad on the front doorstep.

On exam night we parked all the way at the end of the lot. Dr. Haley was already there. He was trotting Whatsy around out on the grass, and he waved when he saw us. There was only one other dog who showed up, an Irish setter puppy in show training. Just Mom, Dr. Haley, and this puppy. And then Mary Crumpet started making this big deal about who would come in third.

She said she'd planned on having only three places anyway. And now with just three taking the exam, the only real challenge was to see who could avoid third.

Each dog had to jog in figure eights, circle Mary Crumpet with her Doberman beside her; and Rambona lost seven points for sniffing.

The dogs had to "sit" and "stay" for three minutes while the owners walked to the other side of the parking lot, and Rambona got nervous and came running after Mom.

The owners then had to unleash their dogs, call them while Mary Crumpet held their leashes, and they had to come running all out. And Rambona did, except that she jumped up on Mom and knocked her onto the pavement.

Dr. Haley rushed over to help Mom up. But Mom got to her feet fast, gave him that look that Mandy, George, and I knew real well, like if you make one more move, you'll be grounded for life. She was mad at him, mad at Mary Crumpet, mad at Rambona. And we sat on the tailgate, afraid to even make the sound of opening the potato chips or popping the tops off any drinks.

When the dogs had to "come" and "heel," which meant "circle" and "sit," Rambona did it better than anybody, except that she salivated on Mary Crumpet's shoe as Mary Crumpet walked around Mom, writing down the score. "You certainly did your homework on that for tonight," she said to Mom, obviously impressed. "But why's your dog drooling? What did you feed her for supper?"

Mom just smiled. "I think she got into the garbage and ate a jalapeño pepper by mistake." She patted Rambona's head.

When Mary Crumpet tallied up the scores, she again made this real big deal about who came in third.

Mom walked back to the car. She was moving fast and jerking the choke collar on Rambona's neck. Dr. Haley was walking slowly in our direction, too. I think he was afraid to get too close to Mom, though. He'd probably never seen her like this.

Rambona spotted us on the tailgate and started running. Mom planted her feet, gave a terrific jerk on the choke collar, and Rambona fell on her back with a little yelp. Mom had flattened her. Rambona got up, stood shaking and watching Mom, then slowly walked beside her as she came toward us.

Mom's face was red, and her arms were moving up and down like she does when she's trying not to yell. She opened the back door and told Rambona to get the hell in. Rambona put her ears back like she does when she's ashamed.

Dr. Haley was standing behind Mom now. He didn't even have the slightest idea what he was about to step in. "I think it might be a good idea for all of us to go out to dinner," he said.

She didn't turn around. She was busy taking the choke collar off of Rambona, anyway. "Why, so you can flaunt your blue ribbon?"

He laughed. "No. Because I'm hungry. Aren't you?"

"No. And the idea of going to eat anything with anybody anywhere makes me absolutely sick!"

If I'd have been him, I'd have stepped back. But instead, he leaned closer. Whatsy reached up and touched noses with Rambona, who was sitting on the backseat.

"Well, how about if I bring over something for the dogs and kids, at least?"

George popped open a Coke and put a whole fist of potato chips in his mouth.

Mom reached out and took the potato chip bag away from George. Then she whirled around and looked at Dr. Haley. "Just look at me!" she said, her voice one note lower than a yell. "I've lied and cheated to get through all these weeks, and now walking across here, back to my car, I even threw my dog to the ground. This whole ordeal has brought things out in me I didn't even know about, or didn't want to remember. I'm so sick of being humiliated! Everywhere I go, I get humiliated. And now I can't even teach my children how to gracefully accept coming in third."

Whatsy's ears were pinned to his head now. But Dr. Haley only reached over and took the car keys out of Mom's hand. "Come on," he said, "I'll drive you to the Skipper's Lounge for dinner." He lifted Whatsy's leash toward the backseat, and the dog jumped in beside Rambona, and then Mandy and I got in beside the dogs. George rode in the front between Mom and Dr. Haley.

Before anybody had time to think of anything to say that might make Mom feel better, George put his hand up around her shoulder and leaned his head on her. I could smell the potato chips on his breath, even in the backseat. And then he said, his voice innocent, because he just didn't know any better: "I'm gonna miss that dog school, Mom, aren't you?"

Luckily Dr. Haley was driving, and the Granny Apple didn't make any sudden stops or run off the road or blow up or anything.

12.
Linda

As the season changed, spring moving into summer, which in Palm Key was more like playing the same pitch of one note, only louder—summer like the fortissimo marked on a musical piece—Mark and I got brave. Started going to the Skipper's Lounge a lot. Sometimes we took the children, sometimes they stayed home and I paid Drew to baby-sit them, or often we'd go when George the First took the kids to his house. Once Mark and George the First met on the steps, Rambona freezing George just as she usually did. (I drove Rambona through McDonald's as a reward for that.) Then when Mark came up, she just licked him.

Rambona had her own brand of secret, it turned out. It wasn't long after the dog school that she went into heat. Either her previous owners had been dumb or just lying, hoping to get her a good home. All night, dogs circled the house, hung out in the bushes, and peeked at us whenever we went out. Drew went with me when I walked Rambona, and carried a big stick. I had a little more control over her now, at least. It seemed, in fact, that she'd timed the whole thing. I couldn't imagine trying to pass the dog school with her in heat.

When I got the money, I said, I was going to get her fixed, though Mandy was begging for me to let her have puppies. (Frankly, I just didn't need anything else to take care of. And with Rambona's reputation, I might not ever find homes for the puppies.)

So it was during all this that Mark and I moved off of the porch and out into the world together—even one night going to a movie. We sat in the back row like a couple of teenagers, holding hands, and then Mark kissed me for the first time there. Right when the pimply-faced kid in front of us finally got the nerve to drop his arm that he'd been inching around the back of the seat next to him, where his girl sat, squeeze her to him, and steal him a kiss. And as he made each move, Mark inched his arm around me, echoing the pimply-faced kid like we were playing Simon Says. We were both just about laughing by the time he turned to kiss me. Only with me, he didn't have to steal anything. I was primed and ready, practically to the point of stealing from him, if he hadn't followed the idea on out for himself.

At work, we pretended like we'd barely even seen each other. Betty knew what we were up to, of course. She lived so close to me, she'd seen Mark and me on the porch together a lot, or walking our dogs side by side. She never did say anything or tease me, though. Only winked, like she knew I was doing fine.

He did sometimes, though—tease me. Brought up my grade in the dog school and my competitive nature and the way I hated to lose.

(I *did* hate to lose.)

But I came to terms with that by reminding myself that, after all, the point was: I had made Rambona fit into the world. Like a good mother, I had gotten her to give up what might have put her back on Death Row or in the Miami police force, chasing drug dealers and maybe getting shot. I had done what I had to. And now without giving up her spunk, Rambona had stopped terrorizing everybody, or at least would let a good many people near her without rolling back her upper lip and growling like a marble stuck in the dryer.

Speaking of losing, and my hatred for that, over the month that Mark and I had started going to the Skipper's Lounge and elsewhere, I knew I was heading for trouble. I felt like the more I liked being with him, the worse I was making it for myself. Because the whole truth of the matter was, I didn't want to get into anything that might make me feel like I wanted him to love me. For I knew now: knew what brought me to my knees, what took the sense and breath out of me. I could not stand finding out that if once someone loved me, they had stopped. And so I didn't want to even mess with getting close to the possibility of losing like that, again. Strange as it seems and sounds, and with a guffaw in my mind at the mere thought (not to mention the belly laugh at what my mother would think): I had decided to try to get him to use me for just sex. Though I wasn't sure if there was such a thing as Just Sex.

We sat in the Skipper's Lounge one night that July—me and Mark, menus between us, lists of fish: Grouper, Snapper, Softshell Crab, Shrimp. There were stuffed fish mounted all over the walls, mixed in with watercolors for sale. One of mine was there once. We even talked about this: an already established safe subject: my art, my dropped art.

We ordered margaritas, frozen *and* salted. I had amused myself, getting ready for coming here—had picked out a black sundress, aware of the skin it would show, wondering if I really wanted to show it, wondering that if I did, would he want to see it (was the skin still *firm* enough to even let out in public?); then finally just saying, So why not, it's a hot night and this is suitable, and pulling it out of my closet and putting it on. Now that I had raised Drew for nearly sixteen years, and another son for almost five, the best way to understand men, I had decided, was to raise one. While raising one, I had realized how I, as a woman, had always put so much weight on their reactions, reading into their movements, comments, tone of voice, something about myself. Drew really was so simple in his desires—so was George the Second, so were they all!—that I knew now that should Drew ask for a hot dog when I had fixed chicken, it did not mean I had made a lousy dinner; it only meant he was craving a hot dog. I had watched Drew and George the Second's joy in simple things: skipping a rock on the Gulf, throwing around a paper airplane until it was practically confetti, and when it landed in a bush, perfectly happy to leave it there as a monument to their good time (and for me to clean up). They had such a natural delight in being by themselves!—it was so pure, so unlike me, so uncomplicated. Maybe now, I told myself, Mark was focusing only on what fish he was going to order, not on my sundress or skin or the fact that I was showing it—that it had nothing to say except that I was wearing it because of the weather.

I looked out of the window of the Skipper's Lounge that was above the street and saw George the First below me, taking the kids and Anne Marie into the hardware store. Instinctively, I felt my hand go up across my neck, as though trying to cover a little of what I had gotten brave enough to show. I looked across at Mark. He was still studying his menu, looking down, but then glanced at me and smiled. I told myself to take my hand away from my shoulder, that Mark was not George, that George was not every man. And I looked out the window again. I couldn't help myself; I was eager to see my children, just instinctively ready to read their moods. George the Second was holding George the First's hand like a carbon-copy midget. Mandy was stuck to his other leg as if their clothes had been taken out of the same dryer and were now suffering static cling. Drew walked behind them all, beside Anne Marie who reached over to hold his hand, and I saw the wooden shape of my son's shoulders, the stiffness of his arms. It had been over a year since George had moved out and left all of us; and I saw, or maybe mostly felt, that his doing so had blown a hole through our children, a space that had been stuffed back up with an eternal longing. I was the most angry with him about that, now. Not with my own wounds, but with theirs; for when our children were born, his love for them had been so total, so solid, so evident. It still was, but he had left the place where we had been a family, our space that we had hollowed out, huddled down in together and shared. Years ago, if you had asked me, I would have said that I could never imagine George putting his desires before his children's. As a mother, I knew an essential part of my love for them was sacrifice, and yet the necessity of so often putting them first had painted my life with such a joy that I couldn't imagine ever questioning what I had given up. I guess I would always be mad at George for changing our family. Seems the least he could have done was to wait until the children were dead.

Now I watched Drew walk between Anne Marie and his father like a line that refused to connect. In the last few weeks, I had even felt Drew moving away from me, as was natural, I knew, calling me "Mother!" as a way to make me take my hand away from smoothing his hair, even "Mrs. Marsh!" when I inquired about a blemish on his nose, or why in the wash that week I had counted only one pair of his underwear.

Sitting now in that restaurant above them, with a man who was not their father, wondering what to order and trying to decide if sex was like riding a bicycle—something you never forget—my children walked into the store on the other side of the street as if we were being filmed for separate movies, not appearing together this week, this time.

"Have you decided?"

I looked up, startled. But he was only asking me if I had made up my mind what to eat.

"I think," I said, as the waitress put down two margaritas in glasses the size of my face. It was like lifting a bowl, and when I did, I was so thirsty, I drank too much. To slow myself down, I took the lime off the side of the glass and squeezed it into the frozen mixture. It squirted into Mark's eye and he yelped and wiped his eyelashes with his napkin. I was already apologizing like I was a maniac let out only on weekends. But he was laughing and wiping his eye and telling me he wished I didn't have such good aim. Then he said, "I meant to tell you, I like that dress. It's nice."

I could feel my hand aiming for my front again, fluttering like a bird deciding on a landing. "Thanks," I said back, and then, like a fool, added: "It's such a hot night."

"Yeah." He grinned. "So you know what you want?"

Since I was thinking about what I really wanted, and that it wasn't on the menu (and how could I get it on the menu?), I'm sure I looked startled again. But then he added: "I was thinking the snapper sounds good, or the Fisherman's Platter."

I laughed. "Yeah. Well, I've decided on soft-shell crab. My favorite." I smiled.

The first time I had introduced him to this specialty of the mud coast, I had told him that eating it made me feel like a witch, like I was eating a spider: the batter-fried crab with its many legs, its round middle about the size of my hand that I ate with my hands, dipping pieces into melted butter, the taste akin to what an angel might whip up—sweet and soft and tough and salty, all at the same time.

He laughed, ordered it, too. Witches food for both of us. And I watched the kids and George and Anne Marie come out of the hardware store with a kite. They were going down to the beach to fly the fool thing! Going to put on a public display on how to have fun. Drew walked two steps behind George the First, so hungry for his presence and so mad at the same time that he was like a crab himself heading across the beach, hurrying, but sideways.

Mark and I ate our crabs, while beside us, the light disappeared from the windows. The water of the Gulf was a solid darkness, then we looked at each other after we ordered Key Lime Pie, our chins shining with drawn butter.

This was the thing, you see: How could you get a man into bed without letting him know that all you wanted to do was to get him into bed? There ought to have been manuals for this. If I had been too forward, too forthright in expressing my desires, I might have turned him off and been as humiliated as all the seven weeks of dog school.

And where? If I took him back to my house, coaxed him into

my bedroom, there were all those memories, plus at any minute the kids might have come in. They were always bopping in, forgetting something they wanted to show George: a school paper, the picture of an advertised toy.

All of this I was mulling over while eating key lime pie.

And the last thing on earth I wanted was to do it in a car. The Granny Apple was out of the question right off the bat: too small. This man I was after was the length of a small tree; I had to remember that. I wanted to make him comfortable. And I didn't think I could see us either going at it in the antique Mercedes; I had had my share of wrecking it once. It wasn't all that big either. Besides: hanky panky in a car would only remind me of what my mother wouldn't let me forget.

How did you broach the subject with a man? I was not the forward type—footsie under the table. I mean, after all, this man was still my boss. One move that might nauseate him, and I could be fired.

But why was I even thinking like that? Why did I assume he might not respond if I dropped a hint? Just because George the First dropped me didn't by necessity mean that I was undesirable. (*Just how could I ever get myself to REALLY believe that?*) And why couldn't I think of anything to say that might put the idea in his mind that *I* thought it was all right for us—as Drew might say—to Get It On. It wasn't fair that men should have any number of things to do and say as the natural aggressors. But if I made one move that was too forward, too quick, I could come off as nothing more than a Bimbo Hot to Trot.

"Sure a nice night," he said, signing the credit card slip.

The moon outside the window was like a china plate, swollen round and luminous, dark crumbs spilled across its face.

"We could take a drive and enjoy it," I said. Shorthand for Let's Find a Place to Park. Or, at least, it was in high school. All the rules were changed now. I didn't know how to be thirty-six. And I didn't know how old he was, but it was even older than that.

"Fine." He stood up, helped pull back my chair. I purposefully put my hand on top of his on the chair back, carefully pretending that it was an accident.

He opened the door for me to get in the old Mercedes. I didn't know a whole lot of the facts of his life, but I was certain that he had been raised in the South: so many of these give-aways—always opening doors for me, even at work; pulling out my chair for me to sit down, standing up when old ladies came into the room (and not just me, but patients). And there was the tiniest remnant of a drawl in the sound of his speech.

"Any suggestions on where to go?" He looked at me.

I was a fool and a nitwit: a regressed teeny-bopper, hyper hormones and no brain. "How about the cemetery?"

Then I sidestepped, trying a smooth move: "I mean, there's a nice point there where the road goes up near the water and if you haven't seen moonlight on water up close, you really ought to."

"Guess I ought to," he said, smiled, started the motor on the third try, and aimed for the cemetery.

You see, it was a weeknight. I didn't think anybody else would be at the cemetery. All I wanted to do was to give him a little hint that might lead us both onto the idea of a place to go where we could really Be Together. And in my opinion there was no way better to get inspired than practicing a little touching in a cemetery. It was easy to get carried away there, thinking about how short life is and what you might miss.

I pointed out the point, and we parked on it. The moon hovered over the water beside us, and I rolled down my window and showed him the silvery movements in the Gulf that looked like nothing you could see anywhere else. It was as if fallen pieces of metal were floating there, riding on the gentle movement of waves as they lapped against the rocks near us. He scooted near me (I knew he would have to), and put his arm around me (I knew he would have to), so he could lean out of the window and get a good look. I could feel his breath on my neck, and the warmth of his long arm across the back of my shoulders, and I waited, not wanting to make any move of my own just yet. I was so primed in my mind for the touch of him that when he leaned and lifted the hair behind my ear so as to kiss me there, I jumped. I grinned and laughed and tittered like a bobby-soxer about to lose it.

We embraced and huddled, leaned against each other and breathed until the pitch of it was higher. And then as we stopped a minute, we saw a car next to us. We froze, as the pimply-faced boy who'd made his move on the girl in front of us in the movies, weeks before, raised his head behind the wheel of his car, coming up for air, too.

•

Mark parked the Mercedes in his driveway. Asked me to come in to see his watercolors. Since he had moved to Palm Key, he had been collecting them, he said. After all I was a retired watercolorist. But frankly I wouldn't have cared if there were no paintings in the whole house.

After a slow tour through the living room, on the walls of which were five nice paintings, the exact number I was sure of, since, as I studied each one, Mark studied me: his mouth against the lowest part of my neck, then the highest, around the curve of my shoulder, behind my ear. We worked our way into the dining room. Seascapes in cobalt blue and prairie gray, sandy ocher, penny amber.

We followed the walls through the doorway of his bedroom. It seemed that my own worries of how to plant in his mind what was in my own weren't even necessary. (Just might be said to be, I guess, great minds in the same channel?)

•

I lay still, drained of life. Yet so full of the sense of living that my skin sang. The length of his body was beside me, way past, down to the end of the bed and beyond. And my skin held memories of fading and being rolled away, while the lower lining of all of me reminded my outer self that I was indeed doing fine. (Nothing like a man to make of you a believer.)

In the light of the room as I got up to go home, I found out that the strangest thing about what we had done was that now the past could no longer be kept silent. About all those photographs—the one on the dresser, the two across the room on the desk, the images of two dark-haired women with eyes that looked beyond the room—I wanted to know. I turned to look at him; he was watching me. His eyes were so solidly meeting mine that neither of us could look away. And without even knowing it, along with the strength of my desire to know, it seemed that we had also released in him his need to tell.

13.
Drew

The summer passed a whole lot better than I did in the ninth grade (all D's and a recommended six-week stay in summer school), which meant that between school and baby-sitting for George the Second and Mandy, my fishing time that summer was just pitiful.

On Sunday nights, Grandma called as usual. Sometimes Mom made me talk to her, while Mom went outside to do something like just water the yard. I could truthfully say then that my mother wasn't there. Once Mom put a load of clothes in the washer and one in the dryer and said she'd be back in time to put the softener in the rinse cycle (George wouldn't wear jeans unless they'd been softened), and she rode my bike over to Dr. Haley's to take him some cucumbers from our garden for his supper.

"Drew?"

"Yes."

"Is that you?"

"Yes ma'am."

"Well, how are things?"

"Fine."

"Where's your mother?"

"Down the street."

"Doing what?"

"Taking some cucumbers to her boss."

"Well, that's good. It'd be smart of her to try to stay on his good side. I don't know how she got a job in a clinic in the first place. She's sure not qualified. How could she be when she dropped out of college to get married? There's something you can learn from that, Drew, you hear. Stay in school. Finish."

"Yes ma'am."

"What's she fixing for supper?"

"I don't know."

"Is there something on the stove? Is something sitting out, defrosting?"

I lifted a top on a pot. "Looks like spaghetti," I said.

"Well, if she doesn't make you a salad to go with it, you call me back. I've got an article here that says if children don't get enough folic acid in their diets, they get pale and weak."

"I don't think any of us have that."

"I know George the Second doesn't, but I don't think it has anything to do with what he eats. And, well, anyway, tell your mother I called."

"Sure. No problem."

When I hung up, I put the softener in the rinse cycle. Mom didn't make it back in time to even fold the ones that got dry. Then she had to stay up late, ironing out the wrinkles.

Over that summer though, I did learn something new, and it didn't have a thing to do with school. It seems that, by itself, time makes things change—at least it takes your mind off certain things by bringing in others. Mandy had started going to the bathroom alone. And George the Second had started swimming without barrettes. And when September came around again, I got The Real Thing: my permanent license. Got to drive me and Mandy and George, who was now in kindergarten, to school every day, even though it was in the bombed-out-looking car, My First Wreck.

But to women, it seemed that wheels were just about everything. Heather noticed me right off, driving up in the car, parking it beside some senior's. Wasn't but four cars in the whole parking lot, anyway. In Palm Key you can bike anywhere, and almost nobody my age can afford a car. So, in a sense, I was pretty hot to just have one.

Right off I noticed the difference: Heather started paying a lot more attention to me. She was talking to me not only on the phone, but in the halls at school, and when I asked her to go out with me on the next Saturday night, she smiled, then hid every bit of her damn enthusiasm, like girls do. Looked at me, twirled the end of her hair and tossed it over her shoulder and said real cool, with about as much excitement as if I'd asked her to clean out my boat: "Yeah, sure. What time?"

Women. Wouldn't let you know what they really thought about you come hell or high water.

And then the problem was, I had to get all this straight with Mom. I mean, I was baby-sitting for her practically every Saturday night so she could go out with Dr. Haley. And now there'd be two of us wanting to get out and shake a leg, as Mom always said: "Will you sit tonight, Drew, while I get out a little and shake a leg?"

Shake a leg, I figured, covered all sorts of things. But to Mom and Dr. Haley I knew it meant mostly going to the Skipper's

Lounge or taking a walk down on the town pier and watching the sun set.

Thing that bothered me, though, was that as soon as Heather said yes, I had a deep rumbling start in the bottom of my stomach, and I couldn't come up with one good idea of what exactly to do with her.

"Mom?"

"Yeah?"

She was rolling out cookie dough, George and Mandy helping her: 8:00 P.M. and she was tired as hell. I saw it in the lines around her eyes and the bags under them. But still she was playing June Cleaver like she was dead-set on an Oscar.

"I was wondering if this Saturday night I could have the night off?"

"Off from what?"

"Baby-sitting George." I didn't mention baby-sitting Mandy. She was right there in the room and she would have felt insulted. Even though she had gotten over the bathroom thing, she was still afraid to stay in the house at night alone, just wouldn't admit it. She baby-sat George some herself now, but never for long; and whenever she did, she called Lucille Duffy and Betty MacHenry about every ten minutes for the least little thing, like if a cat howled outside or if Rambona barked, which could some nights be about every second, especially when the armadillos were on the move.

Mom gave George a cookie cutter and let him go at the dough like he was a tailor cutting out pants legs on a tight schedule. Mustard sat on a kitchen stool, and Rambona lay under it.

"Sure. I suppose so." Mom looked at me, then away real quick like she didn't want to embarrass me. Good thing, too. Good mom. She could be quick on the draw like that sometimes, didn't pick up the subject or beat it to death like she usually did.

Then later in the living room, after George and Mandy were in bed: "Wonder if I could ask you something, Mom."

"Sure." She was reading a medical journal, one she had borrowed from Dr. Haley.

"I was thinking maybe I wanted to take somebody somewhere Saturday night. You know, shake a leg."

"Oh?"

"Yeah."

"I see."

"You do?"

"Sure."

I hoped to hell we were talking about the same thing, because it was the details that were killing me: like what should I talk about with Heather, or what should I *not* talk about. And should I pay for everything, absolutely everything? Like if we went down to the Good Time Café and played video games—should I even pay for every little game, have with me about a million quarters? And should I pull out her chair—every chair, when she sits down—and open the car door—all these things I saw Dr. Haley doing for Mom and Dad for Anne Marie? And then, how did I make sure that Heather would end up liking me? How did I get her to want to go out with me again? I had to ask somebody these things. I figured the other stuff—the stuff I had on my mind about all the time, like kissing her and so on—would have to be worked out on my own in between all the details. I couldn't ever bring myself to ask anybody that. And I knew anyway, it was the details that led you into doing all that. So it was the details I had to get down first.

I looked over at Mom, glancing down at her medical journal, flour from rolling out the cookies dusting one side of her hair like she was already gray and old and about to kick the bucket when she'd barely even lived.

I'd thought about asking Dad everything I wanted to know about women. But when I thought about Anne Marie and how he'd traded in Mom for her, about like she was a car he was tired of driving—like maybe her clutch had been sticking, or she didn't start right off anymore—I figured, hell, his advice wasn't anything I'd ever want to follow. So the only person I had left to ask was Mom herself. But I figured that since she'd once been a girl, she ought to know how they liked to be treated.

"Where are you planning to go?" she asked me outright.

"I don't know. I was thinking about the show, or the Good Time Café, or the Dairy Dip, or the beach to fly a kite; or maybe even the Skipper's Lounge, at least for a hamburger; or McDonald's for fries, or the Baptist Church Barbecue Supper; or, got any suggestions?"

"Sounds like you've covered everything in town."

"Well, if it were you. I mean if you were the one with all these choices, what would you choose?"

"Why don't you ask her."

"Is that what I should do? Should I just give her the whole list?"

"Well, on second thought, the last thing a woman really likes is a man who's wishy-washy, who comes off as uncertain. I guess when you get right down to it, most of us really like to feel that the man is ready and willing to make decisions, even if they're not exactly the ones we'd make right off. So why don't you just decide what you think you'd both like to do, and then ask her opinion on it."

"So how do I say it?"

"Just start out and tell her what you thought would be fun to do, and then ask her if that's all right with her."

"Oh."

"Yeah. It's just real important to always ask their opinions, take them into consideration, respect them." She smiled. "You'll do fine."

Sounded sort of complicated though: taking charge and yet letting them vote all at the same time.

So that was my plan. Tell her, then ask her.

I was supposed to pick up Heather at 6:15. I'd settled on black Bugle Boy pants with a plaid shirt, a little Brut after-shave. Her father greeted me at the door. A big guy, close to three hundred pounds, at least, ran a tree-cutting service, looked like a damn mountain man. He shook my hand, and, I swear, he squeezed it so hard that at sixteen I was sure I was on my way to arthritis. He invited me to sit down in an over-oiled recliner so that when I did, the foot thing flew out and I was practically bucked off. Then he asked me how I was doing, how was my mom, and then my dad. Fine, I said to everything.

When Heather came out, I couldn't get out of the chair. And while I was trying, he asked me where I was taking her.

I had made my list for her, not him, but I told him my first idea: that we were fixin' to go to the Skipper's Lounge for a hamburger. (Thought the Skipper's Lounge, which is a real grown-up place, would impress the hell out of Heather, and probably him, too.)

Well, fine, he said, then mentioned, "Curfew's 11:15, kids."

Then tapped me on the shoulder and grinned; "Give you an extra ten dollars if you can keep her out till then."

Heather squealed: "Oh, Daddy!"

We headed out to The Wreck, and as we were walking toward it, I added the rest of the list: the Good Time Café for a couple of hundred video games, then out to the Dairy Dip for a sundae. Figured I'd fill her up, if nothing else. Then I said, as I opened the car door for her: "Okay with you?"

"Well . . ." She dipped her head, that cute little move that made her hair fall over one shoulder. "I hate video games. I personally think they're stupid and violent and ruin your mind."

"Okay."

I opened The Old Wreck's door for her. If we scratched the video games, that meant the whole night we would eat. And then as I watched her get in the car, I knew why opening doors was thought up as the thing for men to do and yet pass it off as the sign of a gentleman, because it gave me one hell of a view at the way she sat down, twirled her feet in; and she had on this cute little mini blue-jean skirt, hiked thigh-high on the final turn onto the front seat.

I got in behind the wheel. As I started the car, I couldn't think of a damn thing to say. When I drove I had to concentrate anyway. I felt her eyes on my arms as I put it in gear. I felt her eyes on my feet as I stepped on the accelerator. George the Second had left a G.I. Joe on the floor and she picked it up, had to lean down funny because of her seat belt. "Oh, I just love G.I. Joe," she said.

"Yeah, me too," I said. Then added quick: "That's my little brother's."

Usually Heather was talkative as hell, but there was something about being out together, just us, in a car alone that made us quiet, and I couldn't think of one thing to say either.

It was a full minute's ride to the Skipper's Lounge. Inside, I pulled out her chair for her. It was not as good as watching her get in the car, but it was still worthwhile. And then I studied the menu for a second, and when the waitress came up, I said, following my plan of Telling then Asking: "We'll have two hamburgers without onions, fries, and two Cokes." I looked across at Heather. "Okay with you?" (It was all I could afford anyway.)

But instead she looked at the waitress and said, "I'd rather have fried shrimp and a side salad with baked potato and sour cream, Key Lime Pie and iced tea—if that's okay with you," she added, looking back at me.

"Oh, yeah, sure," I said. It was obvious Heather was going to be way ahead on that folic acid thing. But then, I was glad she wasn't going to be pale and weak. And I said to the waitress, "On second thought, just bring me some redfish chowder and a glass of water."

Heather looked at me. "That's all you're going to have?"

The waitress looked at me, too. "Cup or bowl?"

"Cup," I said, which was a dollar and a half less. Then to Heather: "Yeah, I forgot, I have this stomach thing. A little flare-up, and redfish always settles it down."

"God, that's awful." She looked at me with real sympathetic eyes, which I liked. (Might be worthwhile to act sick the whole night.)

Then by the time dinner was over, she didn't want to go to the Dairy Dip, and the stomach flu I had, which we had talked about almost the whole time through dinner, wouldn't let me want to go to the Dairy Dip anyway.

I was dying to ask her if she wanted to reconsider the video games. But I didn't want to push something she thought rotted the mind. It was only 7:15, though, and we had practically a whole night to do something and I couldn't think of anything, or at least anything that I ought to be doing.

Then out the window of the Skipper's Lounge, I saw the full moon, just sitting over the water of the Gulf like a giant white basketball, its face wearing fingerprints. I remembered something Mom used to do with us—with me and Mandy before George was born: take us to the point beside the cemetery and let us try to step on moonbeams. Skipping on silver, she called it. Splashing the reflections of the moon up onto our legs with our bare feet.

Of course there were other things, too, that were done at the cemetery.

"Wanna just take a drive?" I asked.

"Sure."

She finished off her iced tea, wiped her mouth. Little pink lips left on the napkin like Mom sometimes did. *God, I love women.*

When I got in The Wreck, Heather let out her seat belt, threaded slack through it like maybe she'd gained five hundred pounds during dinner. But she was only doing it so that she could slide on the seat closer to me. *God, I love women.*

I drove all over town. I made a one-car parade through all the streets, showed off Heather next to my shoulder to the guys hanging out near the window of the Good Time Café. I headed out to the airport, but nothing was landing—thank God—so I had a good excuse to just ease The Wreck on up toward the cemetery.

Heather seemed to know what I had in mind, didn't say a thing, just chattered on about the weather and the last ball game that the Palm Key Manatees lost like hell and how her cheerleader uniform got Gatorade spilled on it, and all this stuff that was really small stuff, and ought to have been boring as hell, but that I found out I loved. Loved the sound of her voice and the smell of her skin and the feel of her hair as it brushed against me.

We sat in the car awhile where I parked it. There were a few other cars there, but not close. And then I put my arm around her and I didn't know exactly how to do it, but I kissed her. And if you ask me, she kissed back. Ran her hand over the top of my head like she was holding on. And I liked it so much it scared me.

I looked past her shoulder at the moon hanging there right over the water. I pointed. Moved close to her side of the car where, out the window, we could lean and look at the moonbeams on the water that were like the sides of fish, floating, just waiting to be caught—like you could just reach down and scoop them up with your fingers. I opened her door and took her by the hand.

We skipped out into the shallow water, and where the moonlight caught a wave, we stepped on it. And sometimes I reached down, threaded the lighted water through my fingers and handed it to her. I had never understood what it was that would make some man, any man, someone like my father, move away from someone like my mother and take up with someone else. But touching Heather, I felt that I might do any number of things I hadn't planned on. I wouldn't have left her for anything, though. And I never would have even taken her home, except that I knew that if I didn't—no matter how her father had teased us about paying me to keep her out—he would kill me, squash me flatter than a bug.

At 11:02, we climbed back in the car, dried our feet, and after a few pretty intense minutes, if you know what I mean, I aimed The Old Wreck toward her house.

14.
Linda

That summer was unlike any time I'd known. Mark and I spent part of every day together, which made me feel like Drew's age and yet, at the same time, very old. Like I'd lived a lot.

It was one of those nights when we were sitting on the porch—Mark's legs crossed at the knee. He talked like someone playing a piece of music with phrases erased. Or like a sketch I might make, a few curves and lines left as white spaces for the imagination to draw. That first night when I had been at Mark's house, he saw me looking at the photographs in his room, and without my even asking—and I couldn't decide on the right words, anyway—he said in a voice as even as when he recited medical terms: "My wife." Then after a little pause, almost the length of a swallow, he nodded toward the other frame: "My daughter."

The girl in the photograph seemed as grown as me: dark brown hair, a face turned halfway to the side, wide-open eyes, a mouth with the smile of a strong, confident woman—right on, with no doubts about it. Even if the roof fell in, it wouldn't even faze her. Inner glow, we used to call it in high school. Real beauty.

And inspired by that, I sat on my own tongue, didn't blurt out a damn thing, even though I was dying to. For I was thinking: *My God! You must be a hundred years old.* It didn't seem possible for him to have a child that old. Then I realized that my own Drew was sixteen. In two years could vote, get drafted, could look out from some picture frame with those same sort of eyes, could pass himself off as a man, no longer needing me. Then true to form, my one great strength took over: wild speculation. And I was off and running.

He'd been divorced like me. Must have been. No wonder we'd felt this common thing, this natural affinity if not outright attraction. We'd undergone the same test by fire, been singed in the same places.

Only thing I said, though, that night in response to what he had told me was, while looking at the picture of his daughter, "She's beautiful. Really beautiful."

"Thanks." He had sat on the side of the bed, the length of his back so evident that I marveled at what it must feel like to reach cups on the top shelf in the kitchen, to change light bulbs without a stool and without a crick afterward.

It was a few days later, when even after we had walked Whatsy and Rambona out to the cemetery, and then stolen another few hours in the same room in his house while the kids were out to dinner with George (I especially enjoyed being with Mark in his bedroom while George was doing nothing but eat), it dawned on me: I didn't have a picture of George just sitting around in the house to be admired. Got rid of every last one that had been sitting around or hung. Only pictures left of him were the ones that remained in the family albums, or framed in the children's rooms. He was their father and always would be. But you think the image of him even came one iota of an inch near my bedroom?

So it hadn't been fitting together: Mark's past and mine. And the funny thing about that was that as I realized that, I also realized how smart my own past had made me. I knew a whole lot more about how the world worked now, what was true and not. Knew the only picture of any man who'd left me, that I'd let anywhere near the place where I slept, would have had to have been of a dead one.

Made sense, too, that Mark might make light of his past as I did when I had told my mother that as far as George and I were concerned, the fat lady had sung. Knew he wouldn't tell me right off how she had died.

So I didn't bring it up. Didn't pry loose what I felt he might want to hold close. Wanted to just let him tell me in his own sweet time, like I would him, about me and George, maybe. But, at least, with me he knew the facts: cold hard facts as if they were on my medical history and he was presenting me at rounds: divorced, three kids, ex-husband still in town.

We sat on the porch, our dogs lying at our feet. The kids were down at the beach with George the First flying his fool kite. The clouds were white and thin and spread out, blending into the sky like spilled cream. The sun blushed through them. And out across the water the channel markers were orange squares on poles. Somewhere out in the Gulf there was a storm. The water was gray-brown that, at a distance, looked blue, the surface like a great wrinkled quilt as the wind blew across it. Mark was looking toward the water, and I was looking at him. And his mouth began working like a metal sieve that only let through what it was supposed to, holding back clumps of emotion that might gum things up.

"At the time we didn't think we were young." His voice was low; he glanced at me. "Met in high school; were in the same class. Went to college together. Got married the first year I entered medical school." He reached for my hand. "We were both twenty-three when Lisa was born."

Then his voice became a staccato, a tap dance that could let you swing your arms and do a few turns, then tap off behind the curtain.

"We were in North Carolina. Then I got a residency in the East. I wanted to be a general surgeon."

I saw he needed questions, needed something to bounce his words against. "You trained in surgery?"

"For a while."

There was the sharp cry of birds as they flew across the water in front of us. The air had a delicious smell to it, a blend of salt and marsh grass. The wind blew across the water so fast that perhaps it carried on it the scent of orange groves from Greece, or the sweetness of grapes from the other side of the world.

"And then Barbara got sick." He checked to see if I was still listening.

I did not say anything. I picked up his hand, put it, with mine, in my own lap. We both looked out onto the water, watched the birds there. Sea gulls fluttered across the water so close, they looked like blown paper. Tiny black birds were going nowhere on the strong wind, only beating their wings in place and moving as slowly as if they were the hands on a clock, counting time.

"She had breast cancer. Worst kind. Really young. I didn't want to leave her every night, working that hard. I dropped out. Did clinic work, manned an emergency room, worked shifts I could count on."

His fingers I moved in between mine. There was only this that I could do: put my skin as though woven with his. I turned and listened. "You see, the thing was, she knew she could not live. And there was no way that I could accept that. We didn't want anyone with us. There was only Lisa. She was eight. When I was gone, out working or buying things for the house—I can't even imagine what Barbara and Lisa must have talked about, or how. It wasn't until the night Barbara died that I knew what she and Lisa had planned for. How they had known I could not have."

His fingers stretched so much farther than mine. I wedged mine against his until there was no space left. "She'd put a list of things in a drawer of the desk in the living room. Barbara's handwriting, printed clear and straight so that Lisa could read it easily. They had gone over it. Practiced it. I hadn't known. Hadn't known that Barbara even knew how sick she was. I heard her that night, barely able to breathe, propping pillows under her head, the breaths harder and then none. Somehow even though it was in the middle of the night, Lisa knew. Could sense, I guess. Or heard me calling Barbara's name. And she went into the living room. Got the list of things her mother had printed out for her to do. Dialed the phone—called all the numbers Barbara had left for her. Then Lisa came and sat with me. It was like she was the one taking care of me, and not me her, and yet she pretended. She asked me right off to do this for her, then that. Kept reminding me that she had to have me with her.

"The only way I could finish raising Lisa alone was to keep on pretending that, even though we both knew she was way ahead of me as far as letting her mother go. It was like they were working as a team together, taking care of me. Lisa recited emergency phone numbers to me every day before she went off to school and me to work: knew every place she could reach me every hour, day or night. Seemed to even think up problems I had to help her with." He laughed. "Once she said she had to have a yellow dress for a school play so she could be a piece of wheat. We had to spend one whole Saturday driving all over two cities to just find it—only one certain color of yellow would do, she said." He laughed again, his voice like a burst of warm sound.

He looked at me, smiled. Squeezed my hand. "She was here last Christmas. Came to visit during her vacation from college. When she went off last September, she talked me into taking this job. Said it was time for both of us to move out of the house, make changes. Leave where Barbara had been, where Lisa thought I shouldn't still be alone, even after all these years." He grinned. "That's why I took a little time off from the clinic this past winter, so Lisa and I could go do some things together. Spent New Year's Eve down at a resort near here. She's in Europe now, on some kind of archaeological dig with her college." He laughed again. "Staying with me's too boring, now, at least for any length of time. She gets a fall break from her college, though, and she's coming here then. Wants me to take her to a beach somewhere while the weather's still warm."

I thought back, remembering Jimmy Wampler and New Year's Eve and how I had assumed that Mark's reluctance to spend time with me had meant that he wasn't much interested. How—so typical of me—I had wondered if maybe it was my fault.

On the light pole in front of us, the osprey stood up, stretched her wings, the wind ruffling her. Her nest was a blend of thick sticks as big as the wound blackness of a tire, secure, even though it looked thrown together and poorly kept by a bird not fond of housekeeping. She sat up there, a plain cousin to an eagle, her wings big enough to bat my face and blind me—taunting in her wildness, her confidence in sitting out the wind.

“Wonder how many storms she’s sat through?” Mark said, looking at the bird, too, and squeezing my hand.

I didn’t know anything to say but only what I wanted to do, and I reached over and took my hand at the back of his head and bent him to me, kissing him so solidly that it was as though I was adding my own punctuation to all he had told me. It was as though I was offering *this* in place of what he had lost. But inside, I felt this round hot sense of pain. For just when I had thought I had gotten myself straight and promising myself that I would never again let my selfhood depend on the approval of some man, here I was: sticking my heart up on a long pole where he could just as easily shoot it to smithereens as grab it.

The wind died down, and the little no-see-um bugs came out. I reached to scratch the back of my neck, then my big toe, where they had found me through my sandal, then my elbow, so that I had become a posse chasing after my own body. But for once I really didn’t mind. I took his hand and pulled, made him stand up. For they were a good excuse now for me to lead him inside.

15.
Drew

I don't know if this happens to everyone or just to me, but I can be eating something, like honey-coated Cheerios, and someone comes in and does something, or tells me something, and from then on every time I eat honey-coated Cheerios, they taste different. Take the time I was sitting in the kitchen, watching the last of the Cheerios floating in the milk, the milk taking on a sort of tan color from the Cheerios by then, and me half asleep—I'm a late waker-upper, hard as pulling out nails to get sleep off me—and Dad sat down at the table beside me and told me and Mandy and George—who were both eating honey-coated Cheerios, too—that he was going someplace else to live. Mom was in the living room, picking up, and then she comes in and sits down, too, says their decision has nothing to do with us or their love for us, then gets up and fries eggs till the yellows are as hard as the centers of the black-eyed Susans in all the ditches around town.

And then there was that Saturday in October when I went out in my boat and right off hooked a speckled trout with a jighead. The day was so beautiful I wished I could just put my tongue on it, taste it.

I was out by Driftwood Island, on the flats, in about three feet of water. My motor had been running sweet all morning. I'd worked on it the night before, then gotten up at 5:00 A.M. while everybody was asleep and put my boat in the marsh behind the house and felt my way out of the channels into the Gulf. The light was dim as smoke, the sun coming up in streaks, turning the pale gray of my aluminum boat to the color of a new nickel. The water around me, too, was moving like polished triangles.

Dad was picking up Mandy and George at about eight to take them to Disney World with Anne Marie for another one of those bang-up Disney holidays. Then the next weekend he was taking us to spend the night over at the beach on the Atlantic, sort of like a last farewell to summer. I was going with them to the beach, but I had asked to stay home over the Disney weekend so I could catch up on my fishing. Fish all day. Then Heather at night. A perfect combination in my mind.

Mom was going to work as usual, even though Dr. Haley was on vacation. It was one of the Saturdays when the clinic was open. And she and Mrs. MacHenry were going to be cleaning it up, answering the phone, catching up on the files, that kind of stuff. She'd been still asleep when I left the house, and, for my sake, had put Mandy in charge of waiting with George for Dad if he didn't come until after she left.

It was two o'clock when I decided to come in, put the string of trout I'd caught in the fridge, get some lunch, refill my ice chest, and maybe go back out for a few hours on the other side of Driftwood Island. I tied my boat up at the boathouse in back, walked through the backyard, saw Mom had left a basket of wet clothes just sitting under the clothesline (the dryer was on the blink again) and that was my first clue that something was wrong.

In the kitchen, I saw all the dishes left just where she'd left them—the real bang-up June Cleaver breakfast she always got up early to fix us whenever Dad was going to come by and get us: French toast and blueberry syrup, fresh-squeezed orange juice, and Jimmy Dean sausage. The half moons of squeezed oranges sat on the counter, under them a film of spilled juice now sticky as Scotch tape. And beside them a note: Drew, Call me at 554-3281, Mom.

It was the number for The Love 'em and Leave 'em Day Care. I recognized that.

I sat on the stool at the kitchen counter, eating a grilled cheese and a pear, the phone receiver under my chin. Rambona sat under me, hoping for crumbs. When I dialed, some woman I didn't recognize right off answered. I asked for Mom, and she said, "Just a minute."

When Mom came on the phone, she sounded like someone I didn't know. Like some new teacher on the first day of school who wanted to get what she said just right. "Drew?"

"Yeah."

"I'm at Lucille's. I'm going to be home in a little while. I'm bringing Lucille with me. I want you to clean up a little and put clean sheets on George's bed and feed Rambona." She stopped talking then, and I sat there for a minute just listening to nothing. It seemed I could hear her breathing or trying to catch her breath, like maybe she'd been running, but she hadn't been anywhere. The thought crossed my mind that maybe she was starting to have those breathing attacks like Mandy had once had. But then she started talking again, and, when she did, she told me she had something awful to tell me and she didn't know how to do it but maybe straight out and quick was the best way after all. (Mom could really ramble when she didn't like heading somewhere.) She didn't leave me any space for any questions, either. She just started telling me how two men had broken into Bill Duffy's Handymart in the middle of the night, had robbed it, had tied up both Lucille and Bill, and then had shot Bill on their way out. She stopped for a minute then, which was obviously my cue to start helping her out by asking questions.

"Is he okay?"

All I could think of was Mr. Duffy giving me that key chain on the day I'd gotten my driver's permit, and how every day I'd used it, and it was in my pocket even then.

"He's dead, Drew." I could hear my mother doing that funny breathing again.

Rambona reached up, took the rest of the grilled cheese out of my hand. The words didn't register, not really. I didn't know what that meant, *dead*, not really. I heard it every day on television and occasionally around town. But it didn't seem to go with Mr. Duffy. It didn't seem to fit with the key chain, or the Christmas tree he'd sold us, or the Granny Apple.

"I'm sorry, Drew. I'm sorry I had to tell you. And I'm sorry I have to ask you to do this, but Lucille and I need you. Can you just put the clean sheets on, and maybe vacuum? I bet the room's full of Rambona's hair."

"Yeah. Sure."

"And I didn't get a chance to finish hanging out the wash. Would you mind doing that? Can you fit that in with everything else?"

"Yeah. Sure."

"Are you okay, Drew?"

"Yeah."

"We'll be over there in a little while. If you want to, call Betty MacHenry. If you need any help, call Betty. She'll be off from the clinic soon. Okay?"

Then it was like she was just waiting to hear *me* breathe. It was like she was counting the spaces between my words and the lengths of my breaths. Mom is like that: leaning over, studying vital signs when she's told you something, or something's happened that she knows has knocked your breath out.

"Yeah. Fine," I said.

"Thank God for you, Drew." Then, "This is too awful to understand, Drew. None of us can believe it yet. We'll be there with you in just a little while. Keep busy. Don't worry."

"Yeah, okay."

And then, like when you pull your finger along the smooth cold surface of a glass window on the way into the dentist's office, when you already know you have about a million cavities, we started talking about fish. "Did you catch anything? How was the fishing, Drew? Did you have fun?"

"Yeah, six trout. All keepers."

"Really?"

"Yeah. I just came in to put them on ice. Should I go ahead and clean them?"

"Why don't you go ahead. That'd be good, Drew. Go ahead and put them in the freezer."

Didn't need to add that Bill Duffy wouldn't have hated anything more than letting six good trout go to waste, lie in the sink till spoiled.

When I hung up, even before changing the sheets and vacuuming and hanging up the wet clothes, I cleaned my trout. I knew even while I was doing it that catching trout would never again be just catching trout.

I had a hard time deciding which sheets to put on George's bed. There wasn't much choice. And I didn't know what would be best for Mrs. Duffy. The decision nearly drove me out of my mind. I just stood there looking into the linen closet for about fifteen minutes, pulling out Snoopy pillowcases and then G.I. Joe. Finally decided to just use some of Mandy's sheets: pink with lollipops. It was a dead shame we didn't have any plain white sheets in twin size. Strange how my mind just thought of everything with the word dead in it: the house deadly quiet. A roach in the corner of George's room that I vacuumed up, dead as a doornail. The stuffed dog on the floor that was deathly white. Didn't seem right to put Mrs. Duffy in a five-year-old's room. I worried about the race cars sitting around and the model airplanes that George and I sometimes made together, and the stuffed animals that were left over from his real baby days. Everything seemed to say something about the beginning of life, and having fun, and all that. Mom hated to throw away anything. She'd hung George's crib mobiles up on the ceiling: pink and yellow rocking horses dangling like a string of prize fish. I put a few of Mom's magazines beside the bed: *Better Homes and Gardens*, *Good Housekeeping*, then took away the *Good Housekeeping* because on the cover it advertised that it had an article inside called "How to Keep Your Man Happy." Replaced it with a *Time* magazine. Then saw that the *Time* magazine had a feature on how much longer Americans were living. I couldn't come up with anything that I thought would be right for her. Then I gave up when I realized that nothing would be right, anyway.

When Mom and Mrs. Duffy drove up in the Granny Apple, and parked in the driveway, I didn't know what to do. Didn't know what to say. Just stood in the doorway, looking, saying, Hey. Mom took Mrs. Duffy in the kitchen. Made her sit at the table there, poured her a glass of iced tea, gave her two pills that Mrs. Duffy said she didn't need but that Mom said she'd gotten from the clinic and that she ought to take them whether she thought she needed them or not. Actually Mrs. Duffy did look a little sick, like she had a cold, like she'd missed sleep.

And then the pills made Mrs. Duffy want to go to sleep. And she went into George's bedroom, and Mom commented on how nice I'd fixed it. Instead of the magazines, I'd set a bowl of bananas beside the bed, and then I'd brought in my own portable boom box in case she wanted to listen to music.

It wasn't but about an hour or two when the house started filling up. Food came and got laid out on the dining room table. Half the town sat around in chairs that I arranged in a horseshoe, with Mom at the top of the curve beside Mrs. Duffy when she came out from her nap, and it was like a quiet, unplanned party that went on late into the night. Mrs. Duffy even started telling stories about Bill. We heard about the article he wrote for Humor in Uniform and sent to *The Reader's Digest*. It came back, though. And when he was nineteen, he had driven to New York City to see if he could try out for the Yankees. They weren't much interested. But everybody there that night in our living room talked, and even laughed, about his spunk and then talked about it even more. He wore a size 14 shoe that he had to get on special order, and he hated cauliflower and slaw. He worked the crossword puzzle in two newspapers every day and knew words like ingot and blesbok. Then Mr. Clark told how Bill had designed his own advertisement for the Handymart and brought it to him to put in the paper, offering a package of fishhooks with every fifteen gallons of gas he pumped.

The next day went on like that, except that for a few hours Mom left and went back to Mr. and Mrs. Duffy's apartment over the Handymart and picked up the clothes that Mrs. Duffy said she wanted to bury Mr. Duffy in. And when Mom went, a policeman had to go with her. They had the whole Handymart closed off from the road with yellow tape.

When Dad and George and Mandy came back, we all went to the funeral together. We stood in the cemetery with Mrs. Duffy, while the preacher said some things about Mr. Duffy and said about a million prayers that seemed to go with the thousands of flowers that were just about everywhere. I'd just as soon pull my toenails off as go to another funeral. Then Dad took Mandy and George to stay with him and Anne Marie for the rest of the week. And when Friday came, Mom said I should go on to the beach with them. Said she and Mrs. Duffy would be fine together in our house, that there was no reason for me to miss what Dad had planned.

The sand over there closed over my bare feet. And I stood and watched it, moving over my skin like it was something alive. I sunk down in it pretty far until I got out to where the tide had left it flat and hard and smooth. And then my toes left prints shaped something like the shells of peanuts. The roar of the ocean reminded me of a ball game crowd. And it seemed that over there what had happened to Mr. Duffy had not happened at all. It was like he was just off at a ball game somewhere, up at Atlanta, or down at Miami, or out fishing at the reef, and would be back in town when I got home.

The water was cold, but George couldn't stay out of it. So I pulled him onto the waves on a Boogie board and climbed up behind him to hold him on. Our teeth were chattering almost the whole way into shore. It didn't seem that I had ever thought as much about Mr. Duffy, or learned so much about him, as in the last few days. Seemed, too, that I understood something about dying and being dead that I'd never thought about before. How they hooked themselves to us: the dead. And forever. That we carried them with us wherever we went for as long as we were alive. And I began to think about and worry about how many things in my own life could be changed like Cheerios and speckled trout. And that by the time I was an old man and about to die myself, I'd be carrying around all these things in my head until nothing would be only itself, but would be instead my whole life with parts of everybody else's hooked to it like a string of caught fish, hanging on.

George and I rode the board up into the puddles the tide had left. Even in the October sun, Mandy was getting red in the face, and Dad made her sit under the umbrella he stuck in the sand. Anne Marie had on a bikini, was oiled up and lying with her eyes closed like a beached mammal, even though I thought it was a little too cool for a bikini before noon.

Here in North Florida the mornings and nights had turned cool, the summer sun backing off and leaving only the middle of the day with a reminder of how it could lean over you and get hot. Almost everybody else on the beach had on shorts, or sweat suits, unless they were brave, or dumb, and going into the water like me and George. And then as I looked away from her and down the beach, I saw Dr. Haley—who could miss the whole long length of him?—jogging down the beach with this babe in red silky running shorts and a tank top, the whole outfit about the size of a Christmas stamp. I sat for a minute, then stood up and jogged a little down the beach after them just to make sure that it was really him.

She was tall, too. Tall with creamy-looking skin and long, dark hair that trailed behind her like a flag.

I couldn't understand it. Mom had only said he was going to be off from the clinic for that week. He hadn't even been there for Mr. Duffy's funeral. And here he was, living it up with somebody who wasn't my mom, and not only did I want to run after him, throw him to the ground, even though I knew he outweighed me by about fifty pounds, at least, all I could think about was how this was going to kill Mom. She'd never make it through this. She had it bad for him, I knew. And I knew myself what that meant. Didn't take much to know for sure. All it took was me thinking about Heather to know how Mom would take it.

Frankly I couldn't watch that again. Couldn't stand to see Mom go through all of that all over again, which made me realize, too, how much she and I were hooked together even now, when one of us wasn't even dead yet.

I stood there, the sand like tiny tacks poking me on the bottoms of my feet, and as he ran, alive and well, into the blast of sun that made him disappear, I don't think I've ever felt so awful, or so alone, and yet so hooked to another life that I knew I had to do something. *Had* to.

16.
Linda

Lucille Duffy and I sat in the kitchen. The October sun was like a low setting on my electric blanket, just warm enough so you could stretch any way you wanted to and not pull anything. She had been with me a week. The kids were with George, were due home from the beach the next day, and Lucille and I both knew we had to make some decisions now. When the kids were back all the beds would be taken.

"Want some toast?" I passed over the plate with raisin slices on it.

"No thanks." Lucille was wearing blue slacks and a sweatshirt. She nursed her cup of coffee like it was a bubble that might break, her hands cupped around the cup, her thumb fondling the rim.

"How about some Marshmallow Puffs? I only let George the Second have those on holidays. And I'll let you have them, too, if you promise to be good."

She smiled. Then I went on: "I mean if you promise *not* to be good." She looked up, smiled, again.

One day for her was okay, and then the next was like the inside of a closed bag. All the while she tried to keep up a tough front.

It was almost like I had to give her permission to grieve. And what made it worse was that no one was really sure what had happened to Lucille that night when the store was robbed. She was tied up and put in the stockroom, but other than that, and joking about that: "Showed them this," she would tell, holding up her arm and flexing her biceps, making the same propeller she had made on the day when, over a year and a half ago now, she had come into my bedroom and offered to aim it at George the First. "And they had to go out front and steal some more rope," she added.

It made a good story, anyway. Any way she said it, it made her seem undefeated, unharmed, when the truth was, we all knew she was harmed and defeated.

Only thing I know to do when someone is so troubled is to share troubles of my own, like if you serve up one kind of something, they'll serve up some, too. Almost like making wagers at cards, matching each raise. Or a bake-off between cooks, each offering up a secret recipe.

Straight out I told her I'd decided that I was going to stop seeing Mark. That soon as he got back in town I was going to tell him.

"Stop? Stop altogether?" Lucille looked across at me, and her thumbs met over the top of the cup as if she was afraid of tipping it over.

"Yeah."

"Why?"

I didn't know how to say it. I wanted to be funny blunt—it'd be good for both of us. But I couldn't. "Because we can't stop . . . you know," I said.

Lucille reared back, laughed anyway. I guess I was funny blunt without even knowing it. "Don't know why you'd ever want to."

"Because it's just too much," I said, then laughed a little, too, and added, "I mean, for me to handle." I stood up, started clearing off the table. "Seems like we're just sneaking around, waiting for the kids to leave, going over to his house, even tempted to do it at the clinic in a treatment room. Lucille, it's like I've become what all along my mother was afraid I was. It's just too much for me to handle."

Lucille twisted around in her chair so her eyes could follow me, eyes so bruised with sorrow, it was as if they'd been punched. I was walking to the sink, putting the dishes in, giving the scraps to Rambona. "So why don't you just get married?" she said. "That'll end it. Slow it down, at least."

I smiled. "That's what I'm afraid I might have to do."

Lucille got up, too, took a rag and wiped the crumbs off the table. The water was running in the sink over the dishes and over my hands.

"So?" Lucille came behind me, rinsed her rag out: "What'd be so awful about that?"

"Everything. If what happened to me with George ever happened to me again, and especially if I didn't have the children living with me, depending on me, to make me go on, I know I wouldn't make it. I couldn't live through finding out that he had stopped loving me."

"So who says he would?"

"It happened once."

"That don't mean it's going to happen twice."

"No, but I'd be worrying about it all the time."

"So?" She looked at me. Lucille's face was soft and swollen, kneaded by grief. She looked so intensely at me, so absorbed in my trouble that she seemed ready to puff at me like her old self. She said straight at me. "I don't know anybody who's left on this earth who's not worrying about something."

Then she turned, gave Rambona the piece of toast she didn't eat, letting Rambona rise up on her hind legs to take it out of her fingers. "Seems to me that's the main test to see if you're alive. In fact," she went on, "the only comfort I have is thinking about the things Bill won't have to be worrying about now. The store insurance, gas prices, the mortgages, the dry months when it seemed that nothing but chewing gum was sold."

I had a coffee cup dangling from my right index finger, ready to set it in the dishwasher. I leaned against the counter, faced her, gave her all my attention as she told me: "And the only way I know now that I'm still alive is worrying about what happened and what I could've done, and how I had to sit back there in the stockroom and not know what was happening and how I'm the only one who knows what they looked like—or, at least, the part of them that I could see." Her voice broke off, then she said quickly, with a few quick sobs like commas, surrounding it: "They had on ski masks, god-awful, like monsters. And now I'm worrying about whether or not I'll ever be able to go back over there again. I got to open up the day care next week. Mothers are worrying about replacing me, maybe skipping work, losing pay—going nuts over their kids."

I reached over, touched her hand. "You don't have to go back to work until you feel like it. And you don't have to go back over there, ever."

She looked at me for a good long while. The silence had a solid feel to it. Then she put her hand on top of mine and said to me so directly that I couldn't even breathe. "And you don't have to give up Mark just because he makes you feel so good it makes you feel bad."

For a split second it seemed as though we were going to laugh. But instead we grabbed each other, and the sound of our combined voices rose so high and loud that we began hurting Rambona's ears. She stuck her nose up, howled, too. We were in the house alone, and all around us, for only the remainder of this one day, there was no one. And knowing that, knowing this was our last chance to give up all of our pretenses, honorable or not, we let pour forth a set of moans that eventually just wore themselves out, so that the only thing to do was to stop. To get calm again. To go back to worrying. To go back to planning on how to get rid of the worrying.

I called down to the Seaside Lodge and asked if I could rent a cot.

We drove down there and got the folding cot in the back of the Granny Apple, then stopped by the hardware store and bought a roll of clear plastic. We brought all of it home, set the cot up out on the back porch, and then tacked the plastic over the screens. With the late afternoon sun coming in, it would stay warm all night.

We fixed her up a place that she began calling her cubbyhole. But before she consented to all this, she made me make her a promise.

She made me agree to imagine a future I might not ever have been able to see if I had listened only to myself.

•

It was dark when I went over to Mark's. The same night when I knew he was supposed to be home. From over on the other coast, he had been calling me nearly every night. He had told me the night before that he was going to take Lisa down to Tampa to catch a plane, then was going to come straight back, and he would call me here.

But I didn't even wait. Instead I walked Rambona up and down the street, waiting to see the old Mercedes round the corner and pull into his drive. Drew and Mandy and George were due back at eight. I had to finish all this business by then. I had to get back home and be ready to be the good mother that I tried to be.

It was as though looking at my life now was like looking at something I wanted to paint—when narrowing my eyes, only the essential lines were left—and I saw that living with the fact that love, that life itself, can, at any given moment, disappear, then I had to live with what I was most afraid of. For the first—and probably only time—I saw a connection about my life that mattered. I saw that nothing else allowed me to feel so alive—filled me with so much hopefulness that the dark sides of all things lost their shapes—as having a physical bonding with a man. I had to remain in touch with this most simple life force. In fact, it seemed that for no better reason than for the procreation of myself should I have stood there, waiting, looking down the street for the old funny, humpbacked car to round the corner, pull up into the drive. I was so filled with the thoughts of this that when it did—its grill still missing, its front end marked by a gaping hole—bouncing over the bump at the end of the gravel driveway and pulling up beside me, my words, even though not exactly decided upon, were definite in their intentions. And I stepped close. "Mark?"

"Hey, there." His smile alone was enough of a greeting.

When he opened the car door, Whatsy jumped out, bounded up on me, sniffed Rambona. I unleashed Rambona as Mark hugged me. We went inside together, and the dogs trotted off into the kitchen, then Mark and I stood, leaning against each other for a minute, breathing together. "Did you have a good time?" I finally asked.

"Yeah. Great."

"How's Lisa?"

"Terrific. How's Lucille?"

"Holding up."

We moved over to the couch, sat there. Me beside him. His hand at my back. Then under the edge of my blouse, against my skin. I put my hand behind me, made him be still. "I have to talk to you about this," I said.

"About what?"

I couldn't be serious, straight. That would feel too dangerous. "About this hand," I said. I pulled it out from where he had been rubbing the skin of my back and turned his palm downward so that the back of his fingers were against my lips. "I love this hand," I said. "And I'm pretty fond of this." I kissed the inside of his elbow, then touched the side of his face, while saying: "And I'm not sure I can live without this, not to mention a few other things it's hooked to."

He grinned, watching me. We'd never said the L word. We'd never talked dirty, either. Now I'd gotten pretty close to both. "And I've got something bothering me," I said.

"What?"

"I'm not sure I can tell you."

"Why?"

"I think it's going to embarrass me."

"Why?"

"Because it's about what we're doing and how it makes me feel and all the things it makes me think about and what I think we might have to do about it to make the feeling go away."

"Which one first?"

"I'm talking about what we do and how bad it makes me feel."

"You don't like it?"

I laughed.

"I thought you liked it!"

God! He had that panicked look on his face.

"I'm not talking about you. I'm talking about the fact that I can't live with myself, or my children, going on the way we've been going on."

"Oh."

"I think we're going to have to do something about it."

He looked at me, his eyes like blue-tinted glass, like round rims of air that I was not sure I could breathe without.

"What do you have in mind?"

"One of two things. Both of which scare me so much, I'm not sure I can say them."

"Name one."

"Quit, cold turkey."

"And two?"

"Get legal."

He sat back, grinned, then stopped. "I don't know. I'm not sure I can do either of those."

I watched him. In so many words I was a woman who had proposed, who had said she might be willing to try to do the one thing that I was most afraid of. And he sat there, one leg crossed over his other knee, leaning back, just looking at me and saying he didn't like my choices. God! What was I: The Disposable Woman?

I got up, called Rambona to me.

"Linda."

"What?"

"I don't know."

He said it again. "I don't know." Then "Jeez!"—a half-mad, it seemed, irritated sort of sound.

I could feel him watching me as I snapped the leash onto Rambona's collar. On the way back home, I knew I might feel the urge to just let her go, coax her to forget everything she'd been taught. Let her tree the whole damn world. And grin.

I opened the door. He just sat there while I went out.

17.
Drew

It was up to me. I had to fix it. I had to fix things for my mom. It wasn't just a thing I wanted to do—I *had* to. My whole frigging future was on the line. If I didn't get a life for my mom, I knew I'd never have much of one of my own.

Ever since I'd seen Dr. Haley at the beach, she'd started wearing dark glasses a lot again and buying brownie mix with coupons till the pantry looked like one long shelf of dark chocolate. And she was baking them every night, sometimes humming "Don't Worry, Be Happy." And starting to lose weight.

Either she'd found out about his other woman, or he'd gone into the predumping mode, and that'd unloosened her.

And even though I wasn't too clear on exactly how I was going to do it, I figured I knew the most about what got the best of him. That probably the quickest way to get him to see the light was to take him out in my boat. Sit there long enough until he knew that sticking with my mom and giving up that other woman was a whole lot better than being out on the Gulf with me.

And if that didn't do it, I knew I could always drown him,

though the thought of murder didn't exactly sit so good—if it ever had—after Mr. Duffy. He'd brought the whole thing of it close to home, though. In fact, the whole idea of how a life could just be jerked away in any split second—could be squeezed out of you for no good reason at all—nearly made me so sick I had to leave whatever room I was in whenever the thought of it came to me. I could feel the whole lining of my stomach turning over when I just thought of Mr. Duffy. And now I was starting to think about how my own and my mom's life were just riding on this six-foot-six-inch dude with a dislike for water. It might just be a matter of him or us.

I didn't want to wait for a calm day, either. Hoped instead for a little wind, a few steady gusts when I took him out, just an inch or two under small-craft warnings.

So I went over to the clinic one afternoon after school. I told Mom I was there to bring her some mail I thought she needed to see right away. Made that up pretty good—gave her one of those magazine subscription letters with the envelope marked: "Important. You're about to let a good thing slip."

She looked at me. "Oh, this is nothing, Drew. Just some magazine thing."

"Well, I didn't know. Couldn't tell for sure."

"Anyway, thanks for thinking it might be important. How was school?"

"Fair."

Then Dr. Haley came in the room, and Mom turned to ice. She said she had to go out back and put up a shipment of drugs that'd just been delivered. She turned her back to us, and I can't say I much blamed her. If she had even any inkling of what I'd seen—

him parading down practically the whole Atlantic beach with a babe dressed in an outfit that could barely cover a mole's ass—ice wasn't enough.

I looked at him—all six and a half feet, cool dude, just crying to be busted. "We're fixin' to go fishing," I said. "Next Saturday. I've got us entered in the Fishing Rodeo." He was looking at his own mail. At that, he looked up. Didn't think I'd even start out with: "Thought I would." Instead I just said my stuff like an act accomplished.

"What?"

It was like he was playing this hard-of-hearing thing. More like he couldn't believe what he'd heard. Next would be praying none of it was true.

"You kept promising George you'd catch enough fish for another fish fry. Just thought I'd help my mother out—what with me and you in the tournament this week, that ought to be enough for a good start. Then next week we'll take George out."

"What exactly is a fishing rodeo?" He set his mail down, was looking at me like—at just the mention of it—he was already getting a little sick.

"It's this thing where two men in one boat go out as teams and the fish are weighed at the end of the day. It's pounds that count, not the kind of fish. The winner gets fifty dollars and a new rig at the Bait and Tackle."

"Oh."

I could be wrong, but the skin under his eyes seemed to take on a green tint, just a shade or two under pea soup. Apparently even the thought of being out in my boat for a whole day was enough to get him going. Which was so fine I was laughing on the inside. Now all I had to do was box him in real good.

I half expected him to cry uncle, call in sick with something unrelated, like an ingrown toenail, so he wouldn't have to go. Then I thought I'd just raise the stakes a little, play pitiful and desperate. "I couldn't find anybody else to go with me," I said. "Dad's got a teacher's meeting. I already paid the twenty-dollar entry fee because I knew you'd probably want to do it, since I couldn't find anybody else."

I'd never been so shrewd or such a lying son of a bitch, but that just shows what lengths family can drive you to.

He sat down at his desk. "What time?" He looked at me. "When you want me to be ready?"

"Six," I said. "They won't let anybody start till 6:30. But we have to check in down at the town dock."

Mom came out of the back and walked through the room, carrying a box of chemicals. Her head did not move; her hips barely moved either. As she did, he looked up, followed her as she walked. He had sort of this shocked look on his face, like he'd maybe been told he had B.O. or something. And he said to her as she passed by, "I'm going to be in the fishing rodeo with Drew."

"That's nice," she said, not even stopping or saying anything else. But I swear, as she passed through one of the treatment room doors, it sure seemed to me I heard her say, "Great. Hope you fall out and drown."

•

It was five to six when I got down at the pier. Already it was crowded with men and fishing gear. I looked for him, but he was not anywhere around. It wouldn't have been like him, though, not to show up. I knew his kind, knew it from my mom; they'd rather have their hair pulled out than give their word on something and then just not show.

I didn't really care either if we were the last ones out. If we didn't catch a fish during the whole damn day, I didn't care. I wasn't after just fish. I didn't know what I was going to say to him, or how I was going to do it, but I had several possible plans. And I was so revved up and ready, I knew only that somehow before the day was over he'd be hurtin' bad or totally committed to my mom.

He came walking up in blue jeans and a windbreaker, his hair slicked back with water. The October sun wasn't really all that bad, but it was obvious that he was going to play it safe; had a big white patch of suntan lotion all down his whole long nose. Parts of it were spattered on his mustache. He carried a cooler and a cup of coffee. "All set," he said, like this was some kind of an operation and he was ready to cut through some poor guy's breastbone.

"I got the boat 'round at the house," I said.

"Fine."

We stood in line together to get our contest number, which we had to show when we came back in with whatever fish we'd caught.

We walked in the fuzzy light through the backyard of our house, knowing everybody inside was still asleep. We skirted the house at a distance, because I was worried about Rambona. She was sleeping on the back porch with Mrs. Duffy, and I didn't want her to hear us and bark.

Over the last few days, she had gone into heat again, and we hadn't been so good at keeping her penned up as before. Mom said soon as she got the money, she was definitely going to have Rambona fixed. But just the day before about four dogs had surrounded the house and stayed all night long, circling about like Jaws, one a white-eyed bulldog, too. Just kept cruising the bushes, skulking around. Howling late at night, driven mad by hormones, and driving us mad, too. And then Mom just opened the door and yelled, "What the hell, Rambona. Go get it."

The next day, when Rambona came back, she just lay around. In fact, she slept through three whole days.

Now as me and Dr. Haley tiptoed through the backyard to the boathouse, even on the back porch with Mrs. Duffy, Rambona didn't seem to get a hint.

The sun was not even up yet, just a glow that splashed one corner of the sky in front of us. The sound of the water lapping in the gray light was so wonderful that I couldn't imagine why I didn't get up this early every day just to hear it, see it like this.

I noticed him glance toward the house, toward the window we both knew was over my mother's bed. Then he sat down on the wood bench nailed into the floor of the boathouse and pulled out a little box from his pocket. He laughed. "Got this just in case. You know, the last time I went out in your boat, I got a little queasy." He put a little round adhesive patch behind the back of his ear.

Damn. Doctors. Know how to treat everything. Or think they do. Got it all under control; not anything going to get away from him. If that damn patch worked, I knew I might have to go to plan B. Might have to cook up for certain a Substitute Misery.

We got in, my boat so small we had to be careful. He eased

down on the slat in the front. I got in back by the motor, turned to crank it. The dawn rose over us like streams of juice, and we putted out into the channel.

"How you know how to get through here?"

"Feel," I said.

The oyster bars rose around us in the low tide like hunks of dumped tires, black and scaly.

We moved out through the channel toward its mouth that opened into the Gulf, so flat in the new light that I was worried. I needed waves, something to toss us around a little, test that damn patch behind his ear. And then I realized that I was going to have to definitely come up with a new plan of Assured Misery, and I aimed the boat to where I knew I shouldn't go.

In his eyes I was a sixteen-year-old kid who couldn't know everything. I could mess up, and he'd have to forgive me, or at least not suspect that I was doing it on purpose.

Already a few other boats were dotting the surface out in the Gulf, heading to their favorite honey holes.

As I aimed out to the wide part of the channel's mouth, I wondered, how was I going to bring up the subject with him, anyway? Start out with something like, And so, just what are your intentions toward my mother, exactly? Or: So, yo, what's happenin' with you and old Mom anyway?

But while I was thinking, he said, turning back so he could face me, "It's really nice we're able to do this. Because I've been wanting to spend some time with you, anyway, and this'll give me a good chance. I want to talk to you about your mother."

"My mother?" I said, surprised, and jerklike. Then realized what he was doing, that he was going to beat me to the subject of her first, and I tried to say gruff, back: "Yeah, been wanting to talk to you about her, too." For no doubt he was going to tell me that he was going to dump her and wanted me to keep her from committing suicide.

Fat chance. She and I both were going to kill him first. Or maybe just contract him out to Rambona.

I aimed for the hidden oyster bar that I knew about so well that it was like heading for the doorstop that you once broke your toe on in the dark, and I slammed the side of my boat into it, good. The force of it nearly knocked him out of the front, over the side. And while he was wobbling and trying to get himself right, I stood up, said, "Uh oh, guess I lost my feel."

"What do we do?"

"Not much," I said. "Just sit tight."

I put an oar over the side, stuck it into the mud bottom and tried to push us off the bar. It was only about two feet deep here. Not anywhere deep enough that when I made him get out of the boat to pull us, that damn patch would get washed off. But there was always the chance that he'd slip on the bottom and fall all the way in anyway, or that the tide would come in before we got all the way off the oyster bar.

"No luck," I said, putting the oar back in, the paddle head black with mud. "It's too shallow. And I can't even work my motor here." I pulled up the prop, so it wouldn't get ruined on the oyster bars. "We got two choices," I said, knowing exactly which one he'd choose. "We can either sit here, stuck, till the tide lifts us off." Then I let him watch me look out into the open Gulf where the other boats were now growing in number like a rash. "Which is going to put us way behind. Or one of us can get out and pull us the rest of the way out of this side of the channel." Then I looked at him. I knew what he'd choose from watching him all those weeks in that dog school. He'd rather jump in shit than get behind, maybe lose the chance to win.

"I'll do it," he said, rolling up his jeans.

"You don't mind?" I said.

"Naaa."

Knew he wouldn't want to ever look like a wuss, have me be the one pulling him. And anyway, I had to drive.

He was over the side, water up to his knees.

"That's good," I said, coaching him. "A little more to the left."

He wiggled us off the bar, and I guided him, calling which direction I thought was the channel. I sent him into a few more bars, just for the hell of it, and kept him pulling us out through the channel like a blind mule with me yelling gee and haw, and letting him bump around a little for a good long while. He was nearly all the way covered in mud, looking like the Tar Baby in Uncle Remus that Mom read to George.

He took his shirt off, threw it in the boat. Finally, as we hit the mouth of the channel and he began swimming, he asked me if it was safe to get back in the boat, and I told him yeah, knowing it was not. For out there with no footing, without a dock or a little sandbar to help him get a grip, my little boat was harder to get into, for someone as big as him, than to hold onto a piece of wet soap. He flailed around for a pretty long time, all legs, asshole, and elbows—half in, half out, half turning the whole damn boat over. And then finally made it in when he realized he had to lie like a flat board across both sides of the boat, then change his weight every few inches, until he bent in the middle and sat down. He was as wet as a chicken in a hurricane.

"Want a drink?" I opened my cooler. The least I could do, I figured, was offer him a Coke or some Gatorade.

"Thanks."

He popped the top off.

I let the prop of my motor back into the water and started it. "Figure we'll fish first over at Turtle Key," I yelled, as I aimed the boat toward the distant island, and opened it up, yelling out over the wind of our speed.

We cut through a group of a couple of boats, and I saw him holding on with each big hand around each side of my boat, his fingers long as rubber hoses, his hair lifted straight up off his forehead as I gunned it, that damn patch behind his ear still riding fine and dry.

I got in close to Turtle Key, right next to a beach and dropped the anchor. Seaweed sat on the sugar-sand near us like lost hair.

"What are we fishing for?"

"Cobia. They like these holes in this shallow water."

"Any chance we can get stuck on the bottom, here?" He half laughed. But looked a little worried. I had given him a pretty good workout pulling us out of the channel.

"Naaa," I said. "Tide's in now, anyway."

I handed him a line and a cigarette minnow to put on it.

We sucked Cokes and sat quiet and eyed the water for shadows that might be fish or the holes they were hiding in.

And then he said, "I'm concerned about your mother's happiness."

Quick I said back, "Yeah, me too."

"I want her to be happy."

I returned, like a ball player warming up, trying to outdo him by throwing just a little beyond his reach. "Best way to be, for anybody."

"Well, I just don't know if what I'm going to suggest is the best thing for either of us. Or for everybody. But your opinion is real important to me."

"I bet," I said. And then I got a bite, and we both stopped talking and watched my line. I pulled in a mackerel a little more than a foot long. He leaned over the boat, netted it for me. We both admired it, and I dropped the fish into my fish cooler, and then behind him, his pole jerked nearly out of the boat. He pulled in a flounder. I netted it for him, and we put it in the cooler on top of my fish.

Then I decided he needed a little more Assured Misery. Because I couldn't think of anything else to say to him. And I didn't know what else to do with him but make him pay for what he was about to do to my mother. At least after this, if he still followed through with dumping her, she and I'd have this little bit of comfort in knowing that for just this little while I had brought him to his knees, made him scream uncle. By the time I finished, I wanted him to know that throwing away his other girlfriend would have seemed as easy as getting rid of chewed gum.

I pulled up the anchor, started the motor, headed for deeper water. Then, "Here," I said, handing him a pinfish that I had slit, telling him how to put it on his line.

"What's this for?"

"Big fish," I said. "Big fish really love this bait." I didn't add that sharks took after it like something horny.

The sun blazed away and his bare back was getting blistered; it was like summer had come back for this one day, was helping me out by hanging around and throwing out one more sizzler that could fry anybody. And I reached into my food cooler and handed him a wrapped cheese sandwich. Figured I ought to fatten him up before I scared the living shit out of him. And by the time he was halfway through with the sandwich, I saw a fin on the other side of the boat and then the shark struck his line, and, just as I hoped, he was pulled halfway out of the boat.

"What do I do?" he yelled at me.

"Hold it," I yelled back. "Reel," I said. I started the motor, pulled up the anchor so I could move the boat against the pull of the fish. It was a pretty big one, a hammerhead, about three feet. It wasn't the kind that was likely to eat him or anybody else, but what he didn't know was, I hoped, likely to kill him. Scare him enough to, at least—which in the long run could have meant a lot to me and my mom.

I looked at him struggling, amazed at how mean I could be. Amazed at how angry and fed up and desperate and in love I could feel, all at the same time. I kept thinking of my mother as me if I were about to lose Heather. And then as the damn shark pulled him in, which was just what I expected would happen—since I knew Dr. Haley would never do what ninety-nine people out of a hundred would: throw in the damn rod and let the frigging fish have it. But no, not him. Game for the fight, he was. When he went over the side he made a big splash, too. And now he was hanging on for dear life, the shark pulling him into deeper water while all the while he was yelling back at me, so that I could coach him. I knew I would have to talk him into it: into letting go.

"I really don't care," I yelled, "if you lose my favorite rod. It only cost three hundred dollars anyway."

"Three hundred?" he screamed back.

"Yeah, my dad gave it to me for my birthday." (A little extra guilt thrown in wouldn't hurt, either.)

He tugged some more. But the fish was a far better swimmer than he was and appeared to be headed for Cuba.

"Let go!" I yelled, again. "It's okay. Let go!"

He gave it a few more desperate pulls, but out there in water over his head, it was pretty hard to get some leverage. "God, I'm sorry," he called back, as he finally turned loose of the whole beautiful rod. And we watched it—me in the boat, him treading water like some kind of big blond dog, like a golden retriever—the rod cutting a line through the water straight as a spear.

And then the shark leaped forward, a streamlined silver shape, getting the hell out with the rod I had said I prized, but that I'd also been primed and ready to sacrifice.

When I reached Dr. Haley in my boat, he had to go through that whole long gymnastics routine of his in getting back in without dumping us both.

The pitiful thing was, I discovered I was good at this. I mean, it was really quite a sorry thing to come to know that the one thing you were really good at—sure enough terrific at—was digging up misery for somebody who deep down was pretty nice but that just happened to get in the way of family business.

Because, you see, as I sat there, looking at him, there was no way I could not see that that whole damn patch behind his ear was sure enough wet now.

And I thought: I just have to test that.

That other woman in his mind was probably only a distant speck, too. He was probably even now ready to ship her to Cuba with the hammerhead.

So how could I quit just when I was getting where I wanted to?

I let him calm down a little. We fished through a late-afternoon snack. He put his muddy shirt on to try to cut the sun. He rubbed on sun block till his face looked like mayonnaise. Then I aimed the boat through a channel that would take us up toward the dock where we would weigh our fish. And I just couldn't help rubbing it in that if we'd been able to get the shark in the boat, we'd probably have outweighed everybody in fish, and won.

I told him, though, that we still had a chance. This channel was full of trout, I said. If we got busy and did our best, we still might could win.

But the fact was, I felt, he'd lost all interest in fish.

We putted along as I started Plan B for a little Side Dish of Misery. I aimed my boat to where I knew the sandbars would break my shear pins.

When the first one went, he looked at me, by now tired, dehydrated, burned more ways than just by sun, and asked me what this meant.

"Shear pin's busted," I said, hauling up the motor.

"What do we do?"

"Nothing big," I said. "We can either wait to get towed or make our own."

"Make our own?"

"Yeah. Hand me that coat hanger over there. I always bring some in case this happens."

He held out the coat hanger, and I got my pliers out of my tackle box and cut off some wire that I could fit into my prop. Then when I got it in, we putted a few more yards, then *bam*. Another shear pin.

I didn't mind fixing them. But I could see he was pissed as hell. We were going back in through this whole long channel with only two fish, the breaking shear pins, and their repair, making us move like a hiccup. It was just not his style, not to mention the fact that that patch of his was getting one hell of a workout.

Only thing I hadn't counted on was that fixing the shear pins kept me busy and gave him plenty of time to do nothing but talk.

"What I wanted to tell you," he began, "is that once I was married. Happily married. And then my wife got sick. And there wasn't anything I could do to stop that, or to help her. And when she died, I didn't want to ever have that kind of pain again."

The shallow water in the channel lapped against the sides of my boat, and he was holding the coat hanger and watching me as I cut another shear pin in my lap. I wasn't saying anything.

"Losing people is not something you can just all at once get over."

I put the shear pin in the prop, set the prop down in the water. "Damn straight," I said, figuring I knew as much about that now as anybody.

I pulled the crank. It started, and we moved a few feet more. This time we hit a sandbar that I didn't even aim for. And we were once again cutting another shear pin out of the coat hanger, and he was talking to me again.

"In fact, I have such a fear of it that I tend to avoid getting involved with anybody. I like to keep everything on the surface, everything safe. I don't like to even think about trying to make something permanent because I know it can't last. That's the worst fear in the world for me: that I will be left here, again, that I will be alone here, hurting like that again."

I put in the new shear pin and started up the motor. I didn't see where what he was saying had anything to do with my mom. She didn't make his wife sick. Why did *she* have to pay for what had happened to him? "So what's this got to do with Mom?" I said.

"A lot," he said. "Now that she and I have gotten so close."

We went a few more yards, then *bam*. When the motor stopped, and it was quiet again, I handed him the other oar and I got one, and I said, "I guess this could be just as fast." And we both started rowing.

"What I was wanting to tell you," he went on, turning his head so he talked back toward me. "Or rather ask you . . ." He was in front of me, his back toward me, rowing like he was on a college team or something, his back so broad and strong that I was admiring and envious. "I've thought about asking your mother to marry me, and then I decided I couldn't. I was too afraid." He held up his oar, rested it on his lap, left me doing the work while he looked back at me. I could have popped him in the head with my oar now, just pushed him over and left him. I even whipped my oar around a little to let him know what I was thinking. I came two inches from knocking his whole long nose off his damn face. He ducked. Then went on talking like he was almost getting used to my torture. "So what I want to ask you is—and I figure it's you I ought to ask because in most ways it's you who's the head of your family now, and it ought to be your permission I get, I figure. So what would you say if I admit that I've decided to try it because I love her too much not to?"

"Try what?"

"I want to marry your mother."

I stared at him. Sure sounded to me he was coming around. I leaned to look at that patch. It was wet and half off and he looked a little green, but not too bad for all I'd put him through. And if he was not on his knees because of me, then I didn't know who else had put him there, and my name wasn't Drew for nothing. I stared back at him, admiring my work at how awful he looked.

"So what's your answer?"

Since I was expecting the question, I didn't realize at first I had to say anything back and that he was waiting for me. Instead I rowed faster, hoping now he didn't get too sick to make it over to my mom's.

"So what do you think?" he prompted me. "Is it okay with you?"

You better, I wanted to say. But instead, out loud, just told him, "Yeah." It was definitely all right now to take him in, and I turned the boat toward a shortcut I knew to the town pier. I stuck my oar in and pushed as hard as I could.

"Only trouble is," he said. "I think right now she's pretty mad at me. She hasn't come to work for three days. And she hangs up when I call. You got any suggestions on how I can get her to talk to me?"

I didn't waste a minute. Took the few fish we'd caught and bought a bunch more at the pier where everybody was checking in. Made *him* pay for them, then took him and all the fish home.

She was sitting on the front porch, Rambona beside her feet, tied to one of the porch posts. "How about fish for supper?" I called, as I led him around to in front of the house after we'd put up my boat.

She stood up and looked at him. Then took the fish out of his hand that he was holding out to her. And I saw her smile. I knew she would—would take him back, at least let him in the house and open up his mouth, now that I'd made sure he had something worthwhile to say.

Mom's always been a sucker for any pitiful-looking creature.

18.
Linda

I was in my bedroom. It was right after Thanksgiving. Boxes around me, the contents of my closet lying on the floor and on the bed—a real mess, about as bad as if a tornado'd passed through.

It was Sunday, and the kids were with George.

Lucille was walking around in the kitchen. I could hear her, picking up, unpacking more of her things, and talking to Rambona. Rambona was so pregnant that she could barely move. Lucille would heat her up chicken noodle soup and pamper her like she was going to deliver gold. I was the only one who got a good look at all the dogs who applied to be the daddy. Black, or white; or skinny brown, starved; a bulldog with white eyes—the list wasn't cute.

But then, cute wasn't what we were after. Lucille had asked for the pick of the litter. She was thinking about even taking two.

She came in behind me, held up one of George the Second's training cups, a Mickey Mouse head with ears. "You want to keep this?"

I turned around on the floor where I was sitting, a box of old purses in my lap. "Oh gosh," I said. "I sure hate to throw it away."

"There're two more." Lucille held it up to the light, looking at the bottom. Rambona lumbered in to check on us, see what we were doing.

"Well, let me keep that one, then," I said, reaching for it. I ran my fingers over George's little teeth marks on the rim. Then put it in the box that I had marked KEEP. Mustard was asleep in the bottom.

Lucille headed back to the kitchen. Since it was Sunday, the day care was closed. She and I had come to an agreement, actually she'd had it in mind all the time, part of her deal to make me promise to ask Mark to marry me, so that if he did and I moved into his house, she could move into mine for good, then set up shop.

She had turned the backyard into a playground, incorporated George the Second's swing set into a bigger one she had moved from the yard of the Handymart. And Drew built a sandbox big enough for ten.

Now I held an envelope of a wedding invitation I never got around to mailing. It was to George and Anne Marie, and I just didn't have the guts. Or more precisely, I guess, rubbing things in had lost some of its fun by then.

Rambona lay beside the box of purses, her eyebrows twitching, and I pulled out one of the old purses, opened it, checked the contents. Funny about purses. It takes me hours just to pick out a new one. My mind set on a certain number of pockets or color or the length of a strap. Then after the new one, I never totally empty out the old one, as if I think on any one day I might pull it out, use it again, and it'll be half packed and ready to go. My purses, anyway, are like my filing cabinets. Couldn't do my income taxes or cure a headache without one. In the box now, there were at least three that George the Second had used in his purse-carrying days.

I was cleaning out the whole house, throwing away the accumulation of years. This Christmas Mark and I would be together in his house. He and I had made rooms for the children, were adding a guest room for when Lisa visited. In two years Drew would be gone, too. One of the best things I ever did, when I got brave, was to drive to the junior college near here and talk to the admissions officer. It was right after that terrible night when Mark had turned me down. I didn't want to go back to the clinic, so instead I called in sick and drove out of town. I needed something to keep my mind off Mark and off myself, and Drew's report card was a good one. I had just found it in his room, sitting out on his desk a printed progress report from his homeroom teacher. It had an X marked in the square, "Needs Rest." I was horrified: I'd been working Drew too hard, using him too much to help with George and Mandy and everything else. I called the teacher, and she said she hadn't marked that square at all. But that, yes, Drew was failing, was practically doing nothing at all in school, anymore. So I figured out then, Drew had marked the box, himself. He had left it lying out for me to see. He was just going to drop out of everything, and try to fool me, keep me off his back. Instead I drove to the junior college near here. I not only needed to get out of town, but I needed to talk to someone who could be objective about Drew. I told the admissions officer there everything I knew about how Drew did in school, and I asked his opinion. I showed him all of Drew's records, his grades, the whole works. Then I explained how I had to do something, help him, fix things for him, think about his future before it was too late.

The man just sat there behind his desk. He looked at me hard a minute, probably because I looked so nuts: dark glasses, brownie mix under my nails, a scarf half over my chin where it was supposed to be decorating the collar of my suit.

He told me about an expert who could test for dyslexia. Even set up an appointment for Drew. The workup was going to be expensive, though. Which then made me know how much more trouble I was in. Because I had decided to quit working at the clinic, couldn't stand to be around Mark anymore. I couldn't stand for him to maybe figure out the truth, either—that I wasn't qualified for the job in the first place—then fire me. Turning me down that night made me feel fired once already. I didn't want to stick around for number two.

The night after the Fishing Rodeo when he came over, he didn't look very good, sunburned pink as a shrimp, day-old beard like he'd been shipwrecked. I wasn't going to let him in the house, either. I didn't even want to talk to him, much less cook his fish. He and Drew had caught so many! Yet still they hadn't won. It didn't make much sense. But Mark didn't seem to mind losing. And neither did Drew. He just went to clean up his motor and work on his boat.

Mark stood on the porch, holding out to me those fish, then asked me to walk down the street with him a minute. Of course at that point, I was still ready to kill him for humiliating me the week before. But then he begged me. And that helped.

We walked out toward the cemetery, to the point where in the dark the moon plays on the water, changing it, throwing its light on the waves so that it does not even seem like water or light, but like something solid and silver. And then Mark looked at me and he didn't even touch me, but started talking as if he were presenting himself at rounds, which made it sound even more distant but more honest somehow, like he was giving me words about a serious condition and what we could and couldn't do about it. He told me that the one thing he didn't think he could ever stand to live through again was to lose someone he loved, someone he loved as much as he had loved Barbara. And that now he loved me that much, and that was what scared him, but that he'd decided that if he lost me out of being such a wuss, then he'd end up about the same, anyway. So he was willing to live with the fear if I was.

About that time I decided that since he was getting so open and honest, I might as well come clean with everything, too. And not only did I tell him that I didn't think I could live through learning that someone had stopped loving me, again, either, but that I didn't have any medical background whatsoever, and that I'd accepted the job he'd offered me on totally false pretenses and that he might as well know I was that kind of a person. That I could get desperate and do dishonorable things.

He rolled back his head. A laugh came up from so far down in him that it was like a long-distant hoot, like Mandy and George using a walkie-talkie made out of tin cans and a string. He looked at me, said he'd known from day one that I hadn't known any more about how to measure blood pressure than George the Second did. "You knew that?" I asked, quick, my voice loud.

"Wasn't hard," he said. "But you got enough of the job done to keep from firing you." He grinned. "And I liked having you around."

"You mean that whole time you knew I didn't have any qualifications and you never called me on it!"

"Yeah."

"I'm that good? I did all right. I really did?"

"Yeah."

Then I looked hard at him, took one step closer, and asked him for a raise.

We did finally get around to answering each other—my proposal to him and his to me, and I added a little footnote. In my mind it was the least we could do to do something about what we were most afraid of—since at any time, I knew only too well, the light could change and the ground tilt, so that nothing would seem as it was, or safe. There was no such thing as safety, I knew. I knew now that there was only what I could do to make myself feel safe. So I told him that since I knew I was a good bit younger than he was, I figured the chances of me kicking the bucket on him weren't real good, and I promised not to. And then I made him promise me that if he ever stopped loving me, he'd go fishing, or start making furniture, or take up golf or something—anything just so long as he would keep it to himself.

Wouldn't likely take up fishing, he said.

But he promised everything else.

The old purse I was now holding up was tan, made out of burlap, a summer purse. I opened it and pulled out a wad of stuff. I laid it out on the carpet.

It had been the Saturday before that we had gotten married out in the boathouse, out near where I saw Mark in Drew's boat when the raccoons came down the tree and disappeared in the sea oats. We had Mandy as my Maid of Honor and Drew to give me away and George the Second bearing the ring, which he threatened to bring down the flower-trimmed walkway in his nose. Betty MacHenry sang. And the day before, Lisa flew in to stand beside Mark. And Mama, with my dad, drove down, too, to stand in the boathouse and, more often than not, look pleased. It seemed that a side effect of marrying Mark—one that I hadn't counted on, either—was that apparently it had made Mama happy. Back home, she was going around telling all of her friends that I was marrying a doctor, one who drove around in a Mercedes. That the car was over thirty years old and had no front grill, she didn't, apparently, bother to add.

Now I unrolled the papers from the old purse onto the yellow shag carpet. Rambona's head was two inches from my knee, her eyes so drooped with the business of making puppies, that she didn't even watch me as I pulled an old mashed piece of candy out of the bottom of the purse. I heard Lucille out on the front porch sanding the sign of The Love 'em and Leave 'em Day Care that she hung up over the door when I got everything moved out. (It looks pretty fitting, if you ask me, on the house that George bought.)

There now in all the mess on the floor, I saw an old postcard, bought at a resort in south Florida. A vacation right after Drew was born. I couldn't remember even carrying that purse or whom I intended to send the postcard to. I remembered the vacation (George, skinny in a red bathing suit, the stretch of his skin and the way it felt when he closed his arms around me on the beach; me still feeling like an overfed cow with Drew's leftover baby fat). But carrying that purse that whole while, I couldn't remember. It was as though the details, the small lines of my life, were wiped away, washed off. It felt as though I had misplaced something. I had all these purses, those mementos inside of them, and yet I could not bring back the time and exact place in which they each belonged. It was as though I was, indeed, losing my own life as I was living it.

Rambona began to snore. I picked up the postcard from that

trip that George and I had taken. I rubbed it against my face, smelled it, felt the slick beach picture on the front, and put it in the box marked KEEP. "Mark's here." Lucille called, coming down the hall to help me.

I picked up a box.

Lucille picked up one.

Mark came in and got two.

We all three of us bumped down the hall with the boxes of my things. Rambona tripped Mark as she waddled on ahead, and I laughed, watching him struggling to stay on his feet.

"How much more do you have?" He glanced back at me.

"Tons," I said.

The truth was, once I would have thrown away everything here. But now the memories of George and me were no stronger than echoes, a life that bounced off the solidness of its ending. And for some reason that I did not fully understand, I wanted to remember it, wanted to remind myself of everywhere I'd been. It seemed that the shadows were arranged now. My own chiaroscuro. In my own life.

Lucille shoved the boxes of old purses I had decided to keep into the back of the Granny Apple.

By the time we finished, we had packed both cars tight as ticks, and, once again, sometime, I knew I'd have to trim it all down even more.

"Is this it?" Mark looked at me, slammed the top to the trunk.

"Yeah," I said, and slipped my arm into his. "For now."

19.

Drew

I remember wondering if Dr. Haley would have gone on and married Mom without me stepping in and twisting his arm a little.

I had my doubts when I stood there in the boathouse at their wedding and that girl who was Dr. Haley's daughter stood beside him and, as she looked over at me and smiled, I felt she looked a little familiar. But then she's got his eyes and the shape of his chin, just like I've got Mom's nose and her hair. So it was like looking at parts of somebody else, somebody I felt I already knew.

She told me that she'd been to the beach over at the Atlantic with her father only a few weeks before, which did raise something of a question in my mind. But that day when I saw Dr. Haley with another woman, I wasn't looking at her face. It was the whole long length of her skin—unwrinkled, tight, creamy-colored skin—that I was looking at and worrying about. My mom couldn't even come close to looking like that.

But it really doesn't matter, I figure. For I know now that you do what you have to do to break through some place where you are—and it doesn't really matter if what you do needs doing or not. For your own sake, you do it. And anyway, it was probably good for him all the way around—that fishing trip from hell.

My hands close over the steering wheel now with my fingers loose. My foot just sits on the floor in front of the accelerator like I'm sitting in a show or something. Got cruise control. A new car. Not too fancy. But nice. Sunroof and all.

Mom and I drive back and forth to school every day. An hour each way. Or, at least, I drive. She always sits beside me, like now—her nose in a book, her finger rubbing her eyebrow like she does when she's thinking hard, a yellow Magic Marker outlining whole paragraphs like her hand has the twits.

I spend the whole day in a junior college—got in after some special tests, took some kind of special stuff, therapy they called it, for reading backward. Now I just about cut out reading altogether. Just listen to stuff. I have a little tape recorder I take to class. And get this: I'm signed up to be an emergency technician. The kind of guy, you know, who comes in the ambulance and jumps out and straps people down and saves their lives. Might even get to do the driving. Might even get to carry Annie all around town and brush everybody up on their CPR.

It is almost dusk. The sun setting in front of us as we head home, reaching the bridges now, the marshes just beside us. I study the light as it leaves the sky and how it does so slowly that you think you are seeing it and then, all at once, it is gone.

Every day, while Mom and me are out of town, Dad and Mark (it only took a little while to stop calling him Dr. Haley) switch off taking care of Mandy and George in the afternoons or during daytime emergencies. And of course Lucille Duffy is always on call. Mandy is just starting high school. And George is in third grade. Which makes it even, if you ask me—all of us somewhere now in school. Me at the junior college while Mom's over at the university. And Dad still the principal of K through twelve; and Rambona's puppies, who got given out to a lot of people in Palm Key, now in the same classes she almost failed.

Mom's signed up for premed. Says she's not sure if, at her age, she'll go all the way with it, or even if, over at the med school, they'll let her in. But at the least, she'll end up a physician's assistant or a medical illustrator, *really* help out Mark or draw up everybody's insides.

I turn on the lights. Mom closes the book in her lap and turns on the radio.

"You like this?" She sets the dial on a station and looks at me. She does a little sit-down, hand-waving dance, lip-synching the music.

"It's fine."

I like to think about what I know about the water we are driving over. I can't write any of it down, but it is here in my head as much as the song playing on the radio. It stays with me as solidly as the bottom of the ocean when the tide goes out, and I can see it. It's then that I memorize quickly exactly where each oyster bar is and every other hazard that might snare my prop. When the tide comes back in, and the water covers up everything, I am one of the few people who can guide a boat straight up a channel and into clear water.

I don't know why, and I can't really say that I'll ever cash in on it, except for fishing, but I like feeling that knowing the channels is good. Something really fine. To know that even in the night, I know where I am. That even when I reach out and can't touch anything, I still know that I have been here before.

If you ask me, that's not a bad thing to remember. In fact, I guess, it even keeps me calm.

Yeah, I take a lot of comfort in memorizing where I've been.

I know it's what I do best.